"WHO ARE you?" Branwen whispered.

"I have many names," said the woman, and something in her voice made Branwen think of water rippling over stones. "But for you I am Rhiannon of the Spring. And my falcon, you already have met. His name is Fain."

Branwen let out a breath, fear clutching her heart as the words of the bard came back to her.

"You are a Shining One."

"I am."

Branwen stepped forward, her eyes grown used to the brilliance but her mind still dazzled. "What do you want of me?"

"I have waited long for you, warrior-child. All of Brython will be your home, and you will gather to you a band of warriors who shall keep the enemy at bay for many long years."

"No! You're wrong. I am not a warrior."

"You can be a warrior, if you choose to be," Rhiannon said, her eyes shining.

"Not me!"

"There is no one else," Rhiannon said. "You are the one who will save this land. You are the Sword of Destiny. The Bright Blade! The Emerald Flame of your people!"

Warrior Princess

Frewin Jones

HARPER TEEN

An Imprint of HarperCollins*Publishers*

HarperTeen is an imprint of HarperCollins Publishers.

Warrior Princess
Copyright © 2009 by Working Partners Limited
Series created by Working Partners Limited

Library of Congress Cataloging-in-Publication Data
Jones, Frewin.
Warrior princess / Frewin Jones. — 1st ed.
p. cm. — (Warrior princess)
Summary: After a deadly attack on her home, fifteen-
year-old Princess Branwen meets a mystical woman in
white who prophesies that Branwen will save her homeland
from falling to the Saxons.
ISBN 978-0-06-087145-1
[1. Princesses—Fiction. 2. War—Fiction. 3. Magic—
Fiction. 4. Saxons—Fiction. 5. Wales—History—To
1063—Fiction.] I. Title.
PZ7.J71War 2009   2008023936
[Fic]—dc22   CIP
                                                   AC

Typography by Ray Shappell
09 10 11 12 13   CG/RRDH   10 9 8 7 6 5 4 3 2 1
❖
First paperback edition

*In Memory of Merlie O.
Great Friend. Much Missed.*

1

BRANWEN AP GRIFFITH sat on the grassy hillside
with her back to an oak tree, gazing out over the
rugged landscape of bony hills and steep, wooded valleys that she had known since childhood. Her raven
black hair hung in curls almost to her waist; her face
was tanned by sun and wind; and her eyes were a
smoky gray blue, like a stormy sea. She was dressed in
a simple marten-skin jerkin and leggings of animal
hide—peasant clothes, suited to the hunt. Behind her
the forest rose up in dense swaths toward stark brown
mountain peaks. At her feet the hill sloped away to a
wide valley, where children played around a pool of
clear, spring-fed, white water.

The voices of the children drifted up to where
Branwen was sitting. They were singing an old nursery rhyme.

Water woman in the well
Stag-man waiting in the dell
Ancient crone in house of stone
Warrior by the north wind blown

Call from wood and hill and deep
Into the darkling forest creep

Child of the Spring
Child of the Wood
Chase flesh, fowl, fish
But spill no blood

Chase them through the twisted trees
Until you fall down on your knees!

Laughing and shouting, the children tumbled onto the grass. They shrieked and wrestled, but watching them play made Branwen feel sad.

Perhaps it was the thought of the coming war. . . .

She looked beyond the children to where the round hillock of Garth Milain thrust up from the valley like the half-buried skull of a giant. The huge mound of rock and earth had been piled here thousands of years ago by a people long departed.

A huddled village of daub-and-wattle huts and wooden buildings topped the hill, circled by a tall fence of wooden stakes. A quiet pride welled in her. This was her home, and had been home to the House

2

of Rhys for eight generations, gifted to them by the king of Brython. From the Great Hall of Garth Milain, Branwen's father, Prince Griffith, and her mother, Lady Alis, ruled a wide cantref of land that stretched from the mountains in the west to the hazy line of cliffs in the east.

A narrow path on a steep ramp of beaten earth led up to the heavy wooden gateway atop the hill. It was the only way to approach the fortified village. Around the flattened summit of the hill, timber palisades jutted into the clear sky like a crown, and only the lofty thatched roof of the Great Hall was visible over the saw-toothed defenses. Her father's guards stood on the ramparts, their spears needle-thin against the pale horizon.

In the middle distance beyond the hill, Branwen noticed a wispy plume rising into the sky. She leaned forward, her eyes narrowing as she stared at the pale wing of smoke.

Is that a farmer's bonfire—or is it them? she wondered uneasily.

By *them* she meant Saxons. She stood up, calling down into the dale. "Cadi! Come here!"

A gangly lad of seven or eight started to scramble up the slope toward her.

Branwen watched the lazy smoke, her heart beating fast in her chest. For the first fourteen years of her life, the cantref of Cyffin Tir had been at peace, but over the last twelve months the Saxons had begun creeping back into her parents' land. They came mostly by night, in twos and threes at first, cutting throats, thieving goods and livestock before stealing away like ghosts. The raids had lessened over the harsh, frosty winter; but with the spring the raiders had come again—and now as the summer solstice drew near, they came in groups of ten or twenty, striking like thunderbolts, leaving death and misery in their wake as they fled back to the borderlands, clutching plundered weapons and driving stolen cattle before them.

Branwen had never seen a live Saxon warrior; the only Saxons she knew were the servants who belonged to her father's household. They were men and women who had been captured in the old wars and dragged from their homes to live among their enemies in unpaid servitude. They had no rights, they were the lowest of the low, and they were as docile and obedient as broken horses.

But Branwen knew that not all Saxons were as humbled. Beyond the edge of sight, the Saxon armies were gathering again under King Oswald of Northumbria. Branwen imagined them swarming like the bees in her father's hives—cold eyed, beating their swords on their shields as they marched in a pitiless swarm that blackened the earth.

"What is it, my lady?" panted Cadi.

Branwen put a hand on the boy's shoulder and turned him, pointing to the curl of gray in the blue sky. "Where the smoke is," she said, keeping the urgency out of her voice so as not to alarm him. "Isn't that your father's farm?"

Cadi wiped his nose on his arm and peered into the distance. "Yes. He's clearing trees and burning them to make room for more pigpens," he said.

Not Saxons. Thank the saints!

"Good. That's all I wanted to know. You can go now."

Cadi gave her a respectful bob of his head and went racing back down the hill to his friends.

Branwen sat down again. She was relieved that the burning was innocent, but at the same time a tiny part of her was almost disappointed. She would like to have seen her father's fine horsemen galloping over the hills to do battle with Saxon invaders, their banners waving and their swords flashing sunlight.

A small movement caught in the corner of Branwen's eye. She turned her head slowly. A fat wood pigeon had landed on a low branch at the forest's edge. The slender branch was still bobbing from the weight. Branwen's mother liked roasted wood pigeon. Branwen pulled her slingshot from her belt. The bird would be a good gift to take home.

At her left hip hung a leather pouch of small, rounded stones. She opened the pouch and chose a white pebble about the size of the end joint of her thumb. She folded the slingshot double and with skilled fingers fitted the stone into place.

5

It would be an easy kill.

Before she had time to take aim, a hand gripped her arm from behind and another hand clamped across her mouth.

Too shocked even to feel scared, she was pulled over backward and dragged, kicking and struggling, into the forest. A single, terrible word hammered in her mind:

Saxons!

2

BRANWEN LASHED OUT with her free hand. Her fist hit something solid; there was a cry, and she was suddenly released.

"Ow! Branwen! That hurt!"

She scrambled to her feet, spinning around to face her assailant.

"Geraint!"

Her older brother was sprawling in the flattened bracken, rubbing his cheekbone with the side of his hand. His dark hair hung in his eyes, and a grin was spreading across his broad, smooth-shaven face. He squinted up at her with sapphire blue eyes. "Were you scared? You looked scared."

She glared at him, her body still tingling with shock. "You mooncalf!" she shouted. "What did you do that for?"

Geraint stood up. Despite the four-year age difference, he was only a thread taller than Branwen; but he was stocky and powerfully built, his shoulders bulging under his tunic. "Oh, calm down, Branwen." He brushed pieces of the forest floor off his hunting clothes. "It was just a bit of fun."

"I wasn't scared. I was taken by surprise, that's all," she told him defensively. "You won't get to do that twice."

"We'll see about that." He took a couple of steps and picked up a bow and a quiver of arrows from where they had been lying behind a tree trunk. "I thought you might want to come hunting with me."

"I was about to bring down a wood pigeon, before you grabbed me!" Branwen said. "So *you* can come hunting with *me*!" She ran back to where she had dropped her slingshot and then loped past her brother and bounded into the forest, intent on being the first to find worthy prey. A young deer, a wild boar, even a plump pheasant would do—just so long as she reached it first!

"You'll catch nothing making all that noise!" she heard Geraint call. "What have I always told you?"

"Be calm, be silent, be swift, be still," she shouted back as she ran. "Right now, I'm being swift!" She leaped a tumble of rocks, her arms raised to fend off low branches and ferns as she headed into the shaded depths of the forest.

* * *

Branwen slithered along on her belly. She was determined not to alert her quarry to her presence. A female grouse was sitting on its nest—a shallow scrape in the earth lined with vegetation—with its tail toward her.

Absolutely silently, Branwen loaded her slingshot. The bird turned her head, and now Branwen could see the black eye, shining brightly in a ring of white on the small brown head. One well-aimed stone and it would all be over, so quickly that the bird would not even know what had happened.

"Hoy!"

It was Geraint's voice.

The bird took to the air and disappeared into the trees.

Branwen jumped up, seething. Was Geraint deliberately trying to ruin the hunt for her?

There was another shout—another single word, Branwen thought, called out with urgency or alarm—but it was farther away now, muffled by distance.

A sense of unease began to grow in her, turning her stride into a run. Was Geraint in trouble? Perhaps a wild boar had cornered him—those creatures could be dangerous. A gouge from the sharp-edged tusk of a full-grown boar could rip a person's belly open!

Branwen saw light up ahead through the trees. She was approaching a patch of cleared woodland, one of many where farmers planted grain or grazed cattle and goats.

She could hear more voices now, shouting and

calling. Horses were neighing, and there was the crackle of flames.

She saw red tongues of fire through the trees and coils of thick, gray smoke.

She came to the hem of the forest, and the sight that greeted her brought her to a halt like the blow of a mattock to her forehead.

There were farm buildings on the far side of the clearing—round, daub-and-wattle huts around a stockade of withies. The conical thatched roofs were ablaze, and horsemen rode cheering across the flames. Other men had dismounted and were running with blazing torches, shouting and whooping. Some of them were tearing down the stockade fences and driving out the cattle. Bodies lay in the dirt—a man, a woman, and four children—their clothes torn and smeared with blood.

The raiders wore billowing cloaks and chain mail jerkins. On their heads were riveted iron helmets with nose and cheek guards and floating white plumes. Some carried round, wooden shields and long, iron-tipped spears; others bore short stabbing swords and heavy, double-headed war-axes. But the most jarring part of their appearance was their full, bristling beards and long, pale hair. The men of Cyffin Tir wore traditional thick, heavy mustaches; but they all had clean-shaven chins. These were Saxons! Their beards made them look to Branwen like wild things— like savages.

In Branwen's lifetime, Saxons had never penetrated

this far west—they had never dared enter the forest. If anyone saw the smoke, they would simply think that it was a farmer burning stubble or bracken.

Branwen knew she should do something; but her limbs wouldn't move, and her chest was so tight that she could barely breathe. She saw her brother running across the clearing with an arrow on his bow.

Follow Geraint! she told herself. *Do something!*

The twang of Geraint's bowstring sang through the air. A horseman wheeled out of the saddle, an arrow piercing his throat. Geraint fitted another arrow. He drew the bow and loosed it in a single, fluid movement. A second Saxon stumbled with the shaft embedded deep in his belly.

Geraint reached behind for a third arrow as yet another Saxon pulled his steed around and came galloping toward him. The rider swung low in the saddle, a battle-ax whirling in his hand. The ax struck Geraint in the stomach, lifting him off his feet and throwing him backward while the blood spurted high.

"No!" Branwen screamed. *"No!"*

The horseman raised his head, and his battle-maddened eyes fixed on her. A grimace of bloodlust transfixed his face as he urged his horse onward. He raised the blood-wet ax and howled as his horse bore down on her.

3

BRANWEN SAW THE leather bridle and trappings of the chestnut brown horse, the foam at its lips, the flexing of muscles under its skin. The man's cloak spread out from his shoulders, as dark as storm clouds, as he rode her down. His mouth gaped like a red hole in the tangled mass of his beard. Deep scars formed a white cross on his left cheek. Strangest of all, Branwen had time to consider, one of the man's eyes was brown, but the other was blue.

Droplets of Geraint's blood spun off the head of the ax as it scythed through the air, spattering warm across Branwen's cheek as she stood and waited for death to come for her.

But at the last possible moment the horse swerved to one side, its hooves hammering the ground. The rider was almost tipped from the saddle. He jerked at the reins, shouting in a language that Branwen didn't understand. The horse circled, rearing up. The Saxon raider's head turned, his strange eyes on Branwen, his ax still raised.

A look of alarm came over his face as he stared at something behind her.

He shouted words that sounded like *Ai ragda!*, and Branwen saw her own fear mirrored in his bloodshot blue and brown eyes for a moment before he galloped back to his companions, shouting and pointing to the forest.

Many of the raiders stared uneasily into the trees at Branwen's back. But then a huge man with long, golden hair and with golden studs on his shield pushed his horse forward, shouting and gesturing with his sword. Their leader, Branwen guessed. A small band of men broke away and began to gather the released cattle. Soon, all the Saxons were mounted again, riding to the edge of the clearing, herding the cattle along the trackway that led through the trees.

The big man urged his horse toward Branwen, drawing his sword but keeping a tight rein. He halted a little way from her and peered into the forest. He let out a shout and then waited, as if expecting a response.

He tilted his head as though listening and then let out a harsh burst of laughter and brought his horse closer, so that it loomed over Branwen. He towered above her, the point of his sword at her throat. She looked up into his ice blue eyes, deathly afraid but also filled with a blazing rage.

Savages! Murderers!

The man let out a stream of words; and although Branwen didn't understand what he was saying to her, the contempt in his voice was obvious. He pulled the sword back and spat in her face before turning his horse around and riding off at a canter to rejoin his men.

They disappeared through the trees, and Branwen was left alone with the leaping flames and the dead bodies and the stench of blood.

"Geraint!" She ran to where her brother was lying. He was stretched on his back, his eyes closed and his face peaceful. But his tunic was gashed and thick, red blood welled from his chest.

He was dead.

Tears flooded down Branwen's cheeks. She caught hold of his hand and pressed his fingers against her burning face.

"Geraint . . . I'm so sorry. . . ."

She doubled up, her forehead touching his chest, his blood smearing her face. She opened her mouth, trying to release some of the pain by screaming—but the scream would not come.

At last she lifted her head, her hair matted with Geraint's blood and clinging wetly to her cheeks. In a daze, she let go of his hand and rested it gently on his chest. She stood up, swaying, and then turned and walked toward the six bodies that lay in the dirt outside the still-burning farmhouse.

She felt a terrible coldness in her chest, as though her heart were encased in ice. The fierce heat of the fire scorched her face as she stood over the bodies. The man was named Bevan. The last time she had seen him, he had been arguing with Anwen the cook over the price of a calf.

His wife lay next to him—Branwen didn't remember her name. And there were the four children, three girls and one boy.

All dead. She stooped and draped a corner of cloth over one little girl's upturned face.

Then she turned and walked back to where Geraint lay. She sat down cross-legged at his side. She gently smoothed his clothes, pulling the ripped edges of his tunic together to try and hide the wound. The dark blood had stopped flowing. She laid her hand on his chest and lifted it to her face, looking at the blood. Then she drew his hunting knife from his belt and, holding it between her two fists, she straightened her back and stared slowly around the clearing.

She would let no Saxon come back to desecrate his body. No animal with cruel teeth and a hungry belly would be allowed to come sniffing his blood. She would not move from her brother's side, not if the world ended and the sky came crashing down around her ears.

4

THE AFTERNOON PASSED with a crushing slowness.
Branwen knelt over her brother's dead body,
her mind numbed with grief.

There was no thought in her head other than
the need to keep Geraint's body safe. She had been
unable to do anything to help him in life, but in
death she would protect him. If need be she would
stay there forever.

The shadows were long and the sky was dark-
ening when two warriors emerged from the forest
on white horses, their white cloaks gleaming in the
failing light. Branwen stood up on stiff and aching
legs. She stepped over her brother's body and stood
between him and the oncoming riders.

"I'm not afraid of you!" she shouted, lifting the
knife high in her fist. "I won't let you touch him!"

More riders emerged from the forest: a dozen or

more warriors followed by two heavily laden ox-drawn wagons covered by skins. One of the riders was carrying a standard—a limp, white banner. White for the Saxon dragon.

A rider broke from the others and cantered toward her, a round, iron helmet on his head, his long, white cloak cracking. He brought the horse up short as a breath of air moved across the clearing and the white banner fluttered open to reveal the red dragon of the kingdom of Powys emblazoned proudly in the center. Not Saxons but men of Brython.

"Branwen ap Griffith, put down your knife," called the rider. "We are not your enemies." He jumped down from the saddle and walked toward her.

"Draw your sword!" Branwen howled, slashing the air with the knife. "I'll kill you. I'll kill all of you!"

The man stopped. "What has happened here, Branwen?" he demanded. "Speak, girl. Who did this?"

Suddenly Branwen looked into the man's face and recognized the wide brow and the dark, deep-set eyes; the war-scarred cheeks; and the heavy, black mustache under the curved, hawklike nose.

It was Prince Llew ap Gelert, lord of the cantref of Bras Mynydd beyond the mountains, her father's closest ally. In the horror of the day Branwen had forgotten that he had been due to arrive at Garth Milain, traveling over the mountains to discuss the Saxon threat with her father and mother.

Prince Llew stared beyond her, and his face twisted with anger. He took a step forward; but Branwen spread her arms, warding him off.

"Don't touch him!"

"Is he dead?"

"Yes. A Saxon cut him down with an ax." She looked defiantly at the tall, battle-hardened prince. "But he took two lives for his own."

"How many were they?"

"Ten. Maybe more. I was in the forest; I heard Geraint shouting. He was already in the clearing when I came out of the trees. The roofs were on fire; Bevan and his family were dead. The Saxons were releasing the cattle. Geraint shot two of them with his bow."

Prince Llew stepped forward, taking the knife out of her fist and resting his hand on her shoulder. "You poor child!" Branwen felt an urge to rush forward and cling to him, but she refused to lose control. Her anger was all that was holding her together; she needed to keep a tight grip on it.

"How long ago did this happen?" Llew asked.

Branwen drew back, looking up into his cavernous eyes, filled now with sadness and sympathy. "It was the middle of the day," she said. She shuddered. "I did nothing to help him," she whispered. "I stood and watched as he was cut down."

"What could you have done?" he said. "A child against armed men?"

Branwen winced. He was right. She had acted as a child would, while Geraint had behaved like a warrior.

"I will send a rider after them," Llew said. "They have a long start on us, but the cattle will slow them down."

He turned and shouted instructions to his men. Some of them had dismounted and were stooping over the bodies of the farmer and his family. One was checking the two dead Saxons.

Two men approached.

"Put the body of Geraint ap Griffith on a wagon," Prince Llew ordered.

"No!" shouted Branwen. "Don't touch him."

Llew gave her a look of deep compassion. "He must be taken to Garth Milain, Branwen," he said. "His body cannot be left here for the carrion birds. And your father must be told of this tragedy as soon as possible."

Branwen stepped reluctantly aside as the two men stooped to pick up Geraint's body. But she couldn't bear to be apart from him. She leaned forward, touching his cheek with her fingertips. She gasped and pulled back her hand, shocked by the unexpected chill of his skin.

A howl of grief rose in her throat. She fought against it. Her brother's flesh was as cold and dead as stone. How could she bear this? Tears stabbed from behind her eyes. Her hands trembled. She felt that her legs were going to give way under her.

But she gathered her strength, gritting her teeth to stop the howl, clenching her fists to prevent her hands from shaking. A single hot tear ran down her cheek as she managed to gain control of herself.

She walked alongside the two warriors, keeping close, making sure they were gentle with Geraint as they carried him to the nearest wagon. She noticed how his head had become rigid on his neck and how his limbs and back were already beginning to stiffen with the rigor of death. She was aware of Llew's men murmuring among themselves; she heard curses spoken against the Saxons and words of ire and grief at the deaths of Geraint and the farm family.

Space was cleared on the wagon, and Geraint's body was laid on the boards. Branwen climbed up next to him. The cart driver turned and looked at her, his face furious.

"There will be retribution, my lady," he said. "Do not fear; Prince Llew will find the Saxon dogs and make them pay!"

She looked at him. "I hope he does not harm them," she said.

The man gazed at her in confusion.

"I want them alive and healthy when I dig a knife into their bellies," she explained with absolute calm. "I want them to die slowly and painfully, and I want to watch."

Hold hard to the anger. Feed the rage. Do not give in to grief. Not yet. Not now. Not in this place and in front of these people. Do not!

The man nodded and looked away.

Room was made for the six other bodies on the second wagon. The warriors mounted up again and Prince Llew led them out of the clearing, following the Great Forest Way toward Garth Milain.

Branwen clung onto the side of the wagon, gazing down at the face of her brother, indistinct now in the dark shadows of the forest. She knew that she would never be carefree again. In the space of half a day—of a single ax blow—everything had changed.

As the night darkened, it seemed to Branwen as if the Great Forest Way was a black tunnel, taking her down into the deepest pits of Annwn. The warriors were subdued and silent around her. The forest held its breath. The night gaped like an open mouth.

The road came out of the forest, and they continued their journey beneath a cold, bleak, star-pocked sky. A gaunt man in a red cloak brought his horse up alongside the wagon, his voice startling Branwen out of her dark thoughts.

"I am Angor, captain of the prince's guard," he said, holding up a water-skin. "May I offer you refreshment, my lady?"

She looked at him, feeling strangely disoriented. He had a long, deeply lined face the color of old leather. His mustache was touched with a gray that was echoed in his heavy-lidded eyes.

"No, thank you," she said. Her stomach was an iron fist in the middle of her body. The thought of food or drink almost made her retch.

Captain Angor nodded. "Call me if you need anything," he said, urging his horse toward the front of the line.

The path skirted a fold of land, and Branwen saw the lights of her home glowing above the palisade and shining brightly through the wide-open doors at the top of the ramp. As they approached the steep earthen slope, there were shouts from the walls.

"Who comes to Garth Milain?"

Captain Angor called up in response: "Prince Llew ap Gelert and men of his court. We bear with us the body of the son of the House of Rhys, slain by Saxons."

There were shouts of dismay and horror from the walls. The lead horses stepped up onto the ramp. Soldiers of Prince Griffith's guard stood in the open gateway, their faces shocked.

"The enemy may still be in Cyffin Tir," called Prince Llew. "Close the gates when we are all safe inside."

The oxcarts lumbered up the steep path. Branwen rested her hand on Geraint's chest to try and save him from being shaken about too much. At last they passed through the tall, split-log gates and into the village fortress.

Branwen blinked tears from her eyes as she stared around at the familiar sights of her home. How could Garth Milain still look the same when the whole world had been turned on its head?

Torches blazed from the palisades; and through the low doorways of the round, daub-and-wattle huts, she saw the homely flicker of firelight.

People were going about their everyday business: cooking the evening meal, telling tales around the hearth, putting their children safely to bed under coverings of furred hide or woven cloth.

Innocent of what had happened.

For the moment.

Guards swarmed around the wagon. More people came running from their homes, crying out in grief as word spread that Geraint was dead.

A guard came up to the wagon. "My lady, are you hurt?"

Branwen shook her head. "No, Owen, I am not." She lowered her head and left a kiss on Geraint's cold forehead before jumping down from the wagon. "Do as Prince Llew says: Close and bar the gates," she ordered. "I must . . ." She swallowed, choking on her words. "My brother is dead; I must tell my mother and father."

She saw Prince Llew riding toward the Great Hall.

It isn't his place to tell my mother and father what has happened. I have to do that. It's my duty.

The Great Hall was her home—Geraint's home— with its soaring walls of seasoned oak timber and its long, high, thatched roof. The doors were open in welcome, and on either side, red flames leaped in iron braziers. Branwen ran forward and drew level with Prince Llew's tall black stallion, smelling the sweat of travel on the great beast's hide.

The prince looked down at her. "Branwen—stay with your brother. I will bring the news to the lord and lady."

"No!" she called up to him, gripping his reins, feeling the supple leather hard in her fist as he looked sternly down at her. As the numbness began to clear from her mind, she was intensely aware of the richness of the clothing of this wealthy and powerful prince from beyond the Western Mountains. Aware of his white silk cloak with its golden brooches, of the golden belt about his waist and the golden bracelets on his wrists. She felt small and humble in her hunting clothes—like any one of the villagers who were standing close by with dismayed and angry and terrified faces.

But she was *not* one of them; she was a daughter of the House of Rhys, and she had an obligation to fulfill, whatever the richly attired Prince Llew might say.

"I will tell them," she said. "It's my responsibility."

Branwen knew that once she stepped into the Great Hall, the news that she carried would shatter the lives of her mother and father for all time. The open doors were like the gateway into hell.

She passed weeping men and women as she strode toward the Great Hall.

"My lady?" A woman caught at her hand, tears

flooding down her face. "Is it true? Your brother?"

She nodded, pulling away as the woman moaned with sorrow. The weeping and cursing of the village folk was like a rising tide at her back as she came to the doors of the hall.

She walked into her home. Rushes crackled beneath her feet. The timbered roof soared away above her head. The central hearth leaped with bright yellow flames, and there was the smell of roasted meat in the air. The evening meal was half finished, and the earth floor was scattered with food bowls and drinking cups. The men and women of the court were gathered there, making merry as they did on many a summer's night.

But the clamor from outside the hall had brought them all to their feet, and they stared at Branwen as she came into the long chamber.

The double throne of the House of Rhys rested on a low dais at the far end of the chamber, but Branwen's mother and father had already risen and were moving forward as Branwen stood swaying in front of them. She said nothing for the moment, her jaw clamped shut, her throat aching, her head pounding. She wished that this final moment of ignorance in her parents' lives would never have to end.

Lady Alis was as tall as her husband, her long, black hair framing her beautiful, strong-featured face. Prince Griffith stood at her side, his brown hair cut at the shoulders, his eyes dark and keen, his cheeks and chin shaven to leave only the long, thick, hanging mustache worn by all men of the kingdom of Brython.

She saw her mother's dove gray eyes fill with fear. Branwen knew that her appearance must tell a dreadful tale: her hair matted with gore, her face and hands streaked with dried blood.

"There were Saxon raiders in the forest—at Bevan's farmstead," she said, her voice oddly calm in the maelstrom of fire and ice that seethed in her head. "Geraint shot two of them before they even knew he was there." She looked into Alis's horrified eyes. "My brother is dead, Mother. Geraint is dead."

Branwen wrung a cloth into a wooden bowl of water and wiped her brother's hands. She tried to hold back her grief by focusing on the details of straightening Geraint's jacket, wiping dirt off his fingers. Trying not to notice the terrible trembling of her mother's hands as she combed out his tangled hair, her face almost as pale as the dead son she tended. Tears were threading silently down Alis's face—but Branwen was emptied of tears for the moment. She had cried herself dry in the clearing; and now she just felt hollow and terribly alone, even among people whom she had known all of her life.

Prince Griffith stood at his son's head, staring down into the ashen face with stricken eyes. Prince Llew was at his side, his warriors mingling with Griffith's men, their heads bowed in sorrow. Occasional sobs and groans broke the silence like small stones dropped in a dark lake.

The bier was laid in the rushes that covered the earthen floor, placed reverently in front of the great iron cauldron that stood over the open fire. Rushlights and candles lit the tall, wooden walls. Trenchers lay on the floor, forgotten now with food half eaten. Goblets and wine flasks stood about, but the warriors of the court and their ladies had no use for wine or mead. They stood in small groups, watching with haggard faces as Lady Alis and Branwen washed the blood from Geraint's body and laid him out with his hands folded gently over his chest.

"When I crossed the mountains to discuss the Saxon threat, little did I suspect that I would bring such woe with me," Branwen heard Prince Llew say in a low, resonant voice. "The passing of Geraint ap Griffith is a sore blow, my friend; and we share your grief."

"And yet the sharing of such grief does not lessen its agony," her father replied, and although his voice shook, it was clear and firm. "Our hoped-for future leaches into the ground with the blood from my son's wounds."

Lady Alis lifted her head and looked into her husband's face. "Our future?" she echoed bleakly. "Our son is dead, and my heart is broken. . . . I cannot think of our . . . *future*."

Branwen rested a hand on her mother's arm, trying to offer some crumb of comfort. Lady Alis took Branwen's hand and pressed her fingers to her lips. The desolation in her mother's face was more than she could bear. Branwen began to sob, and suddenly she was clinging to her mother, all hope of holding back the agony gone as they wept in each other's arms.

Branwen felt her father's arms around her as he crouched beside them, and through her tears she heard his voice.

"We have not lost all," he said, his voice cracking with emotion. "We have hope still."

Lady Alis pulled away from Branwen, wiping the tears from her face and straightening her back. "Yes, we do," she said, her hand warm in Branwen's. "All our hopes and wishes rest in you now, my precious daughter."

Branwen felt a pain like a knife in her chest as she heard her mother's words. How could she live up to such faith? Geraint had been the hero; she was just a child.

Prince Griffith rose to his feet again. "Stand, daughter," he said.

Branwen got up. Her legs trembled, and she could feel the eyes of the warriors and their ladies burning into her.

"The years of peace are gone," said Griffith, his voice carrying so that everyone in the hall could hear him. "The Saxons gather on our border.

The great King Cadwallon is dead, and Oswald of Northumbria wishes to gorge himself on the blood of the men and women of Brython. We have not looked for war, yet war is here, and we must fight for King Cynon and for our homeland." A murmur of agreement and approval ran through the hall. "My son is dead, but we must put aside our grief and face the threat that is coming. But a prince must also think of his family."

He turned and looked at Branwen, and she saw with agonizing clarity the pain that lay behind his eyes. "Branwen, you are now the future of the House of Rhys. I cannot keep you here when such peril beats at our gates. You shall be sent south to Gwent immediately—and there you will marry Hywel ap Murig of the House of Eirion, as has long been arranged. By this marriage an alliance shall be forged between Powys and Gwent that not even cold Saxon iron can break."

Branwen reeled. "No, Father! Don't send me away!"

There was sad understanding in her father's eyes. "I know this is against your wishes," he said. "But the danger here is too great."

"I don't care," Branwen cried. "I want to stay. I *have* to stay."

Her mother stood behind her with her long-fingered hands on Branwen's shoulders. "You came close to death today," she said. "Only the protection of the saints saved you from suffering your brother's fate. You must go, not only for your own safety, but because you have a duty to the House of Rhys."

Branwen turned and looked into her mother's eyes. The pity and fear she saw there were too much to bear. Her shoulders slumped. She turned back to her father.

She was not a great warrior like her mother. She did not have the courage of her dead brother. What use would she be if she stayed? To be burned in the Great Hall while the battle raged around her?

She bowed her head, tears pouring again down her cheeks and her voice barely above a whisper.

"As you wish, Father," she said.

5

B RANWEN LONGED TO blot everything out in the
oblivion of sleep, but a torch burned with a fierce
white light in her mind and sleep would not come.

She felt broken, like an earthenware pot dashed
to pieces on a stone floor.

All Garth Milain was sleepless that night. With
no word from Prince Llew's rider, Prince Griffith
sent more men out to seek news of the Saxon raiders.
The gifts that Llew had brought over the mountains
lay forgotten under the skins on the wagons. Instead
of a great feast of welcome for Llew's men, the warriors had eaten a simple meal together. The outer
gates were closed, and armed men walked the torch-
lit ramparts staring uneasily into the darkness.

Branwen abandoned her bed and sat on the
rampart, huddled in her cloak, staring into the west

with sore and aching eyes.

Below her, in the vale where that morning she had watched children playing, men were constructing Geraint's funeral pyre. Timbers were brought down the path from the fortress while other men, working by torchlight, felled more trees on the forest's eaves.

Come the dawn, Geraint's body would be anointed with sacred oils and laid on top of the pyre; and as the sun rose over the eastern hills, a flame would be thrust into the woodpile and his spirit would soar into the sky as his body was consumed by fire.

A hand rested gently on her shoulder.

"Branwen, why aren't you sleeping?" her mother asked. "You should rest."

"I can't," whispered Branwen.

Lady Alis sat at her side, gathering her cloak around herself against the cool of the night. "We have sent a messenger to King Cynon at Pengwern," she said. "If war is coming, then we must all band together."

"And I will be sent on the southward roads," Branwen said quietly. "To safety and to a long, slow death."

Lady Alis looked sharply at her. "Why do you say that?"

Branwen avoided her mother's eyes. "I'm not complaining," she said. "It's what I deserve. I should have died at Geraint's side."

"I give thanks to Saint Cadog that you did not!" Alis exclaimed.

"You don't understand," Branwen mumbled.

Lady Alis stood up, taking Branwen's hand. "Come, walk with me, and tell me what I don't understand."

Branwen rose, gripping her mother's hand tightly, her eyes fixed on her shoes. As they walked the ramparts she began to tell her mother what had happened at the farmstead. Her voice cracked and quavered, but she managed to get to the end.

There was a long silence. Branwen lifted her eyes. They had come around to the far side of the hill, and beyond the wall of sharpened staves all of the eastern world lay shrouded in shadow. Just over the horizon, the Saxons were preparing for war. Branwen shivered, and her mother opened her cloak and brought it around her daughter's shoulders.

Finally, Branwen dared to look into her mother's eyes, expecting to see disappointment or reproach. She was surprised to find that her mother's face was full of love and understanding.

"My poor child," she murmured. "You must not think ill of yourself."

Branwen swallowed painfully. "I always thought I would be brave," she whispered. "Why wasn't I brave?"

"It is not cowardice to avoid certain death," Lady Alis told her. "There was nothing you could have done to save your brother. It wasn't lack of courage

33

that stayed your hand but rather good sense. And I thank the saints for it or else we would be building two pyres this night."

Branwen put her hands up over her face. "I wish I had died."

Her mother dragged her hands down again. "No!" she said sharply. "Never say that again. *That's* coward- ice, Branwen! You must have the courage to face what happened today and to live with it in your heart and to use the memory of it to grow and be strong."

"And how do I do that if Father sends me to be Hywel's wife?"

"Remember, Branwen, I too was sent by my father to become the wife of a man I hardly knew. Courage and strength come from within; and when you go to be Hywel ap Murig's wife, the strength you already have will travel with you."

"But I don't even *like* Hywel," Branwen said, her voice sounding weak even to herself. "The only time we met, he pulled my hair and knocked me into the mud."

"The boy was only six years old, Branwen!" her mother said. "And I daresay he had little enough reason to like *you* at the time. But that was ten years ago. He will have changed as you have changed." She gave a pale smile. "I didn't think much of your father when I first met him. He was sullen and moody and would not even speak to me. But over time, love and respect grew as we got to know each other. And from that love, two children were born. Geraint is dead, and now you are our heir. In your father's place, Branwen, what would you do? Would you have your only child put on armor and face a Saxon army—or would you send her away to be the mother of heroes and to keep the House of Rhys alive?"

Branwen didn't reply.

Lady Alis turned, bringing Branwen around with her so they were both looking down into the huddled village. Many lights still burned.

The Great Hall looked so safe and so proud, standing in the middle of a gathering of lesser wooden buildings—dwellings for her father's warriors and their families. Branwen could not imagine what it would be like to leave her home.

She let out a long, sad breath. "And what about you and Father?" she asked. "What will you do?"

"We will fight for this land," her mother said, her fingers closing over the hilt of the golden knife that she always wore at her waist. "No Saxon warrior has ever set foot within Garth Milain, and none shall while I draw breath. And I will fight better knowing that you are far from here and safe from harm."

"I would rather fall in battle than live in exile," Branwen said bitterly.

"It is not exile," Lady Alis said. "You may yet have to fight, Branwen, although if Saint Cadog wills it, and I have my wish, that day will never come. But for now, your duty to the House of Rhys must come first. You will go south, and you will marry Hywel ap Murig."

6

BRANWEN'S EYES STUNG as she stared into the bitter dawn. The night sky had drawn all the heat away from the land; and even with a thick cloak around her shoulders, she felt cold.

Torches guttered and sparked in the wind as the first light of day began to seep over the hill, but the vale below Garth Milain was filled with a lake of clogged darkness as the funeral procession wound its way down the ramped pathway. Four warriors of Cyffin Tir carried Geraint at shoulder height on a wooden bier, his body draped with a purple cloth that covered him to the chin. Branwen walked between Prince Griffith and Lady Alis, their faces pale and set as they followed the warriors. Her heart ached to see her brother's upturned face so white and waxen; it was awful, but she could not look away.

Keep a steady pace behind the warriors, she told herself. *Don't fall apart in front of everyone. Stay on your feet! Do proper honor to Geraint!*

Behind the family, the warriors of Garth Milain walked in silence, followed by Prince Llew and his own warriors. Every other soul from the garth was already gathered around the looming pyre of interlocked logs. It had been built with painstaking care through the night, and now it reared up five times Branwen's height.

They halted at the side of the pyre. A ladder led up. Two warriors scaled the pyre, and ropes were used to lift Geraint's body. The bier rose with jerky movements, catching on the edges of the logs as it was pulled slowly to the summit. He was placed on an altar of leafy branches. The warriors climbed down again, and for a few moments, time held its breath.

Then Prince Griffith turned to the east, raising his arms toward the still-hidden sun. His voice rang out clearly over the hiss of the wind.

"I bow to the east, to the coming sun, to the new dawn, to new life. Shine now upon this, our child, formed from the green forests, formed from the bones of the mountains, formed from the sweet wild waters, formed from the rushing wind. He is laid upon the lap of the green forest; his body will kindle to the flame of the firestone of the mountain; he is anointed with the sweet water; and to the rushing wind will he be given."

He held out a hand, and one of his warriors placed a torch in his fist. He turned to face the pyre. Branwen stood shivering at his side.

Her father turned to her. "Daughter, you were with our son when the life left him," he said. "It is only fitting that you should kindle his journey into the Land Beyond the Summer Stars."

Branwen found herself gripping the torch, the wood rough and cold beneath her fingers. The flames leaped and spat in the wind, as if the fire were trying to escape.

"Go," Lady Alis murmured to Branwen. "Don't think of yourself; think only of Geraint."

Branwen's legs shook as she took the first steps toward the foot of the ladder. The heat of the flames drew tears from her smarting eyes as she began to climb. The ladder seemed to stretch up to the clouds. She climbed rung by rung, clinging on with one hand as the wind picked at her clothes and pinched her body with cruel, chill fingers.

She would never reach the top of the ladder. She would be climbing forever, chilled by the wind, scorched by flame, a pain like knives in her heart, her limbs water-weak, her mind clouded in a red fog. This was worse than the terror she had endured in the clearing. This was worse than seeing her brother cut down. Worse than watching the bloody ax swinging at her head.

But she had to do her duty by her brother, light the oil-soaked logs under his bier and help him on his way to the Land of Forever.

She came to the top of the pyre, walking carefully on the creaking timbers to where he lay. Gold disks covered his eyes, and a gold circlet was on his forehead. Branwen stood gazing down at him for a long while. She could smell the oil that had been poured over wood and cloth. She was acutely aware of the watching crowd that stood far below her.

Geraint, wake up now! You're frightening me! Geraint! This isn't funny anymore! Wake up!

"Branwen? What a strange dream I had! I dreamed that I was dead and that you were here to light my funeral pyre."

That is why I'm here. I'm sorry, Geraint. I'm sorry I didn't help.

"Don't weep, Branwen. There was nothing you could have done."

Filled with agony and loss and despair, Branwen thrust the torch into the piled wood and held it there. The oil-soaked kindling caught, and flames began to leap.

Branwen released the torch and stood up straight, her eyes fixed on Geraint's face.

You must have the courage to face what happened today and to live with it in your heart and to use the memory of it to grow and be strong.

"Good-bye, Geraint," she whispered.

She turned as the flames leaped and with slow, deliberate steps climbed down to the ground. She stood between her parents as the rim of the sun climbed above the eastern hills and the flames of Geraint ap Griffith's funeral pyre were turned in an instant to burnished gold.

7

THE FIRE BURNED fiercely all through the morning, the smoke swelling upward like the blooming of a dark and dreadful flower. As the sun stood at the top of the sky, its disk pale and weak through the smoke, the great mass of timber suddenly caved in on itself with a shower of sparks.

At twilight, Branwen stood alone on the ramparts, watching small flames licking among the blackened remains of the pyre. She kept her lonely vigil into the darkest part of the night when the embers glowed as red as dragon-breath in the dale.

Branwen was shaken out of sleep by a hand on her shoulder.

"My lady."

Groggy from too brief a time in bed, Branwen

turned over, pushing off the hay-stuffed quilt. She stared up into the eyes of Inga, an elderly Saxon woman who had served Branwen's family for as long as she could remember.

"The lord and lady would have you attend them in the great chamber," Inga said with long-practiced mildness and respect.

Branwen sat up, knuckling her eyes, wondering what her mother and father wanted of her. She had a blissful moment of forgetfulness before cruel memory stabbed into her mind. The world she knew had ended. Geraint was dead. She was going to be sent away.

She stared at the old woman, sparrow-thin in her shapeless gray dress, her hair like cobwebs on her shoulders, her face pinched and anxious. A Saxon woman—a woman of a race that Branwen hated above all others.

"How long have you been with us, Inga?" she asked.

"Many, many years, my lady."

"Did you bear sons before you were captured?"

Inga's brow wrinkled as if she was trying hard to remember the life she had led before captivity. Branwen got up and picked some clothes from the chest at the foot of her bed. Inga had still not replied.

"Well?" Branwen demanded. "Did you have children or not?"

"I had a son, long ago . . . but he was killed in battle, my lady."

Good! I'm glad! Branwen thought.

Branwen looked into the old woman's frightened face. The malice she had been feeling melted away, leaving her feeling empty and sick at heart. Was this what true hatred was like—the need to lash out at people simply because they were born Saxon? Even people as helpless as Inga?

"Go away," she said. "Tell them I am coming."

She must look her best for her audience with her mother and father.

It was her duty.

She put on her white shift with its long, narrow sleeves and then chose a woolen gown of pale olive, dyed by club moss and greenweed. The gown was fastened at either shoulder by a pair of golden brooches and then bound at the waist by a silken sash—an expensive adornment that had been a betrothal gift from Hywel's parents all those years ago on the only occasion that they had met.

As was the custom, Branwen attached a few special personal objects to the sash, among them a golden hair comb given to her by her mother. She seldom spent much time dressing her hair, but she liked to keep her mother's gift close by. She also had a small leather pouch with some pieces of crystal in it—crystal that Geraint had found for her in the mountains. The glossy stones were translucent white with a sparkling surface; and if they were held to the sun in exactly the right way, a flickering rainbow could be seen at each crystal's heart. There was also a pouch that contained two firestones and a scrap of dried moss for kindling. The final item was a small golden key that her father had given her on her tenth birthday. It had been found in the ruins of an old Roman temple. Branwen liked to imagine what the key might be for, what treasures might be discovered if the lock it fitted were ever found.

It was still early and the air was cool as Branwen stepped from her room into the main chamber of the Great Hall. The doors were open, and the courtyard beyond was striped with long shadows from the slanting sun. Her father and mother were seated on the double throne. Several warriors of the court stood close by; and Prince Llew was with them, seated on a chair brought in especially and flanked by a few of his own men.

Branwen was aware of how plain and simple her people's clothes seemed against the opulence of Prince Llew's and his men's. But the prince was a good man and a true friend to her father, and she felt no envy of his wealth and power. Besides, she had a fierce pride and loyalty to her home and to her parents; after all, they lived on the disputed borderlands of Brython—they had more important concerns than jewels and finery.

"Branwen, come here," Lady Alis said, holding out her hand. Branwen saw that the sword of the House of Owain hung from her mother's belt. Branwen knew her mother had wielded that deadly weapon in the wars that had raged across Brython before she herself had been born, but she had never seen it at her mother's hip before. It was an ominous sign of the conflict that was coming.

Branwen stood in front of her parents, knowing that her fate was already decided. Waiting for the hammer-blow to fall.

"Most of our riders have returned," her father told her. "The news is not good, Branwen. I had hoped to send you on the direct road south, but bands of Saxon marauders have been seen all the way from here to Hen Drewyn and beyond."

"Let no one be in any doubt that Oswald is mustering an army," said Prince Llew. "These raids are intended to test our defenses."

"And each day they carry off more weapons and cattle," Lady Alis added. "By this thievery they would weaken us and strengthen themselves—using our own weapons against us, their army made strong on our meat so that they would swallow us in one gulp as the hunting owl swallows a mouse." Her fingers gripped the arm of the throne till her knuckles were white. "But they will find us a hard morsel to get down!"

"Am I to stay, then?" Branwen asked, a gleam of hope coming into her mind.

"It is clear that the direct way southward is too dangerous to attempt," her father said. "But there are other roads that may be less perilous." Branwen's spirits sank. There was to be no reprieve.

"Prince Llew has agreed to take you over the mountains to his own land," her father continued. "You will reside for a few days in the citadel of Doeth Palas. And when the next party of traders leaves for Gwent, you will accompany it on the safer roads to the west of the mountains."

"Have no fear, Princess Branwen," said Prince Llew. "You will find a warm welcome in Doeth Palas. My daughters will be glad to share their chamber with you while you are under my roof." He looked at Lady Alis. "And for a brief time perhaps, my wife, the Lady Elain, will be as an aunt to your daughter before the princess goes south to her new life."

A roaring sound filled Branwen's ears. She thought she had been prepared; but now that it came to it, the idea of being torn from her home was almost unbearable. But she kept her emotions off her face as she turned to Prince Llew and gave a bow.

"Thank you for your kindness," she said, struggling to keep her voice level. "I hope I will not be a burden to you."

"A burden, Princess?" Llew replied with a smile. "Yes, you will be a burden—a burden of care that I am honored to take, the burden of the jewel of the House of Rhys."

Branwen bowed a little lower. "The honor is mine, my lord."

"Then it is settled," said Prince Griffith. "Prince Llew will be departing at dawn tomorrow, Branwen. Make sure you are ready."

"I will, Father." Branwen turned and walked slowly down the length of the chamber. She clenched her fists at her sides until her nails dug into her palms, but her stride never faltered until she came to the door of her own room. She stepped inside and closed the door. The air was thick with a silence like deep, cold water.

Branwen sank to her knees, her head falling into her hands.

No! No! No!

Branwen sat cross-legged on the hay-filled mattress that lay on the rush-strewn earth floor. She watched with little interest as Inga took garments from the wooden trunk that stood at the foot of her bed.

"I'll take that," she said of a linen shift. "Yes, that can go." It was a yellow woolen cloak with a cowl, warm enough for the bitterest of winters. As Inga folded and packed the cloak, a fresh wave of grief beat over Branwen's spirit; she had last worn that cloak in the deep snows of winter, wading waist high with Geraint and many others, shouting in plumes of white breath and beating swords on shields and spoons on iron pans to scare off the wolf packs that a raging hunger had driven down from the mountains.

The items she approved were folded into a smaller

chest that would accompany her on her journey.

"All that I leave you may take for your own," she told Inga.

"Thank you, my lady," Inga said, her face revealing her surprise at this unexpected generosity. Her bony fingers traced over a woolen tunic. "This will keep the chills out, my lady."

"Don't bother thanking me," Branwen said. "I shan't be needing them. I won't be coming back anytime soon."

"Will you not, my lady?"

Branwen looked into Inga's timid eyes. "I suppose I will be allowed to come here with my husband now and then to visit, once the Saxons are defeated and the roads are safe again," she said dully. "But that could be years from now, and even then the garth won't be my *home* anymore. My home will be in Gwent." An odd thought entered her mind. "You were taken from your home, weren't you, Inga?" she said. "Do you hate us for doing that?"

The woman's eyes widened. Her mouth opened and closed a few times, and her thin fingers plucked nervously at the tunic. Branwen couldn't tell whether the question had confused her or whether she was simply too frightened to give a truthful answer.

"Oh, never mind," Branwen said. "I daresay I already know."

"Yes, my lady. Thank you, my lady." Inga shuffled about, picking up the discarded clothes while

Branwen watched her.

Lady Alis came into the room with a bundle of cloth in her arms. Inga dropped to her knees with her head bowed low.

"Continue with your work," Lady Alis said.

"The packing is almost done," Branwen told her mother.

"I have gifts here for you to give to Lady Elain and the two princesses," Lady Alis said, holding out the bundle of fine violet cloth.

Branwen looked curiously at it—there was enough cloth to make a gown or a light summer cloak. Enfolded in it were a pair of golden brooches encrusted with deep red garnets and a long, silver spoon. "The cloth is for Lady Elain; the other things are for the princesses," Lady Alis said. "Meredith is a year older than you; and I would suggest you give her the spoon, as she will understand its value. Her sister, Romney, is fourteen—old enough to appreciate the brooches, I think."

"Have you ever met them?" Branwen asked.

Lady Alis thought for a moment. "You were one year old the last time I was in Doeth Palas. Meredith was a toddler, and Lady Elain was a moon or so from giving birth to the little one." She looked keenly at Branwen. "If you're asking me what kind of companions they'll be, I can't tell you. But if they are anything like Lady Elain, then they will be both sophisticated and cultured." She paused before continuing. "Doeth Palas is a much grander place than Garth Milain, Branwen; you must try not to allow yourself to be overawed by it. Remember that you are a princess of Cyffin Tir, the child of a long and noble line of warriors."

"I'll try," Branwen said. She was wondering whether she would get on with the two princesses.

"Good." Her mother put the bundle of lilac cloth in Branwen's lap. "But I don't think you'll need this," she said, slipping Branwen's slingshot out of her waist-sash. "I doubt very much whether Lady Elain will give you leave to go hunting."

Branwen frowned. "Why not?"

"Because in Doeth Palas that is not a thing that princesses do," Lady Alis said.

"Please let me keep it," Branwen begged. "Just to remind me of . . . *here*."

Her mother looked into her face for a long time, then handed back the slingshot. "Keep it hidden," she warned. "Lady Elain will not understand."

Branwen clutched at the soft strip of leather. "I will," she promised.

Her mother touched her hand gently against Branwen's cheek. "I know you will," she said, and Branwen saw tears shining in her eyes as she turned and left the room.

A few moments later, the door opened again and Prince Griffith strode in. "Well, Branwen?" he said, smiling at her as she got to her feet. "Is all well with you?"

"All is well, Father," she replied. It was rare for the prince to come to her private chamber.

He turned to Inga. "Woman—go, now. Finish your work later."

Clutching her bundle of clothing, Inga shuffled from the room.

Prince Griffith stood awkwardly in the middle of the floor. Branwen was puzzled. It was unusual for her father to seem so distracted . . . so uncertain.

"Father, is there . . . ," she began.

"Branwen," he said suddenly. "I would not have you leave with anger in your heart." He touched his chest. "Anger for me, I mean."

Branwen lifted her eyebrows. "I don't feel anger toward you, Father," she said.

"But you would not marry the boy, Hywel, if you had your choice, I think."

She gave a half smile. "If I had my choice, I wouldn't marry anyone at all," she replied. "At least, not yet."

The prince frowned. "What would you do?"

She took a step toward him and looked up into his troubled face, knowing she could not say anything that might hurt him or cause him concern. "I would do my duty to the House of Rhys," she said. "I would make you and Lady Alis proud of me. Even Hywel ap Murig may be bearable as a husband once I've knocked him into shape."

"You are your mother's daughter!" the prince said,

almost laughing as he looked down at her.

"I am," Branwen said proudly. "And I am your daughter too." She gave him a questioning look. "Mother told me she didn't like you very much when you both first met. She said you were sulky and wouldn't talk to her."

Her father looked at her in astonishment and then smiled and opened his arms. Branwen stepped forward and pressed herself against his chest, feeling his arms strong around her back.

"She spoke the truth," he said. "But it was not all one-sided. I doubt that she told you of the time she became so angry that she threw stones at me." He laughed. "I had the bruises for many long days. Your skill with a slingshot and your love of the forest remind me of Alis ap Owain when she was much younger." He held her face between his hands. "I have lost one child, Branwen. I could not bear to lose another. I send you south to keep you safe. You understand that, don't you?"

"Yes, Father," she said, hugging him tightly. "I do understand."

Branwen stood in Geraint's room in the chill time before dawn. She was dressed in her shift and holding a beeswax candle. The candle burned pure and clear in the stillness of the night, lighting up the corners of the room and revealing her brother's familiar things. His mattress on the floor in one corner, and three chests: one for clothes, one for other possessions, and the third for his sword and battle gear.

Branwen knelt at the third chest and heaved it open. A gray cloth covered the things within. She drew it aside. She ran her hands gently over her brother's bow and the quiver of arrows. She could almost hear the whine of a loosed arrow, the singing of the string and the *thunk* as the barbed shaft struck its target. With the bow and quiver of arrows, lying half-wrapped in a scrap of cloth, was his hunting knife—as long from tip to base as her forearm. It had a brown bone handle pierced by iron rivets that held the slender, triangular blade in place.

She picked up the knife, remembering how she had held it in her two fists as she had sat over Geraint's dead body. She thought back to the first time Geraint had put the knife into her hands, and how he had taught her to gut and dress deer and grouse and salmon. How she had raised the bloodied knife for his approval, and how he had smiled and praised her.

Long, long ago.

She laid the knife in her lap and continued to look through his possessions. A dark green cloak with the golden brooches still attached. A leather fighting jerkin, sewn with hundreds of small iron disks to ward off sword blows. Thick leather boots with thongs that tied to the knee. His round, wooden shield and his sword. The sword was an old weapon, simple and functional, the leather-bound hilt worn from generations of hands, the dull blade notched and scratched.

Branwen had been struck with envy when her father had presented him with the sword on his tenth birthday.

Guard it well, my son, for it was borne by me in my youth and by my father before me and by his father before him and by his grandsire and his father's grandsire.

For four years Branwen had waited impatiently for her tenth birthday, convinced that she too would receive a sword. After all, her mother was a great warrior—why should she not be given some prized weapon? The lavish gifts of clothing and jewelry that she received on the longed-for day did nothing to stem the bitter tears that she shed alone in her room that night.

I am a warrior! I am! I will be a warrior when I grow up. No one can stop me!

Branwen smiled bleakly as she gazed at her dead brother's sword.

Did I really believe that?

She placed the ownerless objects back into the chest and closed the heavy lid. Then she realized that the hunting knife was still in her lap. She picked it up and turned the blade so that the flickering candle-light shone on the polished iron. She ran a fingertip along the blade, feeling its keen edge. Her parents had no need of one more knife; why should she not take it? She wrapped the knife in the length of cloth and stood up, holding it close as she left the room.

She returned to her own room. Closing the door, she walked over to the traveling chest. She lifted the lid and pushed the knife deep in among her clothing.

She would keep the knife secret and safe. And maybe one day she would have the opportunity to look into the face of the Saxon raider who killed her brother and thrust the blade deep into his murderous heart.

8

THE FOLLOWING DAY dawned bright and fair; Branwen sat astride her bay stallion with a warm south breeze in her hair and the rising sun as fierce as flames in her eyes. She had ridden Stalwyn up onto the hill that overlooked Garth Milain—the same hill from which only a few brief days ago she had sat and watched the children playing by the pool of white water. But her mood was so changed from the last time that she might have been a different person.

Prince Llew's warriors and wagons were gathering at the foot of the sloping pathway. Branwen tried to fix in her mind every detail of what she was seeing.

Geraint's pyre lay in the dale in the deep shadow of Garth Milain: no more now than a black stain from which thin wisps of faint smoke rose and drifted. Her eyes followed the hazy trails of smoke high into the sky. "Why did you let yourself be killed?" she shouted into the air.

The breeze brought her no reply.

A tiny movement caught her attention. At first she thought it was just part of the smoke—a fleck of ash or soot borne upward by the wind. But as she watched, it circled and descended, moving with a definite purpose.

A bird.

It cut slow arcs down the sky.

A falcon.

Branwen could make out the narrow, scythe-shaped wings, colored like wet slate, and the dark-hooded head and cream-colored chest and throat. It was an adult male, its eyes like bright black beads and its curved beak like a splinter of flint.

It came at her out of the white disk of the sun. She suddenly realized that it was not going to swerve aside and she ducked with a cry as the falcon swept by, its claws grazing her back.

She twisted in the saddle, her heart thumping. The falcon adjusted its wings and flew across the face of the forest. Its yellow claws reached down; and a moment later it landed on the same low branch that the wood pigeon had perched on three days before, when Geraint had grabbed Branwen from behind and dragged her into the forest.

Was that only three days ago?

It felt so very much longer.

The bird turned and stared at her, its head held high, its eyes filled with sunlight.

Branwen had never known falcons to behave in that way. Why had it flown at her? And why was it staring like that?

Her mother and father owned hunting falcons, but Branwen knew them all and this was not one of them. It had none of the jesses or leather leashes that would be tied to the legs of tamed birds. It must be wild.

The falcon moved from leg to leg, lowering its head and ruffling its feathers.

She swung down from the saddle and began to walk along the slope toward the bird. It lifted its head, its eyes still on her, but now with a haughtier look. It let out a series of shrill cries. Branwen expected at any moment that it would rise from the branch in a flurry of wings and go soaring off into the sky.

But it didn't move.

"Have you escaped from somewhere?" she murmured, stopping at the foot of the tree. She couldn't believe that this was not a tame bird. A wild falcon would never allow anyone to come so close.

The falcon gave two sharp, carping caws.

Branwen reached up, and to her amazement the bird allowed her to run her fingers gently down its flanks. "There now," she crooned. "Who do you belong to? I know you're not one of ours. Have you come from far away?"

The bird gave a single croak.

Branwen lifted her arm higher and held her wrist out toward the bird. It spread its wings, scooped the air, and made the jump to her wrist. The needle-sharp talons bit into her skin as the bird settled. The creature was obviously used to being with people.

"So you *are* tame," Branwen whispered.

Only high-born families kept falcons; the bird must have come from a neighboring cantref. But that didn't explain how it could have slipped its leashes—unless it had been set free on purpose.

"Are you looking for a new master?"

The falcon let out another single caw.

Branwen half smiled. It was almost as if the bird was responding to her words.

The high-pitched floating call of a horn came up to her. She looked over her shoulder. "I'm sorry, but I have to go now," she told the falcon. "I'm afraid we'll never see each other again. I'm going a long, long way from here." She swallowed hard. "I don't know if I'll ever come back."

The bird fluttered from her wrist back to the branch.

There were tiny beads of blood on her wrist from the pressure of the bird's claws. She turned and walked back to where Stalwyn was waiting. She mounted the horse, looking back to see the bird still on the branch, still staring at her. "Good-bye," she called.

She nudged Stalwyn with her heels, and he began to walk down the hillside. She could see her mother and father with Llew's men. They were waiting to see her off.

She shivered. But she would not cry; she wanted their final memories of her to be ones they could cherish.

Summoning up every scrap of courage, she rode her horse down to the ordeal of parting.

9

THE PROCESSION OF horsemen and wagons left the dappled green shade of the Great Forest Way and began to climb High Saddle Way. The dense trees fell back on either side, the packed-earth path widening as it forged its way up the steep slopes, the ground baked hard by the summer sun.

They had been traveling for half the day and were now beginning the series of steep climbs that would, by evening, take them up onto the forested mountainside. Branwen rode quietly among the men, lost in sadness. The parting with her parents had been harder than she had even imagined it would be. She had not looked back; that would have been too agonizing. She had stared between her horse's ears, her eyes fixed on the ground in front of her while the images of her mother and her father and of Garth

Milain raged like fire in her mind.

"Do not grieve, my lady." The voice shook her out of her lonely reverie. She turned her head. Captain Angor had ridden his tall, black horse alongside hers. "Your brother died a noble death," he said. "You should be proud."

"Yes, I suppose I should," she replied. "I am proud of him. But I wish . . ." Her voice faded. *I wish he had been less brave! I wish he had kept himself hidden in the forest till the Saxons had gone away. I wish he were still alive!*

"What do you wish, my lady?"

"Nothing," Branwen said. "I wish for nothing."

"I met your brother once, a few years ago," the captain said. "He came to Doeth Palas with your father to meet with the prince. He would have been about twelve years old. A big lad for his age. Very strong, I remember."

"Yes, he was strong," Branwen said. "But not very quick. I could always beat him in a race."

"There was something about him," Angor said, his eyes narrowing as he gazed into the distance. "A kind of strength, unusual in so young a lad. I saw it in his eyes. I remember thinking he would make a good prince when his time came—a good leader of men. There was one night in particular. We were feasting, and your father asked him to recite part of one of the *Songs of the Eleven Heroes* for us. He stood there, so proud and tall with his back to the firelight.

61

Every word rang out clear to the roof beams. It was as if he were living the tale as he told it. I've never forgotten that."

"He loved the old tales," Branwen said with a faint smile, remembering how Geraint would eagerly recite the traditional stories of gallant warfare and heroic deeds. She looked at Angor, suddenly glad of the opportunity to talk about her brother. Perhaps it was because this man was a stranger to her that she felt able to open up to him.

"He used to tell me old nursery stories, too," Branwen said. "There were so many of them. Stories about the pooka of the forest, who rode to war on dragonflies with acorn-cup helmets and swords made from rose thorns. And about the coblyn who live in caves and the goraig of the rivers and the lakes and the gwyllion who dwell high up in the mountains." She glanced sideways at Angor. "He even told me about the Shining Ones."

Angor frowned. "Your father allowed such tales?" he said.

"My father didn't know," Branwen replied. "Besides, Geraint knew that I liked to be scared by his stories of the Old Gods."

The Shining Ones, Branwen! The terrible, glorious spirits of nature that watched over the land of our ancestors. Wild as a thunderstorm, dangerous as a rockfall in the mountains, merciless as deepest midwinter! Rhiannon of the Spring. Govannon of the Wood. Merion of the Stones.

Caradoc of the North Wind. The lost gods, banished for five hundred years. The forgotten ones. The forbidden ones.

"All the same," Angor said grimly. "You would be wise not to speak of this again. It will not honor your brother's memory if people knew he talked about such things."

"How so?" Branwen asked, surprised by the uneasy tone in Angor's voice.

He leaned toward her, speaking in a hoarse whisper. "It is unwise to name the Old Powers," he said. "Let sleeping gods lie, my lady. Trust me in this. It is for the best." He kicked his horse into a trot and went riding up to the head of the column, leaving Branwen gazing after him, mystified by his dark words.

"Look at that falcon!"

"He's been following us since we entered the forest."

"It's a wild bird; there are no trappings that I can see."

"By the saints! If he flies any closer I'll be able to snatch him out of the air!"

Branwen turned at the sudden chorus of voices at her back.

"He's a bold one, for sure, if he's truly wild."

She looked up, following the gaze of the excited horsemen.

A falcon was dancing on the air, rising high and then turning and stooping with folded wings. There were no other birds in the sky, and it was as if the falcon was playing at the kill for the sheer joy of it. At the lowest part of each rushing descent, the bird would twist and turn like a scrap caught by the wind before climbing again and soaring on wide, sickle-shaped wings.

The ghost of a smile touched Branwen's lips. It was the same falcon that she had met on the hillside that morning. She could not have said how she knew, but she was certain that it was. How strange that it should be following them.

On a sudden impulse, Branwen stood in her stir-rups and raised her arm toward the bird. "Come to me! Come!" she called.

She almost laughed aloud when she saw the falcon spiraling down toward her. At the last moment it cupped the air with its wings, its claws outstretched, and came to land quite gently on her wrist.

"By Saint Cadog, I have never seen such a thing!" said one of the riders. "The princess is a bird tamer!"

Branwen was aware of the men watching her in amazement as she lowered her arm. "Hello, my friend," she said to the bird. "I didn't expect to see you again."

It stared at her, its black eyes jeweled with dia-monds of light. It was odd how gently it gripped her wrist with its fearsome talons—falconers usually required thick leather wristbands to prevent injury, yet Branwen only felt a slight pricking where the points of the long claws dug into her flesh.

"What is going on?" It was Captain Angor's voice.

"Lady Branwen called a wild falcon down to her wrist, Captain!" exclaimed one of the men. "I've never seen the like!"

Angor rode up to Branwen. "Is this your own bird, my lady?" he asked. "Has it followed you from Garth Milain?"

"No," Branwen said. "I've seen it once before, but it doesn't belong to me."

"Then it is not tame?" Angor asked sharply.

"I don't know. I don't think so."

The captain urged his horse forward and reached out for the falcon with his gloved hand. Shrieking raucously, the falcon took to the air.

"You startled him!" Branwen said, frowning at the captain. "Why did you do that?"

"By your leave, my lady," he said. "A wild bird cannot be trusted. He could have injured you."

"He would not have harmed me."

"Nevertheless, my lady, your safety lies in our hands," Angor said with quiet authority. "I would not have you delivered to your husband with half your face stripped bare to the bone."

The captain turned his horse and rode back to the front of the procession. "If the bird returns, the man whose arrow shoots it from the sky will be rewarded!" he called.

Branwen looked up anxiously. She understood Angor's concern for her, but she didn't want the bird killed.

To her relief, the sky was clear. The strange falcon was gone.

Higher and higher they climbed, the road running along the rising slope of a valley that lay between the flanks of two great hills. The looming slopes were striped with green and brown and capped with rows of rugged rock like an exposed spine. Trees clung to the southern slopes—forests that Branwen had never seen before. She was now beyond the world that she knew, and in happier circumstances the beauty and the wildness of the unfolding landscape would have filled her with joy.

If only Geraint could have been at her side. If only this were a merry adventure—brother and sister riding together into the mountains. If only there was the chance of turning back and arriving at Garth Milain just as the evening fires were kindled.

Mother! Father! We've seen such things!

She pushed the thoughts away. They only brought her pain. She must think of the future . . . no matter how little she desired it.

Prince Llew brought them to a halt for the night on a plateau overlooked by a rearing escarpment of bare rock. The men set the horses free to graze and then laid fires and kindled them with firestones and set tripods to cook the meats they had brought with them.

Once she had seen that Stalwyn was being looked after, Branwen helped with the meal. She speared joints of meat on iron skewers and joined in with the others to turn them slowly as the juices dripped. The delicious aromas of roasting chicken and pork and beef spread through the camp, along with the enticing smell of the flat loaves made warm on the stones that ringed the fires.

Branwen sat at the fireside, wrapped in her cloak, staring into the leaping flames, drinking from a wooden bowl and gnawing a roasted chicken leg.

Prince Llew came over and crouched at her side. "Is all well with you, Branwen?" he asked. "Do you have all that you need?"

"Yes, thank you, my lord," she replied.

"You look weary," he said. "You have had little rest over the past few days."

"I am tired," Branwen admitted.

"I cannot offer you pillows or a mattress for your bed," Prince Llew said. "But you may sleep in one of the wagons, if you wish."

"No, thank you," Branwen replied. "I'll be fine here."

"Well, good night then, my child," said Prince Llew. "If you need anything, speak with Captain Angor. He will see to your comfort."

"I will." Branwen watched the prince move off through his men.

She threw the bone into the fire and then moved a little way off. She wrapped her cloak around herself and lay down, pulling a fur pelt over herself for warmth, her head pillowed on her arm.

Vivid memories came spewing into her mind. Blood and cloven flesh and leaping flames. She tried to blot them out by focusing on the present, on the fact that she was on the first stage of the long journey south to start a strange, new life. She struggled to draw up memories of Hywel ap Murig, but the only image in her mind was of a podgy, spiteful face above rich silk clothing. Was she really on her way to be married to him? It was impossible to grasp.

Utterly impossible!

Eventually, she fell asleep to the crackle of the fires and the low murmur of voices.

10

WHEN BRANWEN AWOKE it was a cool, damp morning. During the night, heavy clouds had come humping in like bloated gray monsters, wallowing low in the sky and cramming their huge bodies up against the mountain peaks. A thick fog slumped in the lowlands, dense as gray water, trickling through the trees and rolling ponderously along the valleys. The high passes seemed to float like cloud-ridden islands on a phantom sea.

The men were already stirring, cutting bread and cheese for the morning meal, drawing ale and buttermilk from barrels. Branwen took a hunk of bread, some strong white cheese, and a cup of buttermilk.

She had slept well; and despite the gloomy look of the morning, she felt refreshed and alert. She had dreamed about Geraint. She could remember almost nothing about it, except that he had been happy and full of life. They had been alone in the forest, and he had recited a poem for her. The only words she recalled were: *Brush back the ivy from your dark locks glowering.* She had no idea what it meant, but the memory of it lightened her heart. She ate her breakfast with unexpected relish, the cheese strong and tangy in her mouth, the buttermilk thick and sweet.

Before long they were winding their way up toward the dank, gray underbellies of the clouds. At first Branwen rode with Prince Llew, but she had no appetite for conversation and so she asked if it would be all right for her to have some time to herself. She didn't mention her dream to him, but she felt she'd be better able to recapture its fleeting happiness if she was alone. The prince agreed; and Branwen gradually fell back through the ranks of horsemen, wrapped in thoughtful silence, trying to recapture the comforting images that had come to her in the night.

Now she was at the hindmost, following the last wagon. She felt sad, but strangely at peace, her heart still warmed by the memories she had conjured of her beautiful dream. It almost felt as if Geraint were close by, his unseen presence soothing her wounded soul.

Occasionally, she looked around, half hoping for a sight of the strange falcon; but if it was still trailing them, it was keeping out of sight. It seemed unlikely that it would follow them once they had pushed up into the cloud. She watched as the foremost riders disappeared into the mist. It was startling how quickly the gray blanket swallowed up men and horses and wagons. They were there, solid and alive; then there was a moment when they were just gray shapes, featureless outlines in the fog—and then there was nothing.

She heard Angor's muffled voice calling as she entered the mist. "Keep together. . . . The way is narrow and the falls are steep. . . . Do not stray from the path."

The back of the last wagon vanished and Branwen was alone, facing a wall of absolute nothingness. Her horse hesitated, unsettled by the blinding fog. She patted his neck.

"Come on, Stalwyn, my brave boy, there's nothing to be frightened of," she said aloud as they rode into the fog bank.

She gave a gasp. The fog was unexpectedly chill. She saw white steam spurting from Stalwyn's nostrils—but beyond the animal's head, the world had become invisible. She pulled her cloak tight around her shoulders as her own breath billowed.

She could still hear voices and the rumble and creak of wheels ahead of her. She tapped her heels against the horse's sides, urging him on, wanting to catch up with the others as quickly as possible.

She would not have been able to say exactly when the sounds of movement faded into an eerie silence; one moment she could faintly hear men's voices calling among the roll of wagon wheels and the thud of hooves—then she could not.

She kicked a little more firmly at Stalwyn's sides

and the horse broke into a reluctant trot, his head down and his ears flat back. Branwen leaned low, but she could see nothing below them. Stalwyn was wading in fog to his fetlocks.

She rose in the saddle and called out: "Wait!" She listened for a reply, but none came. "Wait for me!"

Nothing.

She brought Stalwyn to a halt and dismounted, coming around to the animal's head, holding the reins and stroking the long muzzle. "It's all right, boy," she said. "There's nothing to worry about. But we need to be careful. Captain Angor said the path gets narrow up here."

Gripping the reins, she walked forward into the fog, Stalwyn following.

Branwen wrapped the reins several times around her wrist; if she lost her footing, at least she would have something to hang onto. Every few steps she paused and shouted. Then listened.

Shout again. Listen again. Then plod onward, her eyes aching from trying to make out anything through the fog.

Pause.

Shout.

Listen.

What was that?

A faint sound, no louder than the pattering of rain on leaves. But there was no rain, and the air was oppressively still.

"Who's there?"

This time she was certain: It was the sound of running footsteps. Something was moving through the fog away to her right. She was about to call out again when she thought better of it.

If it were a person, then surely the individual would have heard her already. If it were an animal, a stag or some other large creature blundering blindly through the fog, then calling to it would be pointless and following it would only take her away from the path.

She patted Stalwyn's neck. "What should we do, boy?" she murmured, rubbing her face against his velvet muzzle. "Keep moving and hope we don't lose the path, or stay here and pray the sun burns the clouds off so we can see where we're going?"

Stalwyn snorted nervously and stamped a hoof.

"No, I don't know either," she said. "And I don't much like the options."

But doing nothing was not in her nature, so she wrapped the reins tightly around her hand again and walked on through the fog. She sang a snatch of an old song as she walked, hoping that the sound of her voice would help to keep Stalwyn calm.

> *Owls fly homeward nightly*
> *in numbers greater than we see here, my child*
> *Filling the skies like rain-clouds*
> *the rumor of their passing is mighty, my child*
> *The mountains hold the sky up*
> *without them our crops would be crushed by*
>   *the weight, my child*

Our hilltop fortress calls us
beware for the owls are circling low, my
child . . .

She stopped singing. It was a gloomy and mysterious song, but she had always enjoyed hearing it in the Great Hall of Garth Milain, the words sending shivers up her spine. But out here in the fog, the haunting melody and the curious words made her ill at ease. She imagined monstrous owls were gliding silently just out of sight, their malevolent eyes bright for hunting, their beaks sharp as new-forged iron.

"Perhaps I should have chosen a more cheerful song, eh, boy?" she said, speaking aloud for her own comfort as much as for the horse's. She drew closer to Stalwyn, her arm curled under his neck, her cheek against the warm side of his head.

She stopped short. Over to her right, a pale flicker of light had shone for a moment through the fog. As she watched, the long, slender glow appeared and disappeared as it moved away from her—as if the light was passing behind trees.

Someone running with a lighted torch?

An overpowering urgency filled her: She had to follow the light. It would lead her to safety. She knew it would. She peered into the fog with narrowed eyes, waiting for the light to reappear.

There it was!

Farther off now—moving away from her.

"No!"

She tugged at Stalwyn's reins, pulling the horse after her. They were passing between trees, the trunks like pillars of smoke on either side.

It was not a torch—the light was too pure and too steady.

And then the light was gone.

Branwen staggered to a halt, gasping for breath. Trees loomed like ghosts all around her. She gave a stifled scream of frustration, her hands knotting into fists. She was brought back to her senses by Stalwyn's nervous snorting. The horse was skittish, his eyes rolling and his head jerking back against the reins.

"Easy boy," she murmured. "There's nothing to be frightened of." She lowered her voice to the merest whisper. "Nothing except that I've acted like a moonstruck hare and led us right off the path."

She couldn't believe she had been so foolish. What had possessed her to follow that light? She looked back the way they had come, hoping that somehow their passage through the fog would have left some trace. It hadn't.

She pulled her cloak around her shoulders and dropped down to sit cross-legged on the ground, one hand raised to hold Stalwyn's reins. She would sit there either till the cloud lifted a little and gave her some chance of finding her way back to the path—or until a better idea occurred to her.

11

B RANWEN HAD NO idea how much time went by, but gradually she became aware that the air felt a little less chill and that the light seemed to be growing around her—not as if the clouds of fog were thinning, but as if they were being illuminated, turned from gray to shining silver by the invisible sun as it climbed into the sky.

She gave a gasp of surprise as the phantom light reappeared.

It stood for a while, hovering about a slingshot's throw away between the ghostly trees. Branwen watched it suspiciously. She felt once more the urge to leap up and chase it, but this time she fought against it. The last thing she needed was to be drawn even farther from the path.

The light drifted closer, hovering just above the

ground. It seemed to be waiting. Tempting her.

"Go away!" Branwen scolded. "I'm not following you anymore."

The slender blade of light shivered and coiled. Branwen shuffled around on the ground so that the light was out of her field of vision.

It came wafting into the corner of her eye, floating across until it hung in front of her again, trembling and wavering, as if it was growing impatient.

"What are you?" Branwen shouted with a sudden annoyance. "Are you real or not? And if you're real, what do you want?"

She heard Stalwyn whickering with unease and felt the horse tugging at the reins.

Branwen stared the light down, willing it to disappear again.

"Are you a gwyllion?" she called. How strange it would be if that flickering light were a mountain-imp from one of Geraint's stories! When she'd assumed all her life that his nursery tales were pure nonsense.

"I don't care what you are," she shouted. "I will not follow you!"

And then the light vanished.

Branwen rubbed her eyes and stared.

Yes. It was gone.

But there were sounds now. So faint that she had to strain to catch them: furtive scurryings and rustlings, as if small creatures were hastening through the trees beyond the edge of vision. And then she heard voices—or something that sounded like voices. High voices calling from far away, and whispering voices from the treetops, and the rumor of low voices that seemed to come out of the ground beneath her.

It felt as though the fog-shrouded forest was holding its breath, waiting for something to happen. Branwen shivered, wishing she had her slingshot to hand, wishing Geraint's knife wasn't locked away in a chest on one of the lost wagons.

And then, just as it felt as if the world were about to crack open under the strain, a dark shape came winging out of the fog, so sudden and swift that Branwen let out a startled yell.

The falcon turned smoothly in the air, then came to land on the ground a little way off. It folded its wings and called to her.

"How did you get here?" Branwen gasped, scrambling to her feet. "Were you looking for me?"

It's just a bird—don't be so foolish!

The bird cawed again and took to the air, circling Branwen's head once before flying off into the fog.

Branwen began to follow, but Stalwyn pulled back on the reins and wouldn't move. The horse stamped hard with a hind hoof and shook his mane, his eyes wide with fear.

"The falcon will lead us true," Branwen said gently. "Come on now, don't be afraid."

Stalwyn allowed himself to be led forward.

"We're coming!" Branwen called.

She led the horse through the trees, expecting at any moment to see the falcon reappear through the fog or to hear its chiding calls, guiding her onward.

After a time she began to doubt that the bird would come back. She even began to doubt whether it had been *her* falcon at all. Her feet faltered.

Now what?

Sounds. Definite, clear sounds in the fog. Something large. The sounds of feet through the undergrowth and of arms brushing branches aside. She spun in the direction from which the sounds were coming. Feet and arms or hooves and antlers? There was only one way to find out; but if the sounds were being made by a man, who could it be and why was he here?

Branwen led Stalwyn to a tree and looped the horse's reins around a low branch. She called on all her wood-craft as she slipped silently between the trees.

She saw a dim shape in the fog.

A man. Definitely a man. She could see long, mousy, golden flecked hair, and a dark cloak that stretched over broad shoulders.

None of Prince Llew's men had such light-colored hair. There were people of Brython whose hair was light brown and even a few of ancient Viking descent who had hair as golden as a field of ripened corn, but it was the Saxons whose hair was predominantly fair.

A Saxon! Was he part of a band of raiders bold enough to try and cross the mountains? Or was he alone, lost in the fog as she was?

The man had come to a halt. She could see the shape of him like a lump of gray rock through the fog. She could hear him breathing hard. She could even see how his head turned from side to side, as though he was searching for a pathway. Or fresh Brythonic prey.

Branwen stooped and picked up a hefty length of broken branch. Gripping it between her hands, she moved forward, lifting the wooden club over her shoulder. Closer and closer she came to the man. His hair was light brown. His cloak was dark green, creased and dirt smeared.

"Saxon swine!" she hissed.

The man gasped, half turning. He received the full force of her blow on his shoulder. The branch broke in two as it hit him.

He stumbled forward with a shout of pain and vanished out of sight.

Panting, Branwen stood holding the remains of her weapon in one hand, staring into the fog and trying to work out what had happened to him.

She took a step forward and saw that the ground fell away at her feet, vanishing into a pool of thick fog. She stared down into the white gulf, her whole body shaking. Her blow had knocked the Saxon off a cliff.

"That was for Geraint!" she shouted down into the mist.

She heard groaning from close below. The fall

had not been as deep as she had hoped. The Saxon was still alive.

But there was something odd about the groans that came floating up to her. They didn't sound to her as if they came from a full-grown man.

A Saxon youth? A scout maybe, or a tracker? She knew that the raiding parties often sent young men out ahead of them to check the lay of the land and bring back news of easy prey.

Clutching the remains of her weapon, she began to slither down the cliff face. She could hear him gasping and groaning below her. And she could hear another sound, too. Water racing over stones.

She stepped into an icy stream, almost losing her balance as the stones shifted under her feet. Down here the fog was much thinner; and she could see the young man sitting up to his waist in the rushing stream, his pale hair plastered down over his face and a trail of red staining the water at his knee.

"I have a knife, you Saxon devil!" Branwen warned. "Surrender or I'll cut your throat where you sit!"

"And if I were a Saxon devil," spluttered the young man, "what makes you think I would understand a word that you just said?"

"Clearly you *do* understand me!" she growled. "So surrender or feel the blade of my knife across your throat. I *will* kill you if I have to." She hoped that she wouldn't be forced to put the threat to the test; Geraint's hunting knife was far from her reach. But she was ready to bring the branch down on the young man's head if he tried to attack her.

"I believe you would," the young man said. "But I'd prefer it if you didn't. I am unarmed, and I mean you no harm. Haven't you done sufficient damage to me by hitting me unawares and throwing me off a cliff? Isn't that enough without cutting my throat as well?"

Branwen glared at him. He seemed to be no older than she; but despite being waist deep in a mountain stream, she could tell that he was tall and powerfully built. He was dressed in simple peasant clothes that had been slept in too many times and were in need of patching. He spoke with an accent that she didn't recognize. She took a step toward him, the branch still raised in warning.

"I didn't hit you unawares," she said. "I called you a Saxon swine first."

The young man laughed softly, then winced and groaned again, clutching at his leg. "Swine I may be, mistress, but don't insult me further than that."

"I thought you were a raider," Branwen said, looking down to where his blood was running in the stream. "If that's not the case, then I'm sorry I hurt you."

"All's well, then," said the young man, looking up at her with a glint of dark humor in his gaze. He had a pleasant face under his wet hair, enlivened by bright, hazel eyes. "A heartfelt apology is as good as a poultice to a broken limb," he continued. "I'll just spring to my feet now and be off on my merry way. Or not."

"Can I do anything to help?" Branwen asked, intrigued that he had answered her back so boldly when he was at such a disadvantage and obviously in some pain.

"That you can, mistress," the young man said. "But only if you have a shred of woodcraft about you. Otherwise you're useless to me."

"I have woodcraft," Branwen said. "Tell me what you want."

"I will need the root of the eringo plant, and a few berries and leaves of mistletoe together with a handful of oak leaves," the young man said. "You'll find the mistletoe and the oak leaves together."

"I know that," Branwen said. She dropped her branch and paddled back to the cliff face. She looked back at the young man. He was watching her with obvious curiosity.

Not a Saxon, then—but not a local boy either, judging from that accent.

He grimaced in pain and made a hurrying gesture with one hand.

"I'm going!" she called back as she began to climb. "I'll be as quick as I can."

She slithered back down the slope to find him sitting on a boulder at the edge of the stream, still surrounded by thin drifts of mist. Through a rend in his leggings, she could see a long, thin cut that ran from his knee to halfway down his shin. Blood was running into his boot. Next time perhaps she would make sure of her quarry *before* attacking.

"Will these do?" she asked, handing him the root and the berries and leaves.

"They look fine," said the young man. "Now I need two rocks. One should be flat, about the size of a small loaf of bread. The other should be rounded and as big as my fist. Can you do that for me?"

"Of course." Branwen hunted along the shallows of the stream and soon found two rocks that fitted his description.

She stood watching as he rested the flat rock on his knees and used the other to pound the leaves and berries to a wet pulp.

He glanced up at her. "The eringo root will draw out the poison from the cut," he said. "And mistletoe is a remedy against all ills. The oak leaves will bind to the berries and the root and will make the poultice hold to the wound." He gave the pulpy mess a final grinding twist with the round stone and then scraped it together with his fingers and packed it along the cut.

"A binding cloth would be useful," he muttered. "But beggars can't be choosers, and I'd rather not tear up any more of my own clothes or I'll end up naked as an eel."

"Here, let me." Branwen stooped and lifted the hem

of her dress, tearing off a strip and handing it to him.

"Thanks," he said. He wrapped the length of cloth around his leg and tucked in the trailing end. "There," he said. "All done."

"Can you walk?" Branwen asked.

"As well as ever," he said. "And I will go on my way—just as soon as the aches and pains of my fall lessen a little."

She frowned. "I said I was sorry."

He raised an eyebrow. "So, Branwen, is it your usual practice to attack innocent travelers, or did you choose me for some particular reason?"

She stared at him in astonishment. "How do you know my name?"

"I'm a Druid seer," he said lightly. "How else?"

"You're a liar, that much is for sure," she said, irritated by his flippancy. "There are no seers anymore—if there ever were any! And you look more like a draggled rat than a Druid!"

The young man rose from the boulder, favoring his injured leg. He bowed low. "Thanks for that at least, mistress," he said. "A rat is a much misunderstood beast, and I would rather be a rat than a croaking white raven."

She looked at him in confusion. "What's *that* supposed to mean?"

He looked mischievously at her. "Are you so ignorant that you don't know the meaning of your own name? *Branwen* means 'white raven.'"

"Are you always this rude to strangers?" she countered. "For all you know I might be someone who could have you whipped."

"*Are* you such a person?" the young man said. "Don't forget that you started the name calling. A liar and rat, I am, if I remember correctly."

For a moment his words left her speechless. "No, I'm not such a person," she said at last.

"I'm glad of that," the young man said. "And in answer to your question, I heard men calling out the name 'Branwen' over and over a little while ago." He pointed upstream. "From that direction." He shrugged. "I avoided them. It's not wise to make yourself easy prey to strangers in these troubled times. But I guessed that you were the person they were looking for, parted from them no doubt by this devilish fog."

"You guessed right," Branwen said. "They were escorting me over the mountains to Doeth Palas."

"Then you had better let them finish their task," said the stranger. "It is a pleasure to meet you, Branwen, and a joy to have been knocked off a cliff by you." He bowed. "I shall cherish every wound and bruise in memory of this unexpected encounter."

Branwen looked at him, confused. "I hope you heal quickly."

The young man grinned. "Oh, I will," he said. "I always do."

Branwen looked up the stream. "I should go," she said. "You can come with me if you want."

"I doubt very much if you are traveling the same path as I, Branwen," said the young man.

"Good-bye, then," said Branwen. She pointed up the cliff. "I need to fetch my horse."

He bowed again but said nothing.

She climbed the cliff. While she had been talking to the young stranger, the fog had lifted. A high south wind had scoured the sky clear of clouds, and the forest was full of hazy sunlight. All thoughts of gwyllion-lights and uncanny forest noises were forgotten as she made her way to where Stalwyn stood waiting patiently for her.

She mounted; and, judging her route from the position of the sun, she rode westward through the trees, the sunlight warming her back as she guided her horse under the fluttering canopy of leaves.

She came to a high ridge that jutted out of the forest.

From its top a wide, new world spread out below her. The ridge fell away into a tumble of forested foothills and heather-clad dales, of green valleys and sunlit hillsides vibrant with silver streams. Her spirits lifted as she gazed farther out and found herself looking across a wide landscape of meadows and woodlands and pasture.

And there, high on a ribbon of roadway that wound its way down to the fertile lowlands, she saw Prince Llew's horsemen and wagons gathered. The main body of wagons and men were stationary, but a few riders were on the upper reaches of the road, far below Branwen's vantage point. They were searching for her, she assumed.

She stood in the stirrups. "Here!" she called, waving to the closest rider, no more than a good arrow-shot below her.

The man acknowledged her with a salute and waited on the road as she encouraged Stalwyn down the grassy slope toward him. Even as she approached the man, it felt to her as if her time on the foggy mountain had been no more than an uneasy dream . . . and the beggarly young stranger just a part of that dream.

She had never even thought to ask his name.

Not that she would ever see him again.

12

As Branwen brought Stalwyn down onto the winding road, Prince Llew rode back along the line of horsemen and wagons. There was profound relief on his face.

"I am glad beyond words that you have returned to us unharmed, Branwen," he said. "I feared greatly for your safety. There are many perils in the high passes. You could have fallen to your death or been killed by vagabonds or wild animals."

"I'm sorry to have caused you anxiety, my lord," Branwen said. "The fog took me by surprise."

Prince Llew smiled. "A sudden fog can be treacherous in the mountains," he said. "And I have never known one to come in so swift and lie so heavy. But you are safe and so all's well! But we must make haste now if we are to reach Doeth Palas by nightfall."

"It is my fault." Branwen gave him a rueful look. "I am being a burden, as I told you I would."

"Not at all," said the prince. "Come, ride at my side, if you will." He turned and cantered his horse to the front of the line, his white silk cloak rising, floating like swansdown on the air.

Branwen urged Stalwyn to follow. The prince spoke briefly to Angor and the Captain gave a shout of command. Horsemen and wagons moved off, following the road as it wound its way down the western flanks of the mountains and out into the rolling hills of Bras Mynydd.

Branwen rode silently alongside the prince for a while, gazing all around. The forested hills and wide, green valleys rose and fell in smooth waves, as though sculpted by gentle, creative hands. In Cyffin Tir, much of the landscape had the look of something hacked into existence by axes and mattocks.

"I've often heard visitors to Garth Milain speaking of Cyffin Tir as a very wild land," she said. "I never really understood what they meant till now. This land looks . . ." She paused, struggling to put her thoughts into words. " . . . so different."

"It has been tamed," said the prince. "Shaped and disciplined by the hand of man."

"Yes! Yes, that's exactly it," Branwen agreed. "In Cyffin Tir, the hamlets and farmsteads have been cut out of the wilderness. But here there *is* no wilderness."

"We have the mountains to thank for that," said the Prince. "Prosperity thrives with peace. Cyffin Tir has no such natural defense and is ever at the forefront of Saxon aggression." His voice lowered. "But I do not think the mountains will guard us in the coming war. We need other stratagems. New alliances maybe with foreign kings from across the seas. For I fear that the old alliances will not . . ." He broke off, glancing warily at her as though he had suddenly realized he was speaking his thoughts out loud.

"Will not what, my lord?" Branwen prompted.

"Will not hold against the Saxon threat, I was going to say," he replied. "But while there is light in Garth Milain and courage and strength in its lord and lady, Brython will not fall. Have no fear, Branwen."

"You have an army, my lord," she said. "And all the lords of Powys will unite behind King Cynon; and every Saxon who crosses our borders will have his head lopped off. And all their severed heads will be sent back to the king of Northumbria as a warning! See how he likes that!"

Branwen smiled as she spoke, imagining herself riding with the warriors of Powys, clad in chain mail with an iron helmet on her head, a shield on her arm, and a sword in her hand.

If wishes could only come true!

"Well said." The prince laughed. "You have your mother's brave heart. I have seen her in battle, Branwen, the fury and the glory of her. None could stand against Alis ap Owain!"

Branwen felt a glow of pride as the prince spoke of her warrior-mother.

If only I did have her brave heart, maybe I too could stand and fight!

Try as she might, Branwen could not shake the growing feeling that by leaving Garth Milain she had run away from something that she should have stood and faced.

They passed hamlets and townships with smithies and tanneries and wheelwrights. So many people— so much coming and going. But strangest and most marvelous of all to Branwen was the cut and shaped stonework that formed the foundations and walls of many of the huts and buildings. There was nothing like it in Cyffin Tir. The only memories harbored by the land east of the mountains were of races from the very dawn of time—the mysterious peoples who had built the hillock of Garth Milain and the lost folk who had raised the standing stones on the hilltops.

"I've never seen houses made of stone," she told the prince. "I've heard stories about the Romans, and their skill with stone. They say that once there were great fortresses in Brython, with tall stone walls and with every building made of stone—even to the roof."

Prince Llew nodded. "And now sheep graze where once the mighty Romans lived," he said. "All that remains in Brython of their power and skill is their enduring stonework, and we use their stones for barns and to strengthen our own walls."

"I can't imagine what the Romans were like," Branwen said as they rode past a lonely ruin, the ancient stone roofs fallen in, the walls crumbling and overgrown. "Why did they come here, and why did they go away?"

"I'm no scholar, Branwen," said the prince. "It's said that they all fled into the east long, long ago, taking ships across the sea. But where they went and why I do not know."

As they rode past those echoes of the long-distant past, Branwen tried to imagine the people who had built such houses, but she couldn't hold them in her mind; their skills were beyond her understanding. Yet the sight of the ruins did make her wonder how so mighty and accomplished a people as the Romans—conquerors, after all, who had ruled over this land for many centuries—were now *gone*, their power broken, their skills forgotten. Would her people vanish one day, leaving nothing but a battered palisade and a handful of brooches?

The long, warm day ebbed into a golden evening.

They passed farmsteads that lay among fields of ripening grain—yellow barley and golden wheat and green swaths of flax. There were cattle and goats in stalls and pigs in drystone sties and herds of sheep that roamed free on the hillsides.

Branwen could not help lifting her eyes to follow the flight of birds as they swooned across the sky, swooping and gliding on the warm air, catching insects in the glowing twilight. She narrowed her eyes, trying to make out the shape of a particular bird. A falcon? *Her* falcon? No. A crow. A magpie. A blackbird. No falcons.

She wondered whether the bird had followed them over the mountains. It seemed unlikely.

"Lights, ho!"

Angor's voice cut through the air. Branwen looked ahead. The road went winding its way up a long, broad hillside. The distant crest of the hill was lined with blazing torches, lighting up the high horizon with a ribbon of white fire.

"Seren, ride ahead," called Prince Llew. "Tell the Lady Elain that her lord is coming. And tell her of our sorrow and of the guest we bring."

One of the warriors broke away from the line and went galloping full tilt up the hillside, dwindling quickly to a dot on the long, pale thread of the road.

"Are we almost at Doeth Palas?" Branwen asked.

"Yes, my lady," said Angor, riding up to her side. "We have made good time."

At the top of the hill the road passed through a narrow gap in a stone wall that stretched away into the darkness to either side. Old stone, crumbling away, overgrown and gnawed by green and gray lichen. Roman stone.

Iron braziers stood on top of the wall—a score of them to either side, the flames leaping and cracking. Warriors lifted their swords in salute as horses and wagons passed through the gap.

Branwen rose in her stirrups to get a clearer view.

Across a gulf of black air, Doeth Palas blazed with a multitude of lights. For a moment the shining fortress appeared to hang rootless in the sky, sheathed in silver and threaded with stars. But then she saw that the hill she was on fell steeply away into a dark, forested valley, the snaking road lined with more torches as it climbed the high crag upon which the fortress of Prince Llew was founded.

Doeth Palas stood atop the huge tooth of rock, its ramparts built of sloping white stone, its rearing walls topped with torchlight. Hanging above the night-black vale, it seemed to Branwen like something out of legends, too marvelous for mere mortals. A place where gods might live.

The horsemen and wagons made their way up the steep incline to the ramparts of Doeth Palas. A slot was cut through the towering fortifications—a narrow chasm overhung with sheer, white stone walls, only wide enough for a single wagon to pass at a time. Branwen stared up at the stone bastions that loomed on either side of the roadway, feeling dwarfed by the scale of the construction.

The road sloped upward to where great wooden gates led into a wide earthen courtyard teeming with people, who let out cheer after cheer as their prince rode in. Many were soldiers, Branwen saw, clad in white linen and with long, white cloaks and helmets of polished iron. But some were simple peasant folk, like the farmers and artisans of Garth Milain—men and women and children gathered to welcome their lord home.

Prince Llew rode among them with his hand raised in salute.

Branwen noticed that the thatched huts and dwellings that surrounded the courtyard were similar to those of Garth Milain—but many of them had drystone walls, or stones pressed in among the daub and wattle. It was clear that Doeth Palas was many times the size of Garth Milain.

The prince turned to her. "Journey's end," he said, his eyes shining. "Lady Elain and my daughters will be at the Great Hall to greet you."

The Great Hall of Doeth Palas stood at the far end of a wide roadway lined with iron braziers. Massive walls of gray stone and oak timbers supported its high, thatched roof, and broad stone steps led up to the open doors. Torchlight shimmered on the door-timbers; and as Branwen came closer, she saw that the doorposts were encased in sheets of beaten gold and silver and that the doors themselves were also sheathed in patterned gold. A rearing dragon hung above the doorway, engraved with exquisite workmanship from a sheet of polished gold.

Three figures stood waiting on the top step. Branwen guessed that they must be Llew's wife, Lady Elain, with the two princesses, Meredith and Romney, at her side. She took a deep breath, smoothing out her skirts, hoping her journey over the mountain had not left her looking too disheveled.

Lady Elain was tall and slender, her chestnut brown hair framing a pale, narrow face with flashing blue eyes. Meredith, the elder of the princesses, was almost as tall as her mother and had the same white skin and glowing brown hair; but she was so thin that she looked as if a breath of air might blow her away. Princess Romney was shorter and sturdier than her sister, her body less graceful and her face broader and rounder and her hair much darker.

Branwen gazed at the elegant purple gowns they were wearing, surprised to see Lady Elain and her daughters dressed so splendidly on such an ordinary day. Her mother had gowns that were almost as fine, but she only wore them on saints' days and at festivals. All three had elaborately dressed hair— braided and drawn up in loops and coils, adorned with golden combs and pins, and hung with strings of jewels. Branwen had never seen a woman's hair dressed in such a way.

She swung down from the saddle and mounted the steps toward them, very aware of her own ragged black hair hanging down past her shoulders and of her travel-stained gown and grubby boots.

Lady Elain smiled and stepped down to greet Branwen, both hands reaching out to her. "Branwen, my child," she said, "it is good to see the daughter of the valiant Lady Alis and the mighty Lord Griffith, although it wounds my heart to have to greet you under such evil circumstances." She took Branwen's hands, her fingers soft and warm as she looked compassionately into Branwen's face. "Our hearts ache for you and for your parents. I met Geraint only twice, once when he was but five years old and again when he was a well-grown lad of twelve. But I remember him fondly. He would have made a great lord of Cyffin Tir."

"Yes," Branwen said heavily. "He would."

Lady Elain looked into Branwen's eyes. "My poor child," she said. "You are tired and worn from the road. But, come, meet my daughters. You will be great friends, I'm sure."

"Thank you for your hospitality, my lady," Branwen said as she was drawn up the final step to meet the princesses.

Meredith smiled and made a graceful bob. "Welcome to our home, Branwen," she said. "All that is ours is for you to share for the duration of your stay."

"Thank you, your generosity does you honor," Branwen replied, longing for these necessary formalities to be over so she could sleep.

"Welcome, Branwen," Romney chirped. "Mama said that you would be dirty and wretched and that we should do everything we could to make you feel at home." She gave an innocent smile. "You do look like a beggar! But a bath and a change of clothes will make you seem less disgusting, I'm sure."

Lady Elain put her hand on Romney's shoulder. "Romney, hush now." She looked at Branwen. "My daughter means well," she said. "Please do not take her remarks amiss."

"Not at all, my lady," said Branwen, controlling her indignation. The young princess had entirely ignored the traditional rituals of welcome; that was no way to greet the daughter of a prince! Still, Branwen was determined to be polite, despite Romney's rudeness. "I *am* dirty from the journey," she added. "And a bath would be very welcome."

"Excellent," said Lady Elain. "I shall leave you in the hands of my two daughters. They will show you where you will be sleeping. Your things will be brought to you there."

"Thank you."

Lady Elain was being a gracious host, but Branwen couldn't help feeling a little overwhelmed. Doeth Palas was an extraordinary, wonderful place—but its splendor only made her long for her own home and her mother and father, and . . . most painful of all . . . for Geraint.

Her heart sank as she thought of her disturbed, rootless future.

Will I ever go home again? she wondered. *Do I even have a home now?*

The two sisters led Branwen into the Great Hall. The vaulted roof soared above her head to ten times her height, supported by a complex lacework of massive oak timbers. The floor was flagged with gray stone, and the high walls were hung with banners and standards and studded with weapons. The main chamber was lined with iron candelabra and lit by a hundred beeswax candles. A great stone hearth stood at the center, filled with logs that burned with a sweet, clear flame. An iron tripod rose above the fire, and suspended from it was a black iron cauldron giving off a haze of aromatic steam. A few Saxon servants went about their duties, tending the fire and sweeping the floor and trimming the candles.

At the far end of the chamber, under a canopy of red silk, stood the prince's throne, an immense, raised chair covered all over with plates of decorated gold.

"Where is your mother's chair?" Branwen asked.

Meredith gave her a puzzled look. "What do you mean?"

"Doesn't the Lady Elain sit with your father when they discuss the business of Bras Mynydd?" Branwen prompted.

100

"What an odd question," Meredith said. "Our father rules alone, Branwen."

"I know why she asked that," said Romney. "Don't you remember what Mama told us? Lord Griffith and Lady Alis rule *together*."

Meredith nodded. "Yes, I remember now." She looked at Branwen. "Does your father have trouble making up his own mind? Does he need the counsel of others before coming to a decision—even that of his wife?" She tilted her head inquiringly. "I'm sorry, but I know very little about the wild lads east of the mountains. Please don't be offended by my questions."

"Of course not," Branwen said. "My mother is wise and well respected; it's quite normal for Father and Mother to make decisions together. I thought it would be the same everywhere."

"Really?" Meredith said in obvious surprise. "Oh, well, Mama did tell us that you had strange ways and customs in Cyffin Tir." She looked over Branwen's shoulder.

Two elderly male servants had come into the hall, carrying Branwen's traveling chest between them. They were Saxons, of course, little more than skin and bone, their stooped bodies clad in gray tunics and leggings, their hair long and their beards ragged.

"Take it to our chamber," Romney ordered. "And see that you don't drop it."

The two men shuffled off toward a side door, their

hooded eyes never lifting from the floor.

"You have to watch them every moment of the day," Romney said, rolling her eyes at Branwen. "I sometimes think these Saxon servants are more trouble than they're worth."

Branwen followed the two princesses in the wake of the stooped old men.

The princesses' chamber was bright and comfortable, with furred animal-skins underfoot and many candles set in iron sconces on the walls. A mattress lay at either end of the room, and six wooden chests were lined up along one wall. Stone shelves jutted from the walls, holding jewelry and trinkets and small wooden or stone ornaments and playthings.

The servants put down Branwen's chest and turned to leave.

"Not so fast, you," Meredith said. The servants turned toward her, their heads down, backs bent, eyes on the ground. "Fetch another mattress for our guest, and be quick about it," Meredith ordered. "And then heat water and lay out some linen in the tub—and tell Aelf and Hild to attend us. Go."

The servants left without speaking.

"Aelf and Hild will help you wash and dress your hair ready for the Homecoming Feast," Meredith explained to Branwen. "They are old, and like all Saxons they are very stupid; but they know what needs to be done."

"Is there to be a feast, then?" Branwen asked.

After two days on the road, she had hoped for nothing more demanding than to be allowed to wash off the dust and fall into a soft bed.

"Of course," Romney said. "There's always a feast when Father has been away." She peered at Branwen. "You're not too tired, are you?"

"Of course she isn't," Meredith said. "Once she's cleaned up and dressed in her finest clothes, she'll be wide-awake. Won't you, Branwen?"

"Oh, yes," Branwen said, trying to sound convincing. "Of course."

Romney dropped to her knees by Branwen's chest. "May I look through your things?" she asked. "I love to see new clothes and jewelry. Mama says the clothes and jewels you wear in Cyffin Tir are quite different to ours."

Branwen smiled. "Of course you may," she said. "Help yourself."

Romney loosened the leather straps that held the chest closed and threw open the lid. She began eagerly to pull out things.

"What is *this*?" Romney asked as she lifted Branwen's hunting jerkin out of its chest. "It looks like something a peasant would wear!" She looked up at Branwen. "Did you let your servants pack for you?" She shook her head. "That's always a mistake; they've left out all your best clothes and filled your chest with whatever scraps they could lay their hands on!"

Branwen crouched down, taking the marten-skin

jerkin out of Romney's hands and putting it back in the chest. "I'm afraid I don't have anything as grand as you," she said, gathering her clothes back together, her cheeks burning with embarrassment. She was uncomfortably aware that the two princesses were staring at her spread-out clothing as if they were looking at shabby rags that someone had thrown on the floor.

Branwen spotted the bundle of violet cloth her mother had given her. "I have some gifts for you," she said. "My mother chose them especially."

She took out the bundle and carefully unfolded it on the floor.

Meredith fingered the cloth. "Quite nice," she said. "I'm not sure I like the color, though. Is it meant for all of us?"

"Oh, no," Branwen said. "The cloth is for your mother." She lifted an edge of the violet cloth to reveal the golden brooches and the silver spoon. "These are for you, Romney," she said, placing the brooches in Romney's hand. "And this for you." She gave Meredith the spoon.

"Thank you," Romney said, glancing briefly at the brooches before getting up and placing them on a shelf. "They're very . . . *unusual*."

It was obvious that she didn't think much of them, and Meredith was staring at the spoon as if Branwen had slapped a dead fish in her hand.

"I'm afraid we had no time to choose gifts for you," Meredith said. "But we have so many lovely things, and you have so little. It'll be easy to find something for you." She gave Branwen a deeply sympathetic look. "It must have been hard for you to leave your home the way you did."

Branwen nodded. "Yes, it was . . ."

"Without even time to pack your jewelry and your best clothes," Meredith continued. She stood up, tapping the bowl of the spoon against her palm as if it were a stick of wood. "I imagine they're being sent separately?"

Branwen looked up at her, trying to work out whether Meredith was making fun of her or whether she genuinely assumed that wagonloads of finery were trundling over the mountains in her wake.

"This is all I have," Branwen said. "Nothing else is coming."

The princesses stared at her.

"How awful!" Romney murmured. "Mama told us that Cyffin Tir was a barbarous place, but I had no idea. . . ."

"Hush!" Meredith interrupted. *"Remember!"*

"Oh, yes. Sorry." Romney put her hand over her mouth.

Branwen gave them a hard look. "Remember *what*?" she asked.

"Nothing," Meredith said quickly. "I'll go and see if your bath is ready." She walked to the door and disappeared.

Branwen looked at Romney. "Remember what?" she asked again.

Romney gave her a coy look. "Mama said not to make you feel bad because you're not as . . . what was the word?" She frowned, then her face cleared. "Not as *civilized* as we," she finished, giving Branwen another of those wide, friendly smiles. "Would you like to see some of my jewelry?" she invited. "I've got lots. I don't mind lending you a few things for the feast, so long as you're careful with them."

"I'll be fine, thank you," Branwen said curtly. "I don't really like dressing up."

Romney's eyes widened. "Really?" she asked. "Oh, I love it." She gave Branwen a patronizing smile.

The door opened and Lady Elain came into the room. "Ah, Branwen, how are you settling in? Are my daughters treating you well?"

If you mean, are they making me feel like a bedraggled beggar girl who has just wandered out of the forest, then yes!

"My mother sent this for you, my lady," Branwen said, avoiding the question and stooping to pick up the bundle of violet cloth.

Lady Elain took it in her arms without even looking at it. "That was most generous of her—and to think of me at such a time. Have the princesses told you about the feast?"

"They mentioned it, my lady," Branwen said.

"She doesn't have anything to wear at the feast,"

Romney said, nodding down at the clothes strewn on the floor. "That's *all she has!*"

Lady Elain glanced at Branwen's things. "Then you will have to lend her one of your gowns, Romney."

"Meredith's will fit better," Romney said so quickly that it was clear she didn't like the idea of Branwen wearing her clothes.

"Then something of Meredith's," said Lady Elain. "You both have plenty to spare." She smiled at Branwen. "But first, we need to get you washed and cleaned up, you poor child." She put a hand on Branwen's shoulder. "Come, your bath is ready. Aelf and Hild will help you."

13

THE LARGE, LINEN-LINED tub was in a room off the main chamber of the Great Hall—a small chamber with its own hearth, over which water was being heated in iron pots.

The Saxon servants looked anxiously at Branwen as she sat in the wooden tub, waist deep in hot water with her wet hair plastered down over her shoulders and back.

Branwen hadn't liked the way the two old women had plucked at her clothes as she had prepared herself for the bath. She liked it even less when the women started trying to wash her. They emptied ewers of hot water over her, then one of them held a bowl of soft soap while the other scooped up handfuls of the stuff and reached forward with the obvious intention of smearing it all over Branwen's hair and body.

"Leave me alone, *please*! I can wash myself."

"But we must wash you, my lady princess," one of them said. "We will be chastised if we do not."

"No one will ever know," Branwen said. "Just give me some soap and then . . . then . . . go and stand in the corner. Preferably with your backs turned."

"Yes, my lady princess," said the other woman, handing her the bowl. "But . . . please . . . forgive my curiosity." Her voice trailed off.

"Yes? What?"

"Do you not have servants to bathe you in Cyffin Tir, my lady princess?"

"Of course we have servants, but they don't *wash* us."

"And, forgive me, my lady princess, but who cuts and dresses your hair?"

"No one does," Branwen replied. "I like my hair the way it is." She rubbed a handful of the soap into her hair and began to knead.

Lady Elain walked slowly around Branwen, her lips pursed and her face perturbed.

"We don't have time to cut your hair properly, Branwen, I'm afraid," she said at last. "But we can do *something* with it, I'm sure."

Branwen was still in the washroom, sitting on a wooden bench wrapped in soft, white towels. The two servant women stood mutely behind Lady Elain as she circled.

"I usually just wear it down, like this," Branwen tried. "I'm not sure . . ."

"No, no." Lady Elain cut her off. "That won't do at all." She turned to the women. "Hild, Aelf, I am giving you charge of dressing Princess Branwen's hair. Do your very best work and be quick; the feast is almost ready."

Lady Elain swept out of the room. Branwen took a deep breath. "My hair is fine as it is," she said. "I don't care what Lady Elain says."

"We will be chastised if we don't dress it, my lady princess," Hild murmured.

"I'll explain."

"We will still be chastised," Aelf said sadly. "But as your lady princess wishes."

Branwen lifted her shoulders and let out a heavy breath. "Oh, very well, then. I don't want you getting into trouble on my account. Do what you must."

"Thank you, my lady princess," said Hild. "We will make you look glorious, don't fear."

"I doubt that," Branwen said, as the two women approached her. "I doubt that very much."

"And who exactly are *you*?" Branwen murmured as she stared at her reflection in a large, round mirror of polished silver held up in front of her by Aelf. It was a good question. The *face* that peered back at her was familiar enough, but that was all.

Her hair had been plaited and twisted and drawn up on top of her head in an elaborate series of ropes and twirls, the whole astonishing pile held together with golden combs and pins and hung with strings of yellow garnets. It was impressive; Branwen had to admit that. But it wasn't *her*.

"Tell me," Branwen said, looking over her shoulder at Hild. "Do women have their hair done like this all the time, or just on special occasions?"

"The Lady Elain and the princesses and other great ladies have their hair dressed every morning, my lady princess," Hild replied.

"And undressed and combed out every night," Aelf added. "My lady princess, are you pleased with our work?"

Branwen regarded her reflection again. "I'm not sure *pleased* is the word I'd use. . . ." She shrugged. "But I look less of a fool than I'd expected, although, if Lady Elain thinks I'm going through this every day, she will have to think again."

"It is the latest fashion," said Hild. "And it makes you look very beautiful, if I may say so, my lady princess."

"Thank you," Branwen said, uncertain of how she felt about the compliment. She'd never given any thought to being *beautiful* before. Geraint would have howled with laughter at the idea.

She stood up. Hild stepped forward and smoothed out the folds of the scarlet silk gown that Lady Elain had chosen for her. Meredith's, she assumed, wondering if the older princess had reacted the same way as her younger sister to the idea of Branwen borrowing her clothes.

The radiantly colored gown had long, wide sleeves with deep yellow cuffs patterned with gold thread. Yellow bands followed the rounded neckline and formed a hem at her feet. Heavy golden brooches were pinned at either shoulder, studded with more yellow garnets, and a belt of finely crafted golden links was clasped around her waist.

Branwen liked the gown. It would have been impossible not to; the silk felt warm and soft under her hands, and she loved the way it shimmered when she moved. They had silk garments in Garth Milain, but not very many; and they were old, handed down the generations, and of a far poorer quality than this. She turned in a slow circle, twisting her head so she could see herself in the silver mirror.

The door to the bath chamber opened, and Lady Elain swept in, dressed in purple silk trimmed with gold. She smiled, holding out her hands to Branwen.

"I knew there was an elegant princess hidden away under that ragamuffin exterior. Come, the feast is prepared, and all we await is the arrival of our most loved and honored guest."

Branwen was uneasy at the thought of being an *honored guest*. She felt more like a bewildered outsider, plucked from the life she had known in Garth Milain, festooned with finery that only made her feel even more awkward and gauche, and expected to behave with poise and confidence in surroundings that disturbed and alarmed her.

14

BRANWEN WAS IN the Great Hall, sitting on soft furs with Meredith and Romney on one side and a taciturn warrior named Daffyd on the other.

Fresh reeds had been spread over the stone floor; Saxon servants moved among the people, laying out communal wooden bowls of food and jugs of drink. The meat was mostly chicken and pork, although there were chunks of roast beef on the bone and platters of sea trout and oysters. With this was served a thick broth from the cauldron and pease porridge and hunks of yellow cheese. The drink was mead and ale for the warriors and their womenfolk, and brimming jugs of buttermilk for the younger people.

The way food was served was quite different from how it was done in Garth Milain. There people gathered in groups of three, each group with its own trencher, a wooden tray from which food would be picked; but here each person had a roundel of flattened wheat bread placed in front of them. Branwen had been about to tear a piece off her bread and eat it when she noticed that all the others were picking food from the bowls and putting it on the bread, filling the disk of bread with food and then eating from that.

I must keep my wits about me, she thought. *It's going to be too easy to make a fool of myself.*

Most of the diners had their own knives, with which they skewered pieces of meat or cut off chunks of cheese; but the rest of the eating was done with fingers—as it was in Garth Milain—and greasy fingers were then dipped in communal water-bowls and wiped on linen cloths.

A trio of musicians had set up near the central hearth, playing sad melodies on harp, pipe, and the four-stringed crotta.

"I don't imagine you have ever seen so much food at one time, have you, Branwen?" Romney commented as they ate. "We have feasts like this all the time in Doeth Palas. This is really quite normal for us."

"We don't go hungry," Branwen responded, keeping her temper in check. "And there's always plenty of food on special occasions." She managed a smile. "I think you have the wrong idea of what life is like in Garth Milain."

"Then you will have to enlighten us," said

Meredith. "We know so little of what goes on in the eastern hill-forts." She frowned at Branwen's hands. "It must be a very hard life."

"I wouldn't say so," Branwen said.

"Really?" Meredith exclaimed. "But look at your hands. They're so . . . *rough*. And your nails are broken, and your skin is . . . well, *look* at it!"

Branwen gazed at her hands, humiliated by Meredith's criticisms. True, her skin was tanned from the sun and her knuckles were scuffed, and there were a few small scars here and there from her adventures in the forest; but they were strong and nimble hands, and she had never before been made to feel ashamed or embarrassed by their appearance.

"They're like peasants' hands." Romney chuckled. "Did you work in the fields, Branwen?"

A spasm of irritation went through Branwen. "I would rather have my hands than yours," she snapped. "Soft and flabby like bread that's been left overnight in a water butt." She regretted her outburst immediately, but the damage was done. The princesses looked knowingly at each other for a moment and then turned back to their food. Clearly, for the time being, at least, their conversation was over.

Branwen realized that making friends with Meredith and Romney was going to be something of a struggle. It didn't help that everything they said reinforced the sense that they thought she was nothing more than an unsophisticated savage from the world's end.

"Princess Branwen, welcome to Doeth Palas!"

The voice came from close behind her. Startled, she turned and found herself looking into the wide, dark eyes of a young man who had come up so silently at her back that she had not heard a sound.

"Thank you," she gasped in surprise. The young man reached out a hand to her; and without quite meaning to, she lifted her arm and put her own hand in his. His grip was warm and strong and dry; and as he held her hand and looked deep into her eyes, she found her heart beating strangely fast. He was about her age, she guessed—maybe a little older. He was tall and slim, dressed in fine linen and with a deep blue mantle hanging from his shoulders. His light brown hair fell about his slender, handsome face; and as he smiled at her, Branwen's mind went entirely and unexpectedly blank.

"My name is Iwan ap Madoc," he said, his voice soft and lilting.

"Oh . . . I'm Branwen ap Griffith . . . ," she blurted. ". . . Princess Branwen . . ."

His smile widened, and Branwen had the uncanny sensation of falling. "Yes," he said. "I know who you are. I look forward to your better acquaintance, my lady, if your stay here permits." He released her hand, bowed, and walked away.

She gazed after him as he circled the room to where a group of youths were sitting. As he sat among them, his eyes turned briefly to her; but she looked away at once, embarrassed to be caught staring at him.

You mooncalf! How could you have behaved like such a fool! They already think you're an uncivilized wretch from the world's end. You didn't need to add to that the impression that you're as dumb as an ox!

She had no idea why the boy had affected her so intensely—beyond the simple fact that she had never before seen a young man with such beautiful eyes and with such a stunning smile. Trying to recover from her confusion, she reached awkwardly for her cup. She misjudged and knocked it over, spilling the buttermilk. She heard a stifled snigger from Romney. Meredith sighed and rolled her eyes. Branwen started to mop the spilled buttermilk with a cloth, but a servant quickly appeared at her shoulder and cleaned up for her.

"Thank you," she murmured, crimson to the ears.

Meredith leaned toward her. "We don't thank them," she hissed.

Branwen nodded and gave her a tight smile. She heard the woman at Daffyd's side whisper under her breath, "Our guest seems to know little of cultured behavior. Let's hope her stay here gives her some understanding of how to behave properly."

Branwen gave her a furious look but swallowed an angry retort.

Keep calm. Say nothing. Show them that you're not an ill-mannered savage.

Branwen turned to her food, watching the others from the corners of her eyes, determined not to make any other mistakes. She was used to feasts in Garth Milain. There, as the night wore on, the children and many of the women would drift off; and the warriors, made bold by too much ale, would start challenging one another to physical contests.

Branwen smiled to herself as she remembered the High Feasts at home, when the hearth was heaped with fresh logs till the flames roared. Warriors would leap through the flames while the others cheered them on. There would be wrestling matches and races and mock sword fights. There would be bruises; sometimes there would be broken limbs, sometimes spilled blood.

She remembered Geraint and her father wrestling to the whoops and yells of the onlookers. Geraint never won those matches. Her father was too strong and too wily a fighter. Sometimes he would over-power Geraint; other times he would slip out a foot, catching Geraint off-balance and throwing him to the ground with a force that shook the hillock! Then he would reach down an arm and haul the dizzy Geraint to his feet.

"One day," he would say, slapping his son on the back. "One day you will beat me, boy! But not today!" And he would bellow with laughter. "Not *today*!"

A voice rose above the others, jogging Branwen out of her bittersweet memories.

"Gavan! Come, Gavan! Entertain us!"

Branwen looked up. It was Llew's voice, but other voices were joining in now.

"Gavan! Get up, Gavan!"

A thickset, grizzle-haired man rose from a couch near to where Prince Llew and his wife were seated. He had a rugged face, like a weather-worn crag, his eyes dark as slate under his brow. He had the usual shaggy mustache of the men of Brython, still thick and dark but threaded with gray. A long, white scar snaked down the left side of his cheek, all the way from his hairline to his jaw. Branwen had the strong feeling she had seen him before—a long time ago, when his hair had been less gray. She vividly remembered the scar.

She turned to Daffyd. "Who is that man?"

"Gavan ap Huw, my lady," Daffyd told her. "Hero of the battle of Chester. He fought at Cadwallon's side when the House of Maelgwn Fawr rose against Edwin."

"Yes!" Branwen said, memory flooding back. Gavan had visited Garth Milain when she had been a small child. Geraint had told her tales of his courage. "He was standard-bearer at the battle of Meigen, when Cadwallon took Edwin's head from his shoulders," she said, her eyes wide as she gazed across the room at the hero. "I didn't know he lived here."

"He was born in Caernarfon," said Daffyd. "But after the death of Cadwallon, he entered Prince

Llew's service; and now he trains our young men for the coming war."

While they were speaking, Gavan had stepped out into the middle of the hall. He walked slowly around the hearth, swinging a long iron sword with casual ease.

"Hearken to me now!" he roared. "Hearken to me as I bespeak the lineage of Cadwallon the Great, sword-master, horse-master, lord of men, he of blessed memory. Cadwallon, son of Cadfan, best of all kings of Gwynedd, whose renown rings forth from valley and hill, shaking the limbs of the Saxon dogs and shattering their swords." Branwen shivered. "Cadfan, son of Idwal Foel, son of Anarawd, son of Rhodri Mawr, whose ancestry can be traced back to Gwrtheyrn and Anna of Legend," he went on.

A murmur of excitement and anticipation grew in the hall as Gavan circled the hearth. "This blade!" He held the sword high above his head. "This blade was ever at my lord's command. It is an ancient blade of glorious lineage. Come, who will try his mettle against it? Whose callow bones will feel its bite? Whose veins will it empty? This blade is hungry; this blade thirsts for a blood sacrifice. Who will try this blade of mine?"

"Not I, by my faith!" called someone from the crowd, and there was general laughter.

"Nor I. I love life too much!" shouted someone else.

"Come, Gavan," called Lady Elain. "You give too

hard a task. Put up your sword and give our young men a fighting chance!"

"Very well." Gavan lay down his sword by the hearth. "There I place it; there let it rest. Give me but a stout wooden staff, and I will match any man who dares to come against me be he armed with sword or spear or knife or ax."

A long staff was fetched for him. He stood against the hearth, swinging the staff around his back and shoulders in a dizzying whirl, bringing it down with a sharp crack on the stones before turning on his heels and cutting the air in a swift arc.

"A gold coin for any man who will stand against him!" called Prince Llew.

A few warriors stood up this time. Prince Llew nominated one and he came out, sword in hand, to face Gavan.

Quicker than the blink of an eye, Gavan sprang, the staff thrusting forward. He gave a sideways twist; and the challenger went sprawling on the floor, his sword chiming as it skidded over the stones. The staff came down, halting a hairbreadth above the man's skull. There was laughter and applause.

A second challenger appeared.

Then a third.

Then a fourth.

Gavan dispatched them all.

"My mother would show him a trick or two," Branwen murmured under her breath, remembering the times she had spent watching her mother practice her skills with sword and spear and staff. "He's strong and quick, but I believe I could avoid that staff of his."

She heard Romney suppressing laughter; she had not realized that anyone had heard her. Romney whispered something to Meredith, and a wide grin spread across the older princess's face. Branwen felt herself go red.

She tried to ignore them, watching how Gavan moved, how he used the staff, how he would catch his opponents off guard. It was curious how similar his fighting skills were to those of Lady Alis. Branwen was vaguely aware that Meredith got up from her couch and wandered off somewhere. The next time Branwen noticed her, she was with the young men in the far corner.

An older warrior had taken up Gavan's challenge, and he had called for a staff as well. The two hardened veterans were trading blows that would have felled an ox, the striking of their staves shivering the air. At last, with both men grunting and panting from the effort, Gavan managed to get in under the other man's guard and gave him such a buffet on the chest with the end of his staff that he was knocked clean off his feet. The cheers rang to the roof as Gavan helped his beaten opponent up and the two of them marched around the hearth with their arms around each other's shoulders.

Branwen was suddenly aware that someone

had come up behind her and was crouching at her shoulder.

She looked around. It was Iwan. Her heart leaped in her chest, but she was determined not to make a fool of herself this time.

"Princess Branwen, how do you like the entertainments we have on offer?" His voice had a faint lilt of amusement.

"I am enjoying them very much," Branwen said, wishing she could think of something quite natural to add. But nothing came.

"I saw you when you first arrived in Doeth Palas," Iwan continued. "If I may say so, you've cleaned up well. You look quite the princess now." He grinned disarmingly at her. "Although I must say I liked the look of you when you rode in with Prince Llew, wild and shaggy haired and feral." He laughed gently and without mockery. "That's just the way I had always imagined a princess from the eastern cantrefs should look."

"I . . . oh . . . thank you . . . ," Branwen mumbled, her hopes of making a good impression on him falling all to pieces.

"Forgive me if I am speaking out of turn," Iwan said. "But am I right in saying that your mother is Lady Alis ap Owain, also known as the Warrior Maiden of Brych Einiog?"

"Yes, that's right," Branwen said, glad that he had finally said something to which she could respond intelligently. "She was born in Brych Einiog, and she learned her fighting skills there when she was very young. She fought in her first battle when she was my age, before she married my father."

"Then I take it you are also skilled in fighting?" Iwan asked.

"Yes . . . a little . . . I suppose . . . ," Branwen stammered. This wasn't entirely true. She had watched her mother sparring with warriors in Garth Milain, and she had practiced the moves herself in the privacy of the forest. But neither of her parents had wanted her to be taught the craft of warfare, and so the only tutoring she had ever received had been from Geraint—and he had only been prepared to show her defensive strokes with a sword of wood, taught occasionally and in secret.

Iwan leaned close to her, speaking in a confidential undertone. "Do you know what would please the prince and his lady?"

"No . . ."

"It is considered a great honor if a guest is seen to challenge Gavan." His eyes sparked. "It is only an idea, Branwen; but I think everyone would be very impressed if the daughter of Lady Alis ap Owain issued a challenge to our best warrior."

Branwen stared at him in surprise. "Do you really think so?"

Iwan nodded.

She looked over to where Gavan was standing, his legs spread, the staff ready in his hands. She knew she had no hope of standing against the great warrior; but if it would help the people of Doeth Palas accept her, then it was worth making the challenge. She just hoped the defensive moves Geraint had shown her would save her from being knocked flat on her back in the first few moments!

She hesitated for a heartbeat more, then stood up and stepped out into the middle of the floor.

"I challenge Gavan ap Huw!" she called, her voice cracking a little with nerves.

Silence came down over the hall.

Branwen looked around, confused. The only sound she could hear now was the cracking of the fire and the thundering of her own heart. Something was wrong. The people were staring at her—and the expressions on their faces were of embarrassment and outrage and amusement.

The silence was broken by Gavan throwing his head back and letting out a roar of laughter. Within moments, everyone in the hall was laughing at her.

Lady Elain hurried up to her, catching her by the arm and pulling her into a corner. "What are you thinking, child?" she hissed. "A girl cannot challenge a warrior!"

Branwen looked around, trying to find Iwan. He was on the far side of the chamber, sitting with his young friends, laughing as loudly as everyone else.

Branwen felt her face burning. "Let me go," she murmured, pulling her arm free. With the laughter ringing in her ears, she walked to the doors of the Great Hall and stepped out into the night. As soon as she was out of sight of the feasters, she broke into a run.

Iwan ap Madoc had made a fool of her! She had allowed herself to be duped by his pretense of friendship. She had been so charmed by his kindly, lying words that the feeling of betrayal was almost worse than the humiliation of having fallen for his cruel joke.

15

D ARK CLOUDS HAD snuffed out the stars and
the night was cave-black as Branwen made her
way through the round huts and wooden buildings of Doeth Palas, walking off her anger and
mortification.

It wasn't so much that she had made a fool of herself in the Great Hall that incensed her; she could live
with that, and she could even survive being laughed
at. What wounded her most was the fact that Iwan
had deliberately tricked her. Guests in Garth Milain
would never be treated so badly. She felt sick at heart
and ached for her home and for the kindness of her
parents.

She reached the outer ramparts, where a long, stone
stairway hugged the towering stone wall. She climbed
the stairs and stared out into the night. There was a

sound from far below, a strange sound that she didn't recognize. It had a regular pulse to it, a kind of slow, rolling boom. But there was a hiss and a sizzling in the sound, too. And something that made her think of swords clashing on shields and arrows skimming deadly through the air. She stood on the very brink of empty space and peered down. She sensed rather than saw an uneasy movement far below, like a restless sleeper turning and turning in a welter of bad dreams.

The Western Ocean.

Was that the sound she could hear: the beating heart of the ocean?

She sat, legs dangling, cool air on her face as the ocean rumbled and purred beneath her.

I wish Geraint were with me.

She could bear it, then.

Perhaps.

A flurry of wings. The click of sharp claws on stone. A single *caw*, so close that it made her jump.

"You again!"

The falcon stared up at her with eyes so black that they paled the sky. Branwen let out a breathless gust of laughter. The bird croaked again and walked across the stones until it was almost at her side. She reached out and smoothed its feathers.

"Where have you come from?" she asked. "How did you find me?"

The bird looked unblinkingly at her with jeweled, predatory eyes.

"I watched out for you, you know," Branwen said. "All the way from the mountains." She laughed again—how foolish to be sitting there talking to the bird as if it could understand her! "The way things are going, you may be my only friend in this place."

Caw!

She smiled, then looked reluctantly over her shoulder. The lights of Doeth Palas burned bright below her. She could see the high roof of the Great Hall.

"I should go back," she said. "I can't sit here forever. I have to go and face them. Mother and Father would want me to."

The falcon was watching her with oddly wise eyes.

"Will you stay?" she asked the bird, stroking its silky feathers again. "Stay nearby for me? Please?"

The bird bobbed its head and gave a single cry.

She sighed and stood up. "I hope that was a yes," she said. "One true friend could make all the difference." She walked down the long stairway and headed back to the feast. She heard the sound of wings behind her. She turned, smiling.

The falcon was following her.

Branwen stood at the doors to the main chamber of the Great Hall.

The falcon had come to rest on the top step. As she paused on the threshold, it looked at her for a moment, then half spread its wings and bobbed its head, its legs shifting so that it swayed from side to side. It was almost as if the falcon were dancing.

She let out a long, slow breath, transfixed by its extraordinary behavior.

Its strange dance completed, the bird sprang into the air and flew soundlessly into the night.

Gathering her courage, Branwen stepped into the chamber. A few heads turned to her. There were one or two mocking smiles. The odd whispered comment. But most of the people were watching a pair of tumblers who were performing in the middle of the floor.

Branwen looked over to the group of young men. Iwan was with them. He didn't seem to have noticed her return. She fought down an urge to go over there and smack him around the head.

Oh, yes, and wouldn't that be the perfect way to prove once and for all what a savage you are!

A better idea occurred to her, if only she could hold her nerve. She made her way around the walls, her eyes on the tumblers. They were good—tucking and rolling, leaping and twisting like salmon. One crouched and the other somersaulted over him, his hand coming down on the crouching man's head. He managed to catch himself so that he balanced one-handed, upside down, his legs high in the air. The lower man rose to his feet and walked around the hall with his partner balanced on his head. There was applause and cheering from the crowd.

Branwen came up behind Iwan. She stooped and

put her hand on his shoulder. He looked up at her, and wariness flickered across his face.

"Iwan ap Madoc," she said calmly. "Will you speak with me a moment?"

Iwan got to his feet, his expression cautious. He eyed her without speaking, as if waiting for her to make the first move.

Branwen reached out her hand. He looked puzzled but took it. She smiled.

She was aware that all his friends were looking at them, and that she had also gained the attention of a few others nearby. "You tricked me very sweetly, Iwan," she said, loudly enough for them all to hear.

"It was meant in fun, Princess Branwen," Iwan said. "Don't people joke with each other in Garth Milain?"

"They do," Branwen said. "Although not usually so unkindly." She lifted her free hand and rested it on his shoulder. "You are a merry prankster, Iwan. You should perform for your lord. I'm sure he'd admire your antics."

"I would not presume to take the place of someone whose mere presence makes us all laugh," Iwan said, inclining his head a little as though the quick jibe had been a compliment. There was a murmur of amusement at this among the others, but Branwen kept her smile steady.

"And thank the saints for the gift of laughter," Branwen said. "But in Cyffin Tir we know the difference between humor and mockery. It's a distinction you'd do well to learn, my friend."

She gave him no time to respond. Instead she broke away from him, fighting the shaking in her legs as she walked away without once looking back.

She came to where the two princesses were sitting and folded herself up on the outspread furs. She didn't even glance at them, although she was very aware of them staring at her. She reached for some food, refusing to give in to the urge to crawl away and hide. She had been made a fool of in front of all these people, but she was determined to stay and claw back all the self-respect she could.

As she ate, she shot a quick look across the hall. Iwan was watching her. There was a smile on his face, but there was also a wary curiosity in his eyes now— and he looked quickly away when he caught her eye.

The tumblers finished their performance, and a harpist came into the center of the hall. The boisterous mood in the hall subsided to an expectant, almost reverent hush. The man was dressed in a long, gray robe, his thin face cragged and riven with age; his hair a thin, snow-white fall; his eyes the blue of a winter's sky. He sat on a hearthstone and began to play a melancholy air, the notes spreading through the chamber like ripples on a deep lake.

Branwen stopped eating, her hand halfway to her mouth.

A citadel of stone stands upon deep-founded rock

A mighty stronghold, girt by the sea
A fine citadel that rises above the waves
Yes, even above the ninth wave that roars
and crashes
And devours the land with salty teeth
A fine citadel upon a deep-founded rock
Fine men dwell there, easy at sunset
Making merry, warriors bold of ancient
lineage
There is a fine citadel that stands above the
waves
On a high tooth of rock
A graceful citadel of white stone
Pure white, as the seagull's wing.
The citadel of Pwyll, old in story
Let me sing you now of the companions of
Pwyll
Let me call their spirits forth from the smoke
Let them live again in this place, those slain
in glory
Eaters of ambrosia, drinkers of honeydew
Great warriors of Brython, glorious and
glad
I sing now of Arawn, of Hagfan, of Hyfaidd
Hen
Of Gawl and Clud and Teyrnon Tyr Liant
of the five lances
Of fiery Cigfa and Euryn of the golden
torque

Of Gwiri the steersman, of Gwyn Gohoyw of
   the slender bow . . .

Branwen had heard many such songs before—
tales of deeds of wonder and renown sung by the old
bards seated at the hearth in the Great Hall of Garth
Milain. Geraint had loved them, those old songs that
told of battles lost and won, of noble warriors slain,
and of the enemy defeated.

But as she let the words roll over her, Branwen
became aware that the spirit of the song had changed.
The bard was no longer singing of the deeds of men
and of the ebb and flow of battle; he was singing of
quite different things.

   I sing you now of the ancient sculptor
   Creator of all that lives and dies
   From years of toil he is old and bowed
   See how he lifts his hands to the skies
   The right hand is firm as the flesh of the
      thunder
   The left is as gentle as rain
   The right molds the mountains and valleys
      hereunder
   The left smoothes the grass of the plain
   The right squeezes diamonds from blood
      clots of iron
   The left shapes the limbs of the tree
   The right hurled the stars that are filling

> *the heavens*
> *The left traces waves on the sea*
> *The right is the hand that created the*
> *warrior*
> *The left guides the flight of the deer.*
> *Now no one can say that they know not the*
> *sculptor*
> *Before you his art is revealed*
> *But hearken now, for others shall follow*
> *The mystical fruit of his seed*

Branwen's mind filled with strange images, the notes like raindrops, like splashes of vibrant color, like the flicker of a stag's eye in the forest, like the flash of a trout in a pebbled stream. The rhythm of blood. The rush of breath. The beat of the heart. The ache of loss. The weight of mountains. The rumor of the sea.

She stared wide-eyed at the bard; somehow she was not surprised to see that his summer-sky eyes, bright as jewels, were staring straight back at her.

> *I sing of Rhiannon of the Spring*
> *The ageless water goddess, earth mother,*
> *storm-calmer*
> *Of Govannon of the Wood*
> *He of the twelve-points*
> *Stag-man of the deep forest, wise and deadly*
> *Of Merion of the Stones*

Mountain crone, cave dweller, oracle, and
*   deceiver*
And of Caradoc of the North Wind
Wild and free and dangerous and full of
*   treachery*
The Old Gods are sleepless this night
They watch and they wait
For the land is in peril once more
And the Shining Ones gather
To choose a weapon, to save the land
The Warrior
The Sword of Destiny
A worthy human to be their tool
Child of the far-seeing eye
Child of the strong limb
Child of the fleet foot
Child of the keen ear

Branwen remembered Captain Angor's words on the road from Garth Milain, recalling his unease on hearing that Geraint had spoken to her of the Old Powers and his insistence that she should not mention them again. She knew that her own mother and father would never allow such a song to be sung in Garth Milain; and yet, here, in the Great Hall of Doeth Palas, a bard was being allowed to hymn praises to the Shining Ones.

Branwen looked around to see how people were reacting. She gave a gasp of disbelief. The great chamber and everyone in it had vanished away like mist under a fiery sun. She was seated on the grassy bank of a river, her legs stretching down and the water flowing fast and cool over her feet. The river ran through a forest girded with mountains; above them, huge white clouds streamed across the cavernous sky. And the voice that sang to her was the voice of the river and the voice of the forest and the voice of the mountains and the voice of the wind-scoured sky.

> *She who will prove her worth in the triple*
> *   hunt*
> *The hunt without bloodshed*
> *And she will drink of the spring*
> *And she will dwell in the forest*
> *And she will cross the mountains*
> *And she will breathe in the north wind*
> *She will know herself*
> *When the Shining Ones send their*
> *   messenger*
> *When the wise bird comes*
> *When the wise bird dances for her*
> *When the wise bird reveals her destiny . . .*

The song ended. The river and the forest and the rearing mountains were gone.

Branwen stared at the feasters who surrounded her. The bard was no longer looking at her. Applause rose, drowning out the dying cadences of his song.

Amazed and light-headed, Branwen joined in the applause.

What had the song meant?

How had it transported her to that faraway place?

And why had that place—a place she had never seen before—felt so much like home?

16

THE FEAST WAS over. Branwen lay on her mattress in the princesses' bedchamber. The mattress had been put against the wall near to the door while the other two mattresses lay close together on the far side of the room. The chamber was lit by the frail glow of rushlights, and the two princesses were sitting facing each other on fur-covered chests while Hild and Aelf knelt behind them to undo the intricate coils of their hair. The girls were talking softly to each other as the combs and pins and strings of jewels were removed.

Branwen had torn her own hairdo apart with great relief, refusing Aelf's help in pulling the braids loose, delighting in the feel of her thick hair tumbling down over her shoulders again. She lay with her hands behind her head, gazing up at the sloping ceiling, her mind filled with the images wrought by the old bard's song.

> *And the Shining Ones gather*
> *To choose a weapon, to save the land*
> *The Warrior*
> *The Sword of Destiny*
> *A worthy human to be their tool*

Branwen lifted herself on one elbow. The servant women had left the room. The sisters were in their shifts, ready to get into bed. Romney was about to snuff out the last of the rushlights.

"That song," Branwen said. "I've never heard it before; is it sung often here?"

"Too often," Meredith said offhandedly.

Branwen sat up, wrapping the blanket around her bare shoulders. "You don't like it, then?"

"It's as dull as ditchwater," Romney said. "Lists of dead people from years and years ago. We get enough of that from our tutor without having to listen to it at feast times, too."

"They always end the feast with one of the *Songs of the Eleven Heroes*," said Meredith. "I hate them all."

"But what about that part at the end, where he sang about how the Shining Ones will pick a hero to save the land?" Branwen persisted.

"What?" Romney gave Branwen an odd look and then snorted with laughter. "I would like to hear the bard who'd dare to sing nonsense like that in front of Father."

"The Shining Ones aren't mentioned in the 'Song of Pwyll,'" Meredith added.

"Yes, they were," Branwen said in surprise. "The second half was about the sculptor and the Shining Ones, Rhiannon of the Spring, and Govannon of the Wood. . . ." Her voice trailed off when she saw the two sisters looking at her as though she had lost her mind. "You must have heard it!"

Meredith gave her a tight little smile. "If you want to fit in here, you really must stop being so *strange*. There aren't any songs about the Shining Ones. And if there were, Father certainly wouldn't allow them to be sung in the Great Hall. We're not *heathens*, you know."

Romney gave Branwen a sideways glance full of mockery. "Do the people in Cyffin Tir still believe in the Shining Ones?"

"Of course not," Branwen said. She lay back again with her hands behind her head.

The rushlights were soon put out. Branwen could hear the two girls whispering in the darkness.

Let them whisper. She knew what she had heard.

The Warrior
The Sword of Destiny
A worthy human to be their tool

She turned over, pulling the blanket up to her ears.

> *She will know herself*
> *When the Shining Ones send their*
>   *messenger*
> *When the wise bird comes*
> *When the wise bird dances for her . . .*

Branwen opened her eyes wide in the darkness as she recalled the curious dancelike movements of the falcon at the entrance to the Great Hall.

The bird's outlandish dance followed her into dreams.

"IT SEEMS THAT no traders are prepared to take the southward roads for the next few days, Branwen," Lady Elain said. "So you will be staying here with us in the meantime."

It was early the following morning. Branwen had been summoned to Lady Elain's chamber and had arrived to find her seated on a low bench while two servant women worked on her hair.

"How many days must I stay, my lady?" Branwen asked, working hard to hide her concern at the news. She wasn't looking forward to the journey to Gwent, but she didn't like the idea of prolonging her stay in Doeth Palas either.

"That I cannot tell you," said Lady Elain. "The traders have expressed fears that the Saxons may be lying in wait for them on the Great South Way. They have asked Prince Llew to send riders along the road to confirm that it is safe. He has agreed to scout the road as far south as the River Hafren. That is two days' hard ride from here, so you will be our guest for four days at least."

Four days! The Saints preserve me!

"Very well, my lady. Thank you."

"Under the circumstances, I think it's only fair that we have a talk about what will be expected of you during that time." She paused as if gathering her thoughts. "I have the greatest possible respect for your mother and for the lord Griffith, Branwen. Life is harsh and uncertain on the eastern borders, and I can only guess at the hardships and the fear under which you have lived."

"It's nothing like as bad as you all seem to think . . . ," Branwen began, eager to put her host right about life in Cyffin Tir.

Lady Elain frowned. "Please don't interrupt me, Branwen. While I know that you have been brought up as well as possible under the circumstances, I feel it is my duty to say that you have not been properly instructed in the ways of the court of Gwent. I do not blame your mother and father for this—they have hardly had the time to teach you the finer points of court manners—but your life will be quite different once you marry Hywel ap Murig. The House of Eirion is as fine and cultured a family as any to be found in Brython." Lady Elain lifted an eyebrow. "You would wish to fit in with the ways of your new husband's family, would you not, Branwen?"

"Yes. Of course."

But what if the court of Gwent is like Doeth Palas? And what if Hywel has grown up as vain and self-satisfied as Romney and Meredith? I'd rather be a vagabond in the forest than spend the rest of my life among such people!

"So, while you are living here under my roof, you will want to make use of your time by learning a little of our ways and customs."

"Yes, my lady," Branwen said. "Any instruction you are able to give me to help me fit in here will be most welcome."

And swallows will fly to the moon to drink buttermilk!

"I'm very glad to hear that, Branwen. I will speak with my daughters and ask them to help you as much as they are able; but a few words of advice from me will not go amiss, I think."

"No, my lady."

"While you are here, I think it best that you share in the pastimes and duties of my daughters."

"Would that include riding and hunting, my lady?"

Lady Elain's expression tightened like a fist. "No, it would not," she said. "Hunting is best left to men."

"But I've always hunted, my lady," Branwen explained. "My brother taught me those skills. I used to go into the forest every day, sometimes on horseback, sometimes on foot. I can bring down a hare

145

at twenty paces with the slingshot. And I can skin it and gut it too—ready for the stew-pot or the roasting stone."

Branwen was aware that the two servant women were giving her uneasy glances, as though Branwen were saying something outrageous.

Lady Elain had closed her eyes while Branwen had been speaking, a pained expression growing on her face. Now she opened them again. "That will not be necessary, Branwen. You will remain within the walls of Doeth Palas for the duration of your stay with us."

"But surely I will be allowed to go into the forest sometimes, my lady," Branwen pleaded. "I would very much prefer that, if you don't mind." She smiled. "I could even teach Meredith and Rom—"

"No more!" snapped Lady Elain. "Would you disobey me, to your discredit and to the disgrace of your noble family?" The two servants pulled away as if afraid that their mistress's anger might be turned on them.

"Not at all, my lady." Branwen gasped. "Never, on my honor."

"Continue your work!" Lady Elain ordered, not even turning her head to look at the servants. Mutely, they returned to the business of dressing her hair. Lady Elain looked at Branwen. When she spoke again, her voice was icy.

"You will do as my daughters do, Branwen. You

146

will dress as they do and behave as they do. Your parents have arranged a fine marriage for you; but if you are to be a worthy consort to Hywel ap Murig, you must shed the free and easy ways of your childhood."

Several biting responses to this flashed through Branwen's mind, but she kept silent.

"I say this not out of anger or reproach, Branwen," Lady Elain continued in a more conciliatory tone. "It is not your fault that life in the east has not equipped you for the great courts of Brython. You will thank me for this in the end." Her forehead wrinkled and her eyes softened. "Look what a fool you made of yourself at the feast last night. Surely you'd rather that didn't happen again?"

"No, I wouldn't want that, my lady."

Lady Elain smiled. "Good, then. We understand each other."

"Yes. I think we do."

"You may go, Branwen," Lady Elain said.

"Yes, my lady."

Branwen stood on the top step of the Great Hall, her hands clenched into fists, her head thrown back, and her eyes tightly shut. Her nails dug hard into her palms. She focused on the pain, using it to quell the anger that was roaring through her. In the past when something had made her wild with rage, she had always been able to burn off her anger with some physical activity—galloping Stalwyn over the eastern heaths or thrusting her way through the forest, alone with her feelings, allowing them gradually to ebb away.

How dare Lady Elain imply that her mother and father had raised her to be a barbarian!

It was only love for her parents that stopped Branwen from seeking out Stalwyn and riding away forever from Lady Elain and her sniggering daughters. Her duty to the House of Rhys calmed her anger, and helped her to find the courage to see this journey through to its bitter end.

"Ouch!" Branwen cried out, wincing as the shears tore at her hair. "Stop it! Stop it! Get away from me!"

Hild backed off. "Forgive me, my lady princess," she said. "Your hair is very thick. It's hard to cut through."

Branwen looked around at the old woman. "I'm sorry," she said. "I didn't mean to shout. Don't be frightened." She gazed into Hild's thin, furrowed face, paying attention for the first time to the deep-set brown eyes that gazed back at her. The face was aged and worn, like a crumpled leather bag; but there was still a spark of life in Hild's dark eyes. How strange it was that she had never really looked into the face of a servant before. She had always taken servants for granted—like two-legged cattle, or like trained dogs, fit only for fetching and carrying.

"How do the women in this place put up with all this nonsense?" she asked. "You say they have their hair dressed every single day?"

"Yes, my lady princess," Hild replied. "It's the fashion."

"Then it's a very stupid fashion."

Hild didn't respond.

Branwen looked inquiringly at her. "It is, isn't it? A stupid waste of time!"

The ghost of a smile touched Hild's thin lips.

"Oh, go on, Hild. Say it—no one will know! You won't get into trouble, I promise."

"I cannot, my lady princess."

"No, I suppose not. But we both know the truth, don't we."

"As you say, my lady princess."

A look passed between them, and Branwen laughed. She was pleased to see the ghost-smile flicker again on Hild's lips.

What a place Doeth Palas was! The only person with whom she could behave naturally was an old Saxon servant woman!

By all the saints, I hope the folk down in Gwent are not like this! I will go out of my mind!

"May I dress your hair now, my lady princess?" Hild asked.

"What happens if I say no?"

"I think you know what will happen, my lady princess," Hild said quietly.

"You'll be chastised, and I'll be laughed at."

"Very likely, my lady princess."

Branwen picked up the silver mirror off the floor. She stared at her reflection. "This is me," she said. "This is who I like being." She glanced at Hild. "Listen, cut as little as possible, and try not to pull. But I don't want to have my hair up. It looks stupid, and it feels uncomfortable with all those combs and pins in it." She frowned. "What's the least you can do so neither of us gets into trouble?"

Hild thought for a moment. "I could weave two braids, one at each side of your forehead," she suggested. "They could be drawn back and held behind with a ribbon of silk. That will keep the hair off your face . . . and I could tie some garnets into the braids. That will make you look very pretty, my lady princess."

"And will it be enough to keep you out of trouble?" Branwen checked.

"I believe so, my lady princess."

"And me from being laughed at?"

"Oh, most certainly, my lady princess."

Branwen smiled. "Then go to it." She rested the mirror in her lap, already tired of looking at herself.

Hild approached her, holding up the iron shears, and Branwen gritted her teeth as more thick coils of her hair fell about her onto the floor.

Branwen was in the bedchamber, kneeling in front of her chest, picking out a few precious things to attach to the waistband of her gown. Here, far from home, those small possessions meant more to her than ever.

She clutched the white crystal stones, remembering how Geraint had returned from a hunt in the mountains, a deer over his shoulders and the crystals in his fist. *I thought you would like them.* His eyes had twinkled with mischief. *I think the gwyllion left them for me to find. If you hold them to the light, you can see all the colors of the rainbow!* "There are no such things as *gwyllion*," she had responded, "but thank you, they're lovely. I'll cherish them always."

Branwen winced. Could she not even remember joy now without feeling pain?

"There is an earring missing!" Romney's voice burst into her memories. "It's been stolen!"

Branwen looked around. Romney's eyes were gleaming with malice as she glared at Hild and Aelf. "One of you has taken it!"

"No, no, my lady princess," murmured Hild. "Let me look for it for you. It must have fallen from the shelf."

"What's the point in looking for it when I know you stole it from me?" Romney snapped, her face twisted with anger.

"But we haven't taken it, my lady princess," wailed Aelf.

"You are a liar! You're both liars!"

Branwen noticed something glinting on the floor beside Romney's mattress. She got up, crossed the chamber, and picked it up. It was a golden earring. She grabbed Romney's wrist and turned her hand over, dropping the piece of jewelry into her open palm.

"Perhaps you should search more carefully before you start accusing people of theft," she said, releasing Romney's hand and going back to her chest.

She was very aware of the way Romney glared at her with hate-filled eyes. She didn't care. She was not prepared to stand by and allow those two old women to be bullied and terrified just to please the spiteful princess.

"Get out! Get *out*!" Romney shrieked at the two women.

As they left, Branwen looked up and saw the gratitude in Hild's eyes.

"Making friends with *servants* now, are you?" hissed Romney. "Why am I not surprised by that?"

"Oh, be quiet." Branwen sighed.

I detest this place, and I'm trapped here for the next four days! she thought with an inward groan. *I shall go mad!*

It was midmorning. Branwen, Meredith, and Romney were in their bedchamber, seated on wooden chests covered by soft furs. The tutor stood in front of them. He was an elderly man with weak, red-rimmed eyes, hair like cobwebs, and a draggled, gray mustache, thin as a rat's whiskers.

Branwen was doing her best to pay attention, but inside she was almost screaming with boredom.

"And now let us come to the kith and kin of your great-grandsire on your mother's lineage," the old man droned. "Anarawd the Nine-Fingered was wed to Llywarch of Bryn Dathyl in Arfon. And of their loins came Iwai Foel and Iago and Idwan Ieuaf and Meurig Cat-Claw. And Meurig Cat-Claw was betrothed to Diflas ap Tywi, who was the brother of Gilla Stag-leg, who was captured by the savage Saxons and strangled at Chester. . . ."

Outside, the sun was high in a cloudless sky. In here the air was thick and stifling, and it was all Branwen could do to stop herself from nodding off.

Her thoughts drifted away from the old man's whining voice. She was in the forest with Geraint. Sunshine poured down as thick as honey through the bright spring leaves that formed a swaying roof above her head. She was running as fast as she could, ignoring the branches that lashed her cheeks. Geraint was chasing her, blundering through the undergrowth like a hornet-bitten ox.

It was pure joy to run deer-swift through the trees, only just outdistancing Geraint's clutching hand. Joy turned to screaming laughter when she let him catch her and they both tumbled to the ground, rolling over and over until they lay panting and exhausted, staring up through the wind-whisked leaves, black against the burning blue sky.

"Princess Branwen!"

A voice broke her daydream like a stone thrown into water.

She looked at the tutor. "Yes?"

"You are not paying attention, Princess," he said testily. "You will learn nothing if you do not pay attention."

"These people you're talking about," Branwen said. "I don't know them. They're not part of my family."

"They are part of the history of Powys, Princess Branwen," said the tutor. "But if you would rather we give over part of today's lesson to the history of your own kin, then I will allow it." He made a rising gesture with one hand, as if wanting her to stand. "Please recite for us the lineage of the House of Rhys, following the male line."

"I don't think they teach such things in the east," Romney put in. "But I daresay Branwen can tell us all about the Shining Ones if you ask her."

Branwen ignored the mean-hearted laughter that came from both princesses. "My father is Prince Griffith ap Wynn," she said. "His father was Prince Wynn ap Mabon. His father was Prince Mabon ap . . . ap . . ." She paused, frowning as the name of her great-grandfather went flitting away over her memory's horizon.

"What did I tell you?" Romney smirked.

"I see that your tutoring has been lax, Princess Branwen," the old man remarked.

"I can revere my ancestors and be a credit to the House of Rhys without the need to recite their names," Branwen said with a flash of anger. "My mother and father taught me that I would do honor enough to my forebears by being loving and courageous and openhearted and dutiful." Now that she had started, it was impossible to stop. "They taught me to welcome friends and strangers alike into our home and to treat them with kindness and respect, whether they were the lowliest bondsman or King Cynon himself. And that is more than can be said of this place, where I have been mocked and humiliated and called a barbarian."

Her outburst had reduced the princesses to wide-eyed silence. Let them stare! What did she care? Summoning all her dignity, she turned and walked from the room, striding across the floor of the Great Hall and stepping out into a day of glorious sunshine.

18

THE WESTERN OCEAN!
Branwen sat on the northern rampart of Doeth Palas, leaning forward to gaze at the blue green ocean. She looked down between her feet—far, far down beyond the place where the stone ramparts were anchored to the cliffs, down and down to where the sea came gliding in with white-foamed lips that kissed the dark rocks before dying. The breeze carried a strange new tang up to her. It made her eyes smart and raised the hairs on her arms and legs.

White birds were wheeling across the stark cliffs, crying out in high, keening voices, singing a song that Branwen found both thrilling and lonely. And rumbling away beneath the shrill voices of the seagulls was the constant pulse of the restless ocean—the sound she had heard last night: the throbbing rhythm of the world's blood.

She wished she were a gull. She wished she could launch herself from this lofty place and open her arms like wings and go swooping and soaring away over that vast stretch of water.

"Fool!" she murmured to herself. "If you have to make wishes, then wish for something possible. Wish for a quick end to your stay here."

She had calmed down now, but she did not regret her anger. Maybe they were right. Maybe she didn't behave the way a proper princess should behave. Was that so very bad, when the alternative was . . . *what?* To be like Lady Elain and her daughters?

Branwen wouldn't wish that on her worst enemy. But what if Hywel's family refused to allow her to hunt and to ride alone into the forests? What if they insisted she idle away the mornings having her hair styled and bejeweled? Shuddering, she lifted her hand and brought it down with a fierce slap on the outer edge of the wall. *There's no way she would live like that!*

One of the stones in the lip of the wall moved under her hand. She picked at the joints between the stones, taking out shards and splinters of mortar until the small wedge of stone moved freely. She used the heel of her hand to edge the stone forward, meaning to prize it out and toss it down the rampart and watch as it disappeared into the foaming waves.

She smiled. If she stayed here long enough, perhaps she would have time to dismantle this whole fortress and send it tumbling into the ocean.

Then she saw that there was something engraved on the inner face of the stone. Intrigued, she dug her nails in on both sides and carefully pulled it out. The stone was very heavy, smooth and white and flawless, and on one side someone had carved an intricate picture.

Branwen ran her fingers over the carving. This must be an old Roman stone. She had been told that the Romans were skilled artists and that they could carve statues of stone that were so realistic it was amazing that they did not come alive.

The piece of stone was no larger than her two spread hands, but the scene on it, broken away at both sides, was perfectly detailed. A woman in a long gown sat astride a horse, half turned in the saddle, staring out of the carving and pointing behind her toward a patch of woodland. Every leaf of every tree had been carved, every blade of grass, every muscle and sinew of the horse's body, every hair on the woman's head.

A bird was perched on the woman's outstretched wrist.

Branwen held the stone up closer to her eyes. Surely that tiny carved bird was a . . .

Caw!

The sound was so close that it made Branwen jump. The white stone tipped forward out of her hands.

"No!" She watched helplessly as the stone plunged

downward, striking the foot of the rampart, bouncing wide, spinning as it dropped into the sea. "No!"

Caw!

She twisted her head to look at the falcon, standing defiantly on the stones at her side.

"Look what you made me do."

The bird edged closer and pecked at her wrist.

She pulled her arm away. "Ow! Don't do that."

Caw! Caw!

The falcon stepped back from her, spreading its wings and bobbing its head. "What do you want from me?"

The bird lowered its head, ruffling its neck feathers.

"I see the barbarian princess has found a new friend!" said a familiar voice at her back.

The bird sprang into the air and floated feather-light on wide wings down the ramparts.

Branwen stared up at Iwan. He was standing a little way off, his arms folded, an amused expression on his face. A twinge of lingering attraction distracted her for a moment, but then she remembered how he had duped her and her eyes narrowed in dislike.

"I heard some of the men talking about the way you took a wild falcon on your wrist on the way here," he said. "Is that the same bird?"

Branwen got to her feet. "What are you doing here?"

"I could ask you the same question. I heard that

you were having lessons with the princesses."

"You seem to hear a lot."

"Do you like them?" he asked, tilting his head. "Meredith and Romney?"

"Very much so," Branwen said. "I aspire only to be as wise and sophisticated as the children of Prince Llew and Lady Elain."

He grinned. "And swallows will fly to the moon to drink buttermilk!"

She stared at him, intrigued that he should use that particular image. "Why did you say that?"

He shrugged. "It seemed unlikely that someone like you would wish to become more like the princesses. I would have expected you to despise them both."

"Then you would have expected wrongly, Iwan," Branwen said. "The art of despising people is not one I have grown up to practice."

"And what have you been taught, my lady?" Iwan asked. "To dispute with passing birds?" The smile widened. "Do birds converse with people in Cyffin Tir?"

"No, they don't." She got up and walked quickly down the stone steps that led from the parapet of the ramparts. "Neither do they speak to vermin!"

She heard him laughing, but she refused to look back.

19

"YOU HAVE GONE too far now, Branwen. I have tried to be understanding, but your behavior toward Reece ap Colwyn was outrageous. Why did you take it upon yourself to leave his lesson without permission?"

"He made impertinent remarks about my mother and father," Branwen said.

"I doubt very much whether a learned man such as Reece ap Colwyn would have done anything of the kind. . . ."

"He said my mother and father had brought me up in ignorance of my heritage!"

"Please do not raise your voice to me, Branwen. I thought we had an understanding, but you continue to prove both disruptive and difficult. Your father and mother would be ashamed of you!"

Branwen felt her face burning. "They would understand," she said between gritted teeth.

Lady Elain threw her hands up. "I do not know what to do with you, Branwen! I would never have expected such . . . such *waywardness* in a princess of Powys. You are beyond me!"

Branwen lifted her chin, her voice shaking with emotion. She could hold her true feelings in no longer. "I will not be spoken to like this, my lady," she said. "I have done nothing wrong."

"So be it," Lady Elain snapped. "I have tried to help you, Branwen, but you will not be helped. Then it shall be the task of another to make something of you. I wash my hands of you. Until you leave for Gwent I want nothing more to do with you, Branwen ap Griffith. Do as you will!"

Branwen sat on the floor in the bedchamber, her traveling chest open in front of her. She was still shaking from her encounter with Lady Elain, and she was desperate to make physical contact with something that would soothe her heart. She pushed her gowns and shifts aside and came to her hunting clothes—her worn and stained marten-skin jerkin and her leggings and boots. Her slingshot lay with them, along with the pouch of stones. She upended the pouch and let the stones fall into her palm.

She spilled the stones from hand to hand, comforted by their smooth feel and by the hard clicking as they tumbled together. She had gathered these stones on the hills of Cyffin Tir. They made her ache for home and for the love of her mother and father. With a sigh, she poured them back into the pouch.

"You have Calculi stones!"

She looked over her shoulder. Meredith was watching her from the doorway.

"They're not . . . *what* did you call them?" Branwen said, closing the pouch and laying it back in the chest.

"Calculi stones. They look just like Calculi stones." Meredith walked over to one of her chests and opened it. She rummaged for a few moments and then drew out a square wooden board marked out with engraved lines. She also took out a small leather pouch. She untied it and spilled out twenty or more stones, half of them black, half white.

"This is a Calculi board, and these are the soldier stones." She looked at Branwen. "Don't people play Calculi where you come from?"

Branwen shook her head. "We play knucklebones. And checkers and lucky sixes. And the men play dice and Terni Lapilii, although my father doesn't approve because sometimes there are fights. But I've never heard of Calculi."

"I could teach it to you, if you like," Meredith said guardedly. "And you could teach me the game your stones are used for."

There seemed to be a genuine hint of friendliness in her voice, but Branwen was wary.

"They're not for a game," she told Meredith. "They're for my slingshot. I use them in hunting."

"Oh." Meredith blinked at her. "We are not allowed to hunt. Are you good at it?"

"Yes, I am. I feel most *alive* when I'm in the forest. It makes me feel that I'm part of something age-old and neverending and . . . and *magnificent*." Branwen knew that her explanation was hopelessly inadequate.

Meredith shook her head. "I don't understand you, Branwen."

"No, I don't expect you do." Branwen attempted a smile. "So, Calculi? I warn you, I'm not good with complicated games."

"Oh, it's really simple," Meredith said, coming over and kneeling at Branwen's side. "There are two players. One takes the black stones, the other the white. The point of the game is to line up five soldier stones in a row, either sideways or diagonally. But it's illegal to make a double-ended three, because . . ."

Meredith's voice stopped short as the door burst open and Romney came charging in.

"Merrie! Have you heard . . . oh!" She stopped in her tracks, staring down at the two of them. "What are you *doing*, Merrie?"

The princess quickly got up. "Nothing," she said, smoothing her gown as she walked away from Branwen.

"Were you making *friends* with her?" Romney asked incredulously.

"No!" Meredith exclaimed. "Of course not. Have I heard *what*?"

"Apparently Branwen has given up talking to people. She spends her time in conversation with birds!"

"I see Iwan's been gossiping," Branwen said. She couldn't bother to be annoyed with Romney, although Meredith's swift denial of what might have been a budding friendship rankled a little.

"Birds?" Meredith gave Branwen a puzzled look. "What birds?"

"Is it only birds?" Romney asked Branwen. "Or do you like to have conversations with other animals?"

"Only birds, so far," Branwen said. "But I'd willingly try other creatures as well. Intelligent conversation is hard to come by here, Romney, or hadn't you noticed?"

Romney gave her a withering look. "Perhaps you should try pigs. You should be used to how they live."

"We do like fresh straw for our bedding at Garth Milain, it's true," Branwen said. "And we like our meat fresh and raw. We drink fresh blood, too, warm from the bodies of our kill." She put her hand down to the bottom of the chest and pulled out Geraint's knife. "The fresher the better!"

She tossed the knife into the air. It turned end over end twice before she caught it by the handle.

The princesses eyed the knife with alarm. Smiling, Branwen began to polish the blade with the hem of her gown. As she rubbed at the shining tongue of iron, she spoke in a low, measured voice.

"I remember the first time I used this knife," she said. "I was about ten years old, and my brother had brought down a deer with an arrow. It was a hot day, and we were a long trek from home, so it was important to dress the deer so the meat wouldn't be tainted. I asked if I could help. Geraint gave me the knife and said he'd explain exactly what to do." She glanced at the princesses, who had moved close together, and as she spoke, she made the appropriate motions with the knife. "You start by making a cut along the belly, down by the back legs, a cut that runs right up to the ribs. But you have to be careful not to nick the entrails or that can get very nasty. Then you follow the cut right up to the neck, using your fingers to hold the cut open so you can see what you're doing and the knife doesn't get caught up in the ribs. You have to do some other cutting now, but I won't go into the details; you look pale enough already." She held the knife up to the candlelight, turning it so the blade glimmered and flashed. "Then you turn the deer onto its side and pull the entrails out with your hands. It's a messy business so it's wise to do it by a source of fresh water so you can wash all the blood off. Then you put the carcass over your shoulders and carry it home."

Meredith and Romney were staring at her with wide, horrified eyes. Branwen pulled the contents of the chest aside and placed the knife carefully down at the bottom again. She rearranged her clothes, slammed the lid shut, and got up.

"It must be time for dinner by now," she said, heading for the door. "Anyone hungry? I'm ravenous!" She pushed through the door, letting it swing closed behind her.

There was not a sound from within the room.

Grinning, Branwen left the princesses to confirm their darkest fears about her.

20

BRANWEN ROSE EARLY the next morning and was on the rampart overlooking the ocean before the sun had climbed above the mountains. She had bread and cheese with her, taken from the storeroom and wrapped in a cloth. She had decided to avoid eating with the others whenever she could.

Solitude suited her mood. She had felt awkward and ill at ease throughout the previous evening's meal. It had not been such a grand affair as the Homecoming Feast; there had been maybe twenty guests in the Great Hall; and although the food had been plentiful, it had not been anything like so lavish. But Branwen had felt even more of an outsider than she had on the previous occasion. Lady Elain and the princesses had pointedly ignored her, and Prince Llew had been so engrossed in conversation with Gavan and Captain Angor that Branwen wasn't even sure if he realized she was there. All in all, she had been glad to get it over with, and she was not looking forward to three more days of such uncomfortable meals.

She sat quietly on the cool stones, biting at the fresh, white bread, enjoying being alone with the salt breeze in her hair.

> *The Old Gods are sleepless this night*
> *They watch and they wait*
> *For the land is in peril once more*
> *And the Shining Ones gather*
> *To choose a weapon, to save the land*
> *The Warrior*
> *The Sword of Destiny*
> *A worthy human to be their tool . . .*
> *She will know herself*
> *When The Shining Ones send their*
>   *messenger*
> *When the wise bird comes*
> *When the wise bird dances for her*
> *When the wise bird reveals her destiny . . .*

When the wise bird comes . . .

She had climbed the ocean-facing rampart in the hope that the falcon would be there. The wise bird. The dancing bird. But it had not come. The wind had come, the salt-heavy north wind, tugging at her

hair and caressing her face with its cold fingers. The
sun had come, lifting above the mountain peaks and
throwing its light and heat down over her.

But the falcon had not come.

*Am I losing my reason? Meredith and Romney didn't
hear the song that I heard. No one sings of the Shining
Ones. The Druid seers who worshipped them have been
dead and gone for five hundred years. Wild birds do not
follow people over mountains. They do not dance for them.
Oh, Geraint—am I going mad? Please don't let me be
going mad.*

"Ho, there, Andras! Lift the bow, lad! You're meant to
be firing at Saxons, not plowing a field!"

Branwen stood up and walked to the inner edge
of the parapet. She found herself looking down into
a wide, unpaved area between buildings. She had
assumed it was a square set aside for market traders
or for cattle, but at the moment it was being used for
archery practice.

Gavan ap Huw stood with a group of seven
young men. Branwen recognized them as the lads
Iwan had sat with at the feast on her first night in
Doeth Palas. And—oh, yes—there was Iwan, leaning against a wall and watching Andras as he struggled with his bow.

Branwen gazed down at Iwan in confusion. How
could such a captivating face hide such an unkind
spirit? And why did her heart beat faster at the sight

of him even when she knew what a wretched trickster he was?

She forced herself to look away. All the lads were dressed in white linen tunics and leggings. Branwen guessed they were about the same age as Iwan, although none were as tall nor as handsome as he. Andras was skinny, all elbows and knees, with a long neck and a face like a startled chicken.

There was a twang. The target was a life-sized human figure made of twisted and coiled wicker. The arrow missed it and sputtered into the ground. Andras gave Gavan a mournful look as laughter rippled around the courtyard.

"You've a long way to go, my lad, before I'd set you against a living Saxon, unless they come for you crawling on their bellies," Gavan growled, silencing the laughter with a flash of his dark eyes. He slapped the boy on the back. "Away now, lad, and stand with the others." Andras crept away with shoulders slumped. "You! Padrig ap Gethin! You're quick enough to laugh. Come, show us how it's done!"

A lad with black hair and a wisp of mustache under his long nose stepped from the ring and took the bow from Gavan's hand. A bunch of feather-fletched arrows had been stabbed into the dirt near one end of the courtyard, about forty paces from the target.

Padrig took an arrow and fitted it to the string. He lifted the bow. Branwen had spent a lot of time watching her brother handle a bow and arrow, and she could tell just from the way Padrag stood and the way he held the bow that he would miss his target.

She nodded as the arrow whisked past the shoulder of the wicker target and bounced off a stone wall. *I knew it!*

"What did he do wrong?" asked Gavan.

"His bow arm was too low," Iwan said. "His elbow was drooping. He had no eye-line along the arrow. I'm surprised he came as close as he did!"

"And can you do better?" Gavan challenged.

"In my sleep, I could do better," Iwan drawled to a murmur of laughter.

Gavan took the bow out of Padrag's hands and held it toward Iwan. Still smiling, the young man peeled himself off the wall and strolled over to where Gavan was standing.

He's very sure of himself! Branwen thought. She felt for the slingshot tucked into her waistband. She had not thought to bring any stones. But there were scraps and shards of stone between the main blocks on the parapet of the ramparts. She quickly found a possible candidate—a little uneven in shape, and not so smooth and rounded as she would have preferred, but it would do the job. She ran along the parapet and down the stairway. She skimmed along the wall, keeping as silent as she could, until she came to a building that formed one of the sides of the courtyard. Hugging the wall, she peered around.

Iwan had taken the bow and was fitting an arrow to the string. Branwen folded the slingshot double and fitted the stone in place. Iwan lifted the bow, his elbow raised high, drawing the string back to his cheekbone, closing one eye to aim the better.

Branwen swung the slingshot around her head. At the perfect moment, she opened two fingers to release one end of the whirling pouch. There was a snap and a hiss as the stone went shooting through the air. It caught the top of Iwan's bow at the very moment that he loosed the arrow.

The thin, pine arrow flew high and embedded itself in the thatched roof.

"Who did that?" Iwan shouted, glaring at the others. "Who threw that stone?"

Branwen put her hand over her mouth to stifle her laughter.

Gavan picked up the stone and rolled it between finger and thumb. "Step from cover, Princess Branwen," he called, lifting his eyes and looking straight to where she was hiding. "There's no need to be bashful, my lady."

Branwen came out, placing her hands on her hips as she gazed at Iwan.

"Well, it seems the princess has hidden talents," Iwan said. "Nicely thrown, my lady, although maybe it was more luck than judgment that sent your aim so true? Perhaps you were not aiming for the bow at all?" He lifted an arm toward the sky. "Perhaps you were hoping to bring down your breakfast? Has your new friend been teaching you which birds are the tastiest?"

"Now, then, Iwan ap Madoc," Gavan growled. "The lady is a princess of Cyffin Tir. Watch your tongue, boy."

"Oh, then I apologize, of course," Iwan said casually. "I thought that perhaps in lands where princesses threw stones from cover, such niceties were not honored." He bowed low, but his eyes remained mockingly on her. "I am your humble servant, my lady princess."

"Humble?" Branwen retorted. "I doubt if that's a trick you could pull off successfully, Iwan ap Madoc. Not if your life depended on it!"

"Can I be of service to you, Princess Branwen?" Gavan broke in. "Would you join us? I'd like to know whether the boy was right or not. Did you aim true, or was it luck?"

Branwen looked at him. "It was not luck," she said. "It was skill."

Gavan opened his hand to her. "Then would you care to test your skill against the young men of Prince Llew's court, my lady?"

Branwen smiled. "I would," she said, walking forward into the courtyard, aware that the would-be archers were all looking at her, some with open hostility, others with scorn on their faces.

Iwan smiled as Branwen approached him, but there was a glint of darker emotion in his eyes, a kind of cool contempt. A look that said: *Not only will I beat you, Princess Branwen, but I will trample you into the dust beneath my feet!*

Branwen smiled back at him.

Iwan plucked another arrow from the ground and fitted it to the bow. Branwen ignored him as she walked around the courtyard with her eyes on the ground, seeking out a good stone or two.

There was some muffled laughter from the lads, and she halfheard some cruel comments aimed at her. She didn't care anymore.

Branwen stooped to pick up a stone. She heard a twang and a thud. Iwan had loosed his arrow. Branwen straightened up and looked across at the target. Iwan's arrow stood out from the center of the woven forehead, the flight feathers still quivering.

There was a shout of approval and a burst of applause from the lads.

Branwen looked at Iwan. "Forgive me, Princess," he said. "Weren't you ready?"

She didn't bother responding. She placed the new-found stone in her slingshot. She swung the sling-shot around her head once, twice, three times—then loosed the stone.

It hissed as it cut through the air. There was a sharp crack. The back half of Iwan's arrow hung by a thread where her stone had broken it in two.

The lads became silent. Iwan scowled.

Gavan broke out laughing. "Nicely done, my lady,"

he said. He looked around. "A lesson learned, I hope. The daughter of Lady Alis ap Owain is not easily bested! Come now, which of you will challenge the princess next?"

No one spoke. Branwen picked up another stone and bounced it on her hand, her eyes traveling from face to face.

"No one?" said Gavan. "Here, Bryn, step up, lad. I'll not have the princess think we breed milk-hearted men in Bras Mynydd."

A tall, wide-shouldered boy with a pale, freckled face and a mop of reddish hair walked up to Iwan and took the bow from him. Branwen noticed that he never once looked her in the face.

Gavan strode across the courtyard. He picked up two stones and placed them one on either shoulder of the wicker target. "My lady, aim for the left shoulder if you will," he called, stepping away from the target. "Bryn, the right."

Bryn fitted an arrow. He had slow and deliberate movements and wasted no energy as he drew the bow and lined up the arrow. Branwen knew he would aim well.

She fitted another stone and swung her sling-shot.

Arrow and stone were launched together. Bryn's arrow stabbed deep into the wicker shoulder, a hair-breadth below target, the impact knocking off the stone. But Branwen's aim was perfect, striking her target true and sending the stone flying.

She looked at Bryn. "You're very good," she said, holding finger and thumb up so they were almost touching. "You only missed by that much!"

He glowered at her and threw down the bow, stalking off the courtyard without looking back. A couple of the others followed him. Gavan stood with fists on hips, his lips pursed as he watched them go.

Branwen frowned after them. "I did not mean to offend him."

"Myself excepted, Bryn is our best archer," Iwan said. "It's hard enough for him to be beaten by a girl without you demeaning him further with your words of consolation." He gazed after the departing lads. "I imagine he hates you quite deeply at the moment. I'd watch your back, Princess Branwen. Bryn is not a good loser."

Branwen was surprised by this implied threat. "Should I be fearful of him, then?" she said.

Iwan shrugged but didn't reply.

"The lesson is over!" called Gavan. "Get you gone from here, and tell Bryn that I would see him in my house at sundown."

The remaining lads left the courtyard in a murmuring huddle. All except for Iwan, who stood looking at Branwen with his arms folded. "*I* would not have missed," he said to her.

"Then try your luck," Branwen replied, holding his gaze.

"Another time." He gave a brief bow, then turned on his heel and strode away.

"These boys are not used to competing against women," said Gavan. His eyes narrowed. "How did you learn to use a slingshot so well? It was no accident that you hit your target with each shot."

"My brother gave me the slingshot, but I taught myself how to use it," Branwen said. "I prefer it to a bow and arrow."

"Indeed? Why so?"

"A bow is too big and awkward in the forest," Branwen said. "A slingshot is better for hunting."

Gavan looked thoughtfully at her. "That would depend on what you are hunting, my lady. What is the largest animal you can bring down with a single shot?" As he spoke, he plucked the arrows out of the ground and slid them into a quiver that hung from his shoulder.

"A roe deer," Branwen told him. "If the aim is true." She walked over to the wicker figure and pulled out the two arrows, handing them to him.

"You say a single stone would kill a deer?"

"Not always. But I do try to kill as quickly as possible. Sometimes an animal has to be finished off with a knife."

"And are you as skilled with a knife as you are with a slingshot?"

"I know how to use a knife on a carcass, if that's what you mean."

"That is what I meant, my lady." He slid the last of

the arrows into his quiver, then gave a small, formal bow. "And now I must attend to my other duties."

Branwen didn't want him to go. This was the closest she'd had to a genuine conversation since she'd been here. "You were a guest at Garth Milain some years ago," she said quickly. "I remember you."

Gavan hesitated. "And I you, my lady," he said. "Although you were but a child."

"You were King Cadwallon's standard-bearer at the battle of Meigen, weren't you? What was King Cadwallon like? Was he as great as people say?"

"He was," Gavan said. "A mighty king and a fearless warrior. His death was a great loss to our land. But we endure, my lady; we live to fight on."

"Some of us do," Branwen said. "And some of us get sent south to be married."

Gavan frowned at her but said nothing.

"My mother is a warrior," Branwen said.

"Yes, my lady, she is. Renowned through the five kingdoms."

"I've never seen her fight—not for real," Branwen said. "People say she was fearsome in battle." She wrinkled her forehead. "It's hard to imagine."

"Believe it, my lady," Gavan said, a faint smile touching his lips. "I knew your mother many, many years ago—long before she was wed to your father." The deep-set eyes burned into her face. "You are the image of her," he murmured. "You have her spirit and her fire; I can see that."

Branwen returned his gaze. "No, sir, in that you're

mistaken," she replied sadly. "I am no warrior." She turned and walked away from him.

The conversation had turned sour for her; she had hoped it would lift her spirits, but it had served only to remind her of the things she had left behind, the things she had lost forever. The things she would never be.

Branwen ap Griffith—proud daughter of a warrior-mother!

No. Branwen the exile. Branwen the forgotten, wife to Hywel ap Murig.

21

ROMNEY WAS IN the bedchamber, sitting on a chest while Aelf dressed her hair. There was no sign of Meredith.

"Don't be so rough!" Romney scolded. "You'll pull my hair out by the roots." Her complaints stopped when she saw Branwen. "Why are you still here?" she demanded. "No one wants you here."

"I'll be gone soon, the saints willing," Branwen said without rancor.

"Not soon enough," spat Romney. "All your talk about hunting and traipsing through the woods, why don't you go and live in the forest like the savage you are?"

Branwen gazed at her. If only she could do just that. Suddenly the urge burst up in her to be away from the fortress and among trees again. She grinned at

Romney. "That's an excellent idea," she said. She tore off her gown and threw open her traveling chest. She cast the upper clothes across the floor, emptying the chest until she came to her marten-skin jerkin and her leggings and forest boots. She pulled them on, wrapping a simple band around her waist and fitting her slingshot and pouch of stones onto it.

Romney was staring at her. "What are you doing? Have you lost your wits?"

"Not at all. I'm taking your advice, Romney."

Branwen drew Geraint's knife out of the chest. She walked across to Romney and dropped to one knee in front of the alarmed girl. She held up the knife in front of Romney's face. "Shall I bring you back something tasty?" she offered.

Romney's eyes bulged.

Branwen laughed and got up. "Good-bye, Romney," she said. "Every time I gut a hare, I'll be thinking of you."

She strode from the room. As she walked through the fortress, she was aware of people staring at her in her unladylike clothes, but she ignored them. There were guards at the gate, but they didn't try to stop her as she made her way into the deep slit that cleft the ramparts. For a few moments she was enveloped in cool darkness, then she came out into the sunlight again.

She began to run down the roadway that led from the fortress. Ahead of her, the road rose toward the ridge crowned with iron braziers; but to her right it was hemmed with trees. She plunged into the welcoming arms of the forest.

"Geraint! Catch me if you can! Come hunting with me!"

She ran until a stabbing pain in her side brought her to a panting halt. She doubled over, leaning against a sturdy oak, sucking in breath. She put her back to the oak and slid down to sit on the ground with her legs folded up. The forest stretched all around her. Branches spread above her head; roots delved beneath her feet.

The fortress of Doeth Palas could have been at the other end of the world. She rested her head back against the knuckled trunk and closed her eyes, breathing in the forest scents, feeling the crumbling earth under her hands. Through her eyelids, she could see the play of sunlight among the leaves, a constant flickering of brightness and shade that made her feel as if her head was filled with a dappled river of rosy light.

She breathed slowly, drawing the forest into her lungs and feeling it tingling in her limbs and sparking at her fingertips. She could hear her heart beating. She could feel her hair growing, spinning out of her glowing skull, creeping down her shoulders to touch the oak bark, needling its way into the living wood. And she felt the tree roots lifting from the ground, waving white in the air, seeking with tender rootlets. Finding her, caressing her, growing up around her until she was clothed in a gentle weave of pale, soft tendrils. Smiling, she felt the roots darken and harden. She felt buds and tiny coiling leaves sprouting. She felt the leaves envelop her. She felt the warm trunk swell out to pull her in. She felt ivy twining through her hair.

> . . . *brush back the ivy from your dark locks glowering* . . .

She felt herself dissolving.

Branwen?

"Geraint?"

Wake up, you mooncalf! You have work to do!

"What work?"

I thought you might want to come hunting with me.

She smiled. "*You* can come hunting with *me!*"

Caw!

"Geraint?"

Caw! Caw!

Her eyes opened. The falcon was perched on a low branch, staring down at her through the leaves. She got to her feet, surprised that the old oak let go of her so easily. She had almost expected to fight against sucking roots and a restraining cloak of leaves.

The forest seemed different, somehow. The colors were deeper and richer, and the scents were stronger. The air burned fierce and wild in her body. The ground was seething with life under her feet. Even the dappled sunlight seemed brighter as it shot arrows of gold down through the canopy of shimmering leaves.

She walked under the falcon's branch and looked up into the bird's glittering black eyes. It stared back at her until she had to blink and look away.

The falcon launched itself from the branch and glided on still wings through the thick, golden air. It came to rest on another branch and turned to look back at Branwen.

Caw!

She followed the bird. As she drew close, it took to the air again. On and on it led her, deeper and deeper into the forest until, in a shallow dell filled with ferns, it vanished.

She stared around, waist deep in a sea of ferns. The silence hummed in her ears.

"Where are you?"

She felt light-headed. The trees leaped like vivid green flames all around her. The sky burned like an oven.

A burst of noise and movement near her feet brought her out of her trance.

A small wild boar squealed as it went plowing through the ferns, its head lowered, its sturdy legs kicking up the soil.

Branwen gave chase, pulling her slingshot out of her belt and feeling for her pouch of stones. The boar came out of the ferns and disappeared into the trees. Branwen grinned, taken over by the thrill of the hunt. The small creature was making such a racket that she had no trouble in tracking it as it zigzagged its way through the trees. Without breaking her stride, she fitted a stone into her slingshot.

She was almost upon the beast now. She could hear its rasping breath, see the bunched muscles of its rump, its back legs kicking as it dived under a hawthorn bush.

Branwen came to a skidding halt. The bush was armored with spikes and thorns, its twisted branches old and tangled. She did not want to risk being scratched; hawthorn scratches could fester and cause fever. She dropped to the ground, sitting on her heels, waiting for the telltale squealing of the boar as it darted from cover.

The boar was strangely silent.

She bent over and peered under the thicket of branches. There was no sign of the boar. "Blood of Annwn!" she gasped. "I've lost it. But how . . . ?"

A brown blur burst from the heart of the bush, almost knocking her over as it took to the air. A full-grown grouse. It swerved, wings working hard as it flapped away through the forest.

Branwen scrambled to her feet and hurtled after it. The boar seemed to have disappeared, but this plump grouse would be hers. She crashed through the trees, the brown grouse always just on the very edge of sight. She felt exhilarated and tireless, leaping over fallen logs, ducking under the hanging branches, pushing leaves aside with both hands as she ran.

At last the bird broke cover, and Branwen burst

into open air and a well of hot sunlight. Oaks hemmed the circular glade. Lush grasses and reeds swayed in the breeze; and in the very center lay a pool of still water, silvered by the sun.

The bird had come to earth in a clump of reeds close to the pool. Branwen could just make out its shape through the thick stems. She stood quite still, watching it. Wings fluttered occasionally. The bird was exhausted.

Branwen moved slowly forward, her slingshot ready. But the reeds were too dense for her to get a clear shot. She needed to be closer.

Creep. Stop. A step. Stop. Almost on top of the creature now. One foot forward. Hardly breathing. Shift the weight. Eyes on the brown shape. Almost close enough to reach down and pluck the bird out of the reeds.

No need for the slingshot. She tucked it into her belt.

One more step.

The grouse took to the air in a blizzard of brown feathers. Caught off guard, Branwen lunged, reaching out with both arms. She caught the bird between her hands; but as she stepped forward she felt the ground vanish under her feet, and she fell headlong into the pool, her hands still gripping the bird as the water closed over her head.

22

B RANWEN'S EYES WERE filled with bubbles, and her ears rang with the churn and surge of the water. She was startled by the fall into the pool, but unafraid. The water was warm and clear—so clear that she could see the weeds waving and billowing beneath her like a secret forest. Bright fish sped away from her like sinuous jewelry, red and yellow and blue and silver, flashing in the spears of golden sunlight that cut through the water.

She still had the bird in her hands—except that it no longer felt like a bird. It felt like a fish.

It *was* a fish.

She realized this with a curious lack of surprise. But she knew she was not dreaming. She had never felt more widely awake.

The giant salmon writhed and struggled in her

grip, thrashing its tail and straining to get free. She managed to keep a hold on it despite the desperate strength in its long, silver body. She pulled the fish toward her, kicking out with her legs to try and push herself to the surface. But the salmon was larger than she had thought. Her hands couldn't keep a grip on it. She had to wrap her arms around it and hold it to her chest as it fought against her.

Even then she could hardly cling on as it thrashed in her arms, the huge head lashing under her chin, the muscular tail flogging her legs.

How had it become so huge?

Her chest began to hurt, as if an iron band was being tightened around her ribs. She needed air.

Let go of the fish. That's the only way.

Never! It's mine!

Then you'll drown.

She was turned over and over in the water as the salmon battled to get free—but still she wouldn't release it. A darkness closed in on her. The pain crushed her chest. A piercing voice howled in her head.

Her foot struck something solid, and she pushed hard against it, her head spinning.

She burst into the air, gasping and coughing, the salmon still in her arms. She kicked for the shore and squirmed onto dry land. She rolled onto her back, digging her heels into the soft earth, pushing herself away from the marshy edge of the pool.

She lay there, gulping in breath, her eyes closed

against the sun, the salmon gripped between her hands.

Smaller than she had imagined.

Much smaller.

She managed to get onto her knees.

The salmon lay quite still in her hands, its sleek body no longer than her forearm. She looked into its eye, and with a gasp of shock she threw it into the reeds.

The eye that had stared back at her had been as black and bright and knowing as the falcon's eye.

"You have won your prize," said a voice. "Kill your quarry and quit this place." It was a woman's voice, soft and musical.

Branwen sat up, staring around, unsure of the direction from which the voice had come. The sun dazzled her, and she could see no one in the glade. She looked again at the salmon. Its tail twitched feebly, its mouth gaping as its life ebbed away.

She couldn't let it die. It had fought too well to gasp out its life like this. She slipped her hands under it and lifted it carefully out of the reeds. She turned and sank her arms into the water. The salmon came alive again in her hands, darting away from her. She saw its silvery shape for a moment, gliding through the water; then it was gone.

"Child, you have passed the test," said the voice. "You have come at last. Why did you resist my calling you for so long?"

Branwen stood up. Was she imagining things?

There was no one there.

Wait!

A white shape through the trees.

As Branwen watched, a tall, white horse moved smoothly into the clearing. Seated on its back was a woman dressed all in silver. Horse and rider seemed to shimmer like the midsummer sun on a hot stone, and beneath them moved a shadow as white as snow.

At first the woman's shape was so bright that Branwen had to shield her eyes. But then the brightness faded a little, and Branwen found she could bear to look.

She had seen the woman and her horse before— carved into the white stone that she had prized from the rampart of Doeth Palas.

Oh, but she was beautiful! So *beautiful*!

The woman's hair was like a fall of pure white water, cascading down past her shoulders and foaming about her waist. The slender face was pale as milk, the wide forehead circled by a band of white diamonds. Her wide eyes were terrible and compelling, the irises ice blue, the pupils like midsummer mist. White eyebrows swept upward, and her nose was hooked like the beak of an eagle. Her lips were full and bloodlessly white. She was dressed in a flowing white gown that sparkled like sunlight on water.

One slim hand held the reins of the horse. The reins and the bridle and all the trappings of the horse were threaded with white jewels that sparkled like droplets of ice, and more jewels hung between its eyes. Its coat was as white as frost under moonlight.

The woman's other hand was raised—and Branwen's falcon was perched upon her wrist.

"Who are you?" Branwen whispered.

"I have many names," said the woman, and something in her voice made Branwen think of water rippling over stones. "But for you I am Rhiannon of the Spring. And my falcon, you already have met. His name is Fain."

Branwen let out a breath, fear clutching her heart as the words of the bard came back to her.

I sing of Rhiannon of the Spring, the ageless water goddess, earth mother, storm-calmer . . .

"You are a Shining One."

"I am."

"Are you *real*?"

"I am as real as a racing river, as real as the pounding sea, as real as a falling dewdrop. Come to me, child; do not be afraid." Rhiannon smiled. "Embrace your destiny."

Branwen stepped forward, her eyes grown used to the brilliance but her mind still dazzled. "What do you want of me?"

"I have waited long for you, warrior-child. All of Brython will be your home, and you will gather to you a band of warriors who shall keep the enemy at bay for many long years."

"No! You're wrong. I'm not a warrior."

"You can be a warrior, if you choose to be," Rhiannon said, her eyes shining. The white horse snorted and pawed the ground.

"Not me!"

"If you turn from me, child, the enemy will sweep over you like a black tide. There is a festering canker at the heart of this land."

"But you don't understand," Branwen protested. "I'm no *good*! I can't do those things. You have to pick someone else."

"There is no one else," Rhiannon said. "You are the child of Alis ap Owain and Griffith ap Wynn. You are the one who will save this land. You are the Sword of Destiny. The Bright Blade! The Emerald Flame of your people!"

"No!" Branwen shouted. "It isn't I you need. It was my *brother*, the other child of my parents. Geraint was the fighter—but he's dead. He's the one you mean, but it's too late now—too late!"

"No, child, it is you," Rhiannon said, her voice rippling. "You have passed the test of the triple hunt. You have chased flesh, fowl, and fish but spilled no blood."

The triple hunt!

> *Child of the Spring*
> *Child of the Wood*
> *Chase flesh, fowl, fish*
> *But spill no blood*

Branwen felt as if iron clamps were tightening around her head. Was she the child in the ancient rhyme? She *couldn't* be.

She felt the weight of Brython pressing in all around her—the mountains, the forests, the rivers and plains, the fields and hills and dales bearing down on her, crushing her. She felt as if all the animals had turned, startled in forest and field, their eyes on her; as if the birds that wheeled in the air were looking down at her. And the people—the ancient people, the stone-movers, the earth-heapers—all turned toward her through the vastness of time. All people, all animals, all of Brython, centered on her—on the *smallness* of her in this place and at this moment.

How could they all be so wrong?

"You are the one," Rhiannon said. "That is why I showed myself to the Saxon horseman in Bevan's clearing and filled his heart with dread. That is why his ax was stayed, why his horse shied away. That is why you were not killed that day."

"It was *you*!" Branwen gasped. "Behind me in the trees when Geraint was killed. The Saxon horseman saw *you*!"

"He did."

"You saved me."

"Your destiny saved you, child."

A terrible anger blazed through Branwen. "Why didn't you save Geraint?" she shouted. "If you saved me, why didn't you save him?"

"His was not the destiny," she said.

"But you *could* have saved him. You let him be killed."

"Peace, child," said Rhiannon. "It was his destiny to die at that time and in that place." She smiled. "Come, Branwen, accept *your* destiny. Come with me now into the elder forest. Come and begin your new life!"

"No!" Branwen howled. "I'll never go with you! You let my brother die!" Her anger was like a red fog billowing in her mind; and she ran forward, drawing Geraint's knife from her waistband, wanting to strike out at this cold-hearted creature.

But she had not gone more than two steps before she was tripped and brought down. The grass beneath her had come alive, coiling around her feet and gripping her ankles, holding her fast. She pulled herself up onto her knees and threw the knife with a yell of anger and frustration.

Rhiannon lifted her hand, and the knife exploded into a hail of silvery droplets.

"Let go of me!" Branwen howled, the grass cutting into her flesh as she fought to get free.

A deep, ground-shaking voice roared from within the forest. "Enough of this, sister! She *must* come!"

The voice stunned Branwen into stillness. Panting for breath, she stared into the trees. She could see nothing.

Or was there something . . . in deep shadow . . . a great, dark bulk . . . and huge, many-branched antlers . . . ?

"No, brother," Rhiannon said, and there was sadness in her voice. "She must come of her own free will."

She made a gesture with her hand, and Branwen felt the fetters of grass loosen.

She stood up. She was still angry, but the wild, red mist had gone.

Rhiannon looked at her. "Child—will you come?"

"No!"

"So be it." She lifted her hand again and pointed at Branwen. "But listen to me, Branwen, listen and remember. As you caught and released the salmon, so I have captured and released you. But there is a price to be paid." As she spoke, her voice grew louder, until it echoed in Branwen's head like a storm. The light around her grew brighter and brighter, until Branwen had to cover her eyes and turn away.

"I do not make the future, Branwen, but I see it as clearly as a picture mirrored in still water. In fire did you leave your home and in fire will you return! Two choices will you be given—two lives to save; but by your choice will one life be lost."

"I won't listen to you!" Branwen blundered blindly into the forest, but the voice followed her.

"You will run in a circle, Branwen ap Griffith, and I will be there. We shall meet again in the place where the men of mud dance beneath the moon of blood. And there you will learn the truth, and perhaps a little wisdom!"

23

H ER SIGHT BLURRED from the dazzling white light, Branwen stumbled on into the trees with the voice of Rhiannon rushing like floodwater through her head. She had no thought but the need to get away from that fearsome creature—to silence the voice in her head, to be free of the Shining Ones and their unwanted destiny.

She tripped and fell with a cry of pain. She lay panting, facedown in the endless stillness of the forest, listening to the drumming of blood through her body, seeing the light, red as embers now, burning behind her closed eyelids.

The Shining Ones were real. Rhiannon of the Spring had called her to some outlandish, impossible destiny; and Branwen had fled from her.

But what did it mean? What did *anything* mean

now? Had the world gone mad—and had it taken her with it?

At last the beating of her heart slowed, and she lifted her head and gazed around. She blinked a few times, and the cloud of darkness that floated in front of her eyes gradually faded away.

It was evening now, and a stifling gloaming had come creeping under the canopy of branches. The air was so heavy with the musty scents of the forest that Branwen could hardly catch her breath. The smells of leaf mold, sap, damp earth, and decaying wood filled her head. She got to her feet and walked toward a place where the glancing light was pouring through the trees.

She came out onto the road.

Thank the saints!

All she wanted now was to get to a human place— a place where the world made sense. She walked quickly along the road, trying not to think. The fortress towered above her like a fire-flecked giant. She labored up the long path between the ramparts. At last the noise and the bustle of Doeth Palas was all around her. She was back in the real world.

She didn't have the heart for another confrontation with Romney and Meredith. In fact, she wanted nothing to do with any of the fine folk of Doeth Palas. She made her way to the knot of servant huts behind the Great Hall. Hild was there, hunched over, sewing by the light of smoldering rushes. Branwen swayed in the doorway, battered and exhausted by her experiences in the forest—weary, worn down, but horribly awake.

"Go to the hall," Branwen said. "Tell the Lady Elain that I will dine alone tonight. Then bring me food and drink here."

"Yes, my lady princess." Hild's eyes were puzzled. "Are you ill, my lady princess?"

"No, not ill." Branwen stepped into the hut. Her legs folded under her, and she sat down heavily on the dirt floor. "Just tired."

"Yes, my lady princess." Hild got up and made for the doorway.

"Do not tell her where I am, please," Branwen called after her. She looked around at Hild's meager possessions. Earthen floor, daub-and-wattle walls. Straw for a bed. Untanned hides for blankets. A small hearth over which thin, yellow flames played.

She sat by the fire, staring into the flames.

She had met one of the Shining Ones. She had refused to do as Rhiannon had wished.

What else could she have done? Rhiannon had let Geraint die! How could that ever be forgiven?

Destiny?

What did she care about destiny?

"You can be a warrior, if you choose to be."

Was it really that simple?

She remembered a conversation with her mother on the night of her brother's death.

"Why wasn't I brave?"

"It is not cowardice to avoid certain death. There was nothing you could have done to save your brother."

And in her grief and misery she had allowed herself to be swept along by events, to be sent away from home and brought to this place.

. . . to find her destiny . . .

Not the destiny of the Shining Ones, but her *own* destiny. A destiny she would forge by the power of her own will. She would not go south with the traders. She would not meekly give into marriage with Hywel ap Murig. She would learn to be a warrior. Not for the Shining Ones, but for herself. She would fight back and avenge her brother's death.

At Doeth Palas she had come to a fork in the road of her life—and the path she would take did not head south.

"You can be a warrior, if you choose to be."

"Yes!" she said aloud. "I choose to be a warrior!"

Branwen gazed at Hild across the flickering yellow firelight. She had eaten a meal of bread and cold chicken, washed down with a cup of buttermilk. The simple food and the bleak but commonplace surroundings of the old woman's hut had helped her to anchor herself back in the world she understood.

A world where boar did not change into grouse, and where grouse did not change into fish, and where white goddesses on shining white horses did not come ripping through reality as though it were no more than a length of threadbare linen.

Hild was busy with her sewing, stitching together two lengths of cloth, her head bowed, her eyes screwed up in concentration in the weak light.

"You must wish us all dead," Branwen said suddenly.

Hild lifted her head, her eyes wide in surprise. "My lady princess?"

"In your heart of hearts, your fondest wish must be for the king of Northumbria's army to come sweeping through Brython and kill each and every one of us," Branwen said. "Then you would be released from captivity. You would be able to go home."

"I don't wish death on anyone, my lady princess," Hild murmured.

"But you must want to go home?"

A wintry smile touched Hild's mouth. "I was taken when I was a child, my lady princess," she said. "I don't remember my home very well. There was a village . . . a river." She lifted her head and gazed past Branwen as she spoke. "I remember mud between my toes. My father spearing trout. Riding home on his shoulders with a basket of fish in my arms. Sleeping warm under furs." She sighed. "Then there was shouting and flames and my mother's screams." She shook her head. "It was all a long time ago, my lady princess. I do not think about it."

Branwen watched the weathered old face through

the flames. It filled her with sadness and horror to think of the little girl this wretched old servant woman had been, and of the life from which she had been wrenched. To end up here, the plaything of a cruel child like Romney?

"If it were up to me, I'd set you free," Branwen said in a rush. "All of you. I'd let you go home."

"No, my lady princess," Hild said. "That cannot be. When the Saxons come, they kill the young men of this land and take the women into servitude. When the armies of Brython go forth into the Saxon kingdoms, they also slaughter and take captives. The world is harsh, my lady princess, and the peoples of both sides are ground like wheat between quern stones." She looked into Branwen's eyes, holding her gaze for perhaps the first time. "Do you think that your people do not weep for the loss of their children? Even the strongest hide a burden of sorrow. The great warrior Gavan ap Huw lost a child to the wars."

Branwen's eyes widened. "I didn't know that. Was the child killed?"

"I do not know." A haunted light came into Hild's dark eyes. "For the child's sake, I would hope she died quickly. There are things worse than death."

Branwen shuddered. "I was brought up to believe that Saxons were savage and stupid and vicious," she began hesitantly. "I was taught that all they were fit for was death or servitude." She shook her head.

"You have had a terrible life, Hild. How can you be so forgiving?"

Hild sighed. "If I am forgiving," she said gently, "then it is *because* of my life. I would not wish it on anyone, my lady princess. No one should have to live like this."

"No," Branwen whispered. "No one should."

It was late night when Branwen walked in through the ever-open doors of the Great Hall. The fire was low in the hearth of the long main chamber, the fading flames glowing on the underbelly of the cauldron. The shadowy chamber was deserted; and apart from the crackling of the settling logs in the fire, all was quiet. Branwen had deliberately waited until everyone would be asleep.

As she passed close to the fire, a low voice growled out of the gloom. "Sleepless awhile, my lady?"

Surprised by the voice, she walked around the hearth. Gavan was seated on the outer stones, his shoulders hunched, his craggy face picked out in red and black by the fire. He was gazing at something in his upturned palm. A small gray stone. Not quite round—but good enough to be launched from a slingshot and to cause an arrogant lad to misshoot with his bow.

"You taught them a fine lesson this morning," Gavan said, turning the black wells of his eyes on her. "Did it please you to do that?"

She sat near him, feeling the fire hot on her back. "A little," she said.

"Then take back the stone. It may serve you again."

Branwen held the stone in her fist for a few moments, feeling the warmth of Gavan's hands on its surface; then she slipped it into the leather pouch. "I'm not going south," she whispered.

"Is that so?"

"People talk to me of my duty. You should do this; you should do that. Wear your hair just so. Behave in this way. You are a princess of Cyffin Tir. Go, marry a boy you don't even know." She looked into Gavan's shadowed face. "No one has ever said: 'Branwen, what do *you* want to do?' No one. Ever."

"If you do not go south, what will you do?"

"I want to become a warrior."

"And how would you do that?"

"I don't know."

There was a long silence. The flames gnawed at the logs. Smoke drifted aromatic to the roof. Branwen's heart was full of sadness, but not solely for herself now: for all the other people who were suffering in the world.

"Do you have a family, Gavan ap Huw?" she asked softly. "A wife? Children?"

"No, my lady."

"But you did once," Branwen persisted. "A child who was killed?"

"I had a daughter." Gavan sighed like a wolf growling. "Perhaps I have her still."

Branwen leaned forward. "I don't understand."

"Alwyn was my only child. She was younger than you when she was taken by the Saxons," Gavan said. "Perhaps they killed her; perhaps they took her away to be a servant. I never knew. Her mother was killed. I begged King Cadwallon to release me from his service so that I could follow the Saxon trail and find my daughter and bring her back. Or, if I found that she was dead, to cut such a path through the men who had killed her that they'd talk of it around their fires for a hundred years."

Branwen guessed what was coming next. "The king wouldn't let you go?"

"'Gavan ap Huw,' he said to me, 'you are my captain; you are my strong right arm. I cannot let you depart on this errand.' I fell on my knees and begged him, but he would not grant my wish. 'Great is the need for you by my side at this time,' he said. 'The Saxons mass at Rhos and must be defeated, or all Brython will be lost.'"

"Rhos?" Branwen echoed. "Cadwallon was killed in the battle of Rhos."

"He was," said Gavan. "And I was at his side when he fell. But despite our loss, we threw back the Saxons . . . for a while. And when the battle was won, and my duty done, I took to the road and sought for my daughter. But the trail was long cold, and after a year in the wilds I gave up all hope." His eyes glinted as he looked at her. "So you see, Branwen ap Griffith, princess of Cyffin Tir, I too know the burden of duty and the pain of loss."

"I'm sorry," Branwen said. "At least I saw Geraint die. At least I was able to mourn for him and light his funeral fire."

"It is cruel. But we endure. We live on. And we fight back as best we may."

"That's what I want to do," Branwen said. She twisted around on the flat stone and asked impulsively, "Will you help me?"

"What would you have me do?"

"Teach me your battle-skills. I have some small ability with a sword—Geraint taught me with swords of willow; but he only taught me how to defend myself. I need to know how to attack. How to kill."

Gavan rested his heavy hand on Branwen's shoulder. "Do you believe you have the heart of a warrior?" he asked.

Branwen held his gaze. "Yes," she said. "I do."

There was a long silence. Gavan stared into the fire, his gaze focused on something much farther away than the leaping orange flames. At last he turned back to her. "I shall help you, Branwen ap Griffith, in what small ways that I can. If I had taught my daughter the skills that I have with sword and staff, perhaps she would not have been seized from me so easily. For your father, and your mother, I shall teach you. But I cannot tutor you openly. Prince Llew would not countenance that." He paused. "Does Lady Elain keep watch on your movements?"

"No, she has lost all interest in me." Branwen almost smiled.

"Are you able to awake early?"

"Very early if the need arises."

"Good. Then rise early tomorrow, when the first cocks crow, and make your way from the fortress. A little way along the road, you will see an old oak tree that has been blasted by lightning. Turn in to the forest at that point. The way is marked with white stones. Follow the stones until you come to a clearing. I will meet you. Now, get you to bed."

Branwen stood up. "Thank you," she said; but Gavan's head was turned away, and his face was lost in shadow.

24

THE EARLY SKY was scattered with a mosaic of white cloud when Branwen reached the lightning-blasted oak tree. Its trunk had been riven in two, the main mass of wood dead and crumbling, the branches just bare claws. But the smaller part of the trunk still had living branches that were garlanded with leaves.

Even a tree struck down from the sky can survive, Branwen thought. She stepped into the forest, scouring the ground for the guide stones.

There! Lying in the leaf mold a few paces in, a white stone the size and shape of a man's fist. She walked past it. Then there was another.

Fain was perched upon the third stone.

Branwen halted, watching the bird watching her. "I don't want anything to do with you," she called, her voice quavering a little. "Tell your mistress that."

There was no response from the bird—just those dark, predatory eyes on her, filled with a knowing light.

"Go away!" Branwen took a step forward, stamping hard.

The falcon did not stir so much as a single feather. The eyes blinked and glinted, hard as flint. Then, with a suddenness that took her by surprise, the bird launched itself into the air and flew straight at her. She put up her arms and ducked as the claws raked her shoulder. It wheeled in the air and came for her again, the curved beak gaping, the claws reaching. Again she managed to bob out of the way at the last moment.

Fain perched on a branch, wings spread, poised for another rush at her. Branwen felt for her slingshot and stones. "Get away from me!" she shouted. "You come near me again and I'll kill you—I will!"

The bird let out a series of rising calls that was almost like cracked laughter.

Branwen slipped a stone into the slingshot. She whirled it and let fly. The stone struck the branch a fraction away from the bird's talons. She had missed deliberately—she didn't want to harm the creature, just to drive it away.

But Fain would not be driven away so easily. It came for her again, screaming.

She dropped to a crouch, fitting another stone to the slingshot. This time she aimed true. The stone struck the bird high on the wing. But it did not fall;

instead, it swerved aside, fluttering away through the trees in clumsy flight, injured but not killed.

Branwen grimaced. Her plan had been to scare it away or to kill it outright—not to hurt it. She loped along after it, not sure what she was going to do but hating to know that it was suffering. It was hard to keep up with the bird in the dense foliage, and Fain soon flew out of sight. Moments later Branwen heard a rustling and rushing sound and the muffled *thwack* of something striking the ground.

She paused. Someone was rushing through the undergrowth to her left—not visible yet through the trees, but coming closer. She stood still, listening hard. Gavan wanted their training sessions to be kept secret; the last thing she needed was to be discovered here by someone from Doeth Palas.

There! A movement in the lower branches, as if something was sweeping them aside as it passed. And then, some way ahead of her, the movements stopped and the forest became still.

Branwen made her way stealthily forward. She saw hunched darkness: a shape—a bent back, low to the ground. Someone was kneeling, and murmuring a lilting song.

> *Three eagles came out of the west—al omla la, al omla la*
> *One brought fire in its breast—al omla la, al omla la*

The second brought frost to line its nest—al
omla la, al, omla la
The third brought solace, peace, and rest—
al omla la al omla la
A talisman to cure all ills
A cure as ancient as the hills
All pain be gone, banished be
By leaf and sap of old oak tree . . .

She recognized the stained and tattered cloak that strained across the broad shoulders, and she knew that voice with its curious accent.

It was the boy from the mountain. What was he doing *here?*

He looked up as she stepped from cover, surprise widening his hazel eyes. He was holding the falcon gently between his hands.

"I thought I'd killed it," Branwen said. "What were you singing?"

"A healing song," he said. "Why did you harm it? Is life so harsh in yonder citadel that hunters are sent out to bring back falcon meat?"

Branwen knelt down and touched the bird's wing with her fingertips. "I'm sorry," she said to it. "I was angry. Forgive me."

Caw!

The bird ruffled its feathers and hopped down out of the young man's hands. It preened and smoothed its plumage for a few moments, then sprang into the air and went sweeping away through the trees.

"An unusual bird," the young man said dryly. "I take it you and he know each other."

Branwen nodded.

He shrugged. "You don't have to tell me about it, if you don't want to."

"You would never believe me if I did," Branwen said.

"Oh, I see," said the young man, a smile sliding up one side of his face. "Trust me, Branwen, I will happily believe anything you might tell me. I have always believed everything I've ever been told. I believe that a thousand pooka can dance on the point of a spear. I believe that the Stag of Rhedenfyre once lived on a rock set on a star, and I believe that Boobach will sweep evil out of your home for a bowl of sweet, fresh cream. So don't underestimate my foolishness, please."

Branwen laughed. "What's your name?" she asked.

"Rhodri."

"Rhodri ap . . . ?"

"It's not important. Rhodri will do, Branwen ap . . . ?"

"Just Branwen."

"There now, one name apiece is plenty to be getting on with." Rhodri stood up, brushing off his ragged leggings.

Branwen stood up as well. "How is your leg?"

"See for yourself." Rhodri pulled his legging aside. The wound was still red and raw, but it was healing well—and more quickly than Branwen would have expected.

"What are you doing here?" she asked. "Are you coming to Doeth Palas?"

"No. I have no wish to be beaten or locked up as a wandering beggar," Rhodri said lightly. "I am just a passing wayfarer, in search of my destiny, as are we all."

"Why do you say that?" Branwen said sharply.

Rhodri lifted his hands. "Why not? Do you think I'm too lowly to have a destiny?"

Branwen backed off a couple of paces. "Are you a servant of Rhiannon of the Spring? Is that why you're here?"

Rhodri seemed about to laugh, but his face became serious when he saw that she was not joking. "I am no one's servant, Branwen," he said. "I was a servant once, but no longer. I fled my master—and I am fleeing still." He looked curiously at her. "Why would you think I was in the service of a dead goddess?"

"Were you telling the truth when you said you would believe anything?" she said. "Would you believe something utterly impossible if I told you it was true?" She desperately needed to talk to someone about the shining goddess of water, if only to say out loud the thoughts that had been reverberating in her mind ever since meeting Rhiannon.

Perhaps this wayfaring beggar boy was the perfect person to tell. After all, he had no idea who she was; and he was certainly in no position to pass judgment on her.

"I'd try," he said.

"The Shining Ones are not dead."

His eyes lit up. "You know this for sure?"

"I have seen Rhiannon of the Spring."

He stared at her in astonishment. "Where? Did she speak to you?"

"Yes, she spoke to me," Branwen said bitterly. "But she is coldhearted and cruel."

"Why? What did she say?"

While Branwen was trying to think of where to start her tale, a sudden brightness flooded the forest. She looked east: Above the latticework of branches, the sun had cleared the mountains.

"There's no time now," she said. "I have to meet someone. Stay here, and I'll bring you food. I'll return by midday at the latest. Will you stay?"

"For food? Of course," said Rhodri. "And will you tell me about Rhiannon of the Spring?"

"Yes, I will," she said, already walking quickly away from him.

"Don't tell anyone about me," Rhodri called.

"No. I won't."

She ran back through the trees until she came upon a white stone lying on the ground, then another, and another. She hoped Rhodri would wait for her.

Rhiannon of the Spring says I have a great destiny!

She says I am the Emerald Flame of my people!

But I won't be what she wants because she let my brother be killed!

25

THE WHITE STONES led to a glade.

It was Rhiannon's glade, lush with grass and reeds, with the pond of still, clear water at its center. Branwen stood at the entrance to the glade, trembling.

The water goddess was not there—but Gavan was. The old warrior was sword fighting with the air, a long, bright blade in either hand, both arms thrusting and parrying, his feet constantly moving as he battled with his invisible enemy.

Branwen watched him, blinking as flashes of sunlight flared off the polished blades. As nimble and supple as a man a third his age, he feinted, drew back, spun on his heel, then lunged hard, bringing the two blades forward in a whirl of sunlit iron.

She stepped into the light. Gavan looked across at

her. "Is this *early*, my lady?" he asked gruffly.

"I'm sorry," Branwen said. "Why did you pick this place?"

"Because no one comes here. Fools avoid it because they believe it is haunted. Others keep away because once it was a sacred place—long ago."

"How was it sacred?"

"The pool is fed by an underground spring," Gavan told her. "Our ancestors revered such places, thinking the water was a gift from the gods of Annwn."

"You don't think that?"

"I do not." He lifted his head, looking intently at her. "Well, my lady, are you ready to learn today whether there is a warrior within you?"

"I am," said Branwen. "Will we be using real swords?"

"We will. Part of your journey must be learning how an iron sword feels in your hand. Wooden swords teach you nothing." An odd smile cracked across his face. "Do not fear injury, my lady. I will not hurt you, and you need have no fear of hurting me." He gestured to the pool. "But it will be thirsty work," he said. "Drink first."

"I'm not thirsty."

"Drink!"

Branwen frowned, puzzled by the sudden stern tone in his voice. She walked over to the pool, moving carefully among the reeds, testing the firmness of the ground. At the farthest edge of solid earth, she came down on one knee and scooped water up in her cupped palm and drank it.

"Good," Gavan said. "You have passed the first test."

She rose and turned to him. "How? What test?"

"A warrior must be ever watchful," Gavan said. "Those least fitted to the task fall on their faces and drink like beasts. Others will go down on their knees and bring water up to their mouths with both hands. But warriors drop on one knee and use only one hand to take up the water. Then they can see if an enemy approaches, and they have a hand free for their weapon."

"Oh. I see."

Gavan walked over to the tree line and drew up two plain, round, wooden shields from the grass. "I need to know what skills you already have," he said. "You say your brother taught you some defensive moves?"

"He did," Branwen replied.

"Bearing sword and shield?"

"Sword only," said Branwen. "But I know how to use a shield."

Gavan tossed a shield to her, and she caught it in both hands. It was surprisingly heavy, its diameter wide enough to protect her chest and shoulders. She pushed her left forearm through the two leather straps stapled onto its back, holding the second in her fist.

Gavan held out one of the swords. "Take this and adopt a defensive stance."

Branwen gripped the leather-bound hilt, trying to remember all that Geraint had shown her. She spread her legs wide, bringing up the shield close to her chest so that she was looking out at Gavan over the upper rim. She held her sword steadily at chest height, the point toward Gavan.

"Are you ready?" he asked. "I want only that you defend yourself against me. Understood?"

"Yes."

Gavan stood with his shield held out and the upper rim angled away from his body. His sword arm was raised to the side, the elbow pointing away from his body, his forearm angled toward his head, his sword held diagonally behind his back.

She had expected him to come straight for her; but instead he stepped in until he was a little over a sword's length away from her, then he began a series of circling moves that meant she had to constantly shift her feet to stay facing him. She watched his expression, trying to guess what he would do next. His eyes were fixed always on her sword hand. He moved in closer. She stabbed at him. He knocked her sword aside with the edge of his shield.

"Put some muscle into it," he growled. "Don't fear to hurt me. That isn't going to happen."

Branwen narrowed her eyes. So he thought that, did he? It was time for him to find out how much she had learned during the days she had spent watching the sparring and training of the warriors of Garth Milain. She gave a yell and ran at him, meaning to give him a nick on the upper arm to show him she wasn't entirely helpless.

He danced back, his shield coming up to block her swing. Her sword glanced off the edge of his shield, and she tottered forward. His shield came down heavy on her back, sending her sprawling. She felt the tip of his sword against her neck as she lay there with her mouth full of grass.

He stepped back and allowed her to get to her feet. She felt foolish and fully expected him to be grinning at her. He wasn't.

"What was that?" he asked. "Did I say attack?"

"No."

"Next time you disobey me, I will give you such a blow on the ear with the flat of my sword that your head will ring for ten days. Do you understand me?"

"Yes."

"Defend yourself!"

She stamped her feet down hard into the grass, her legs spread, watching him intently over her shield. She lifted her sword arm, elbow cocked away from her body, forearm toward her head, her sword angled down her back. Exactly as Gavan held his sword. At least he would see she was paying attention.

He came for her, but again he kept sidling around her, making her turn and change her footing; and every time he darted in close and she swung her sword at him, he deflected it with his shield and was away out of sword reach before she could swing a second time.

The end came so swiftly that she hardly knew it had happened. He leaped in. She swung at him. His shield deflected her blow. His sword arm came hurtling down; and if he hadn't brought the scything blow to a sudden halt, his blade would have taken her head clean off her shoulders.

She stood staring at him, panting, shaking all over, her muscles cramped and aching, her hopes of proving her skills to him in tatters. All she had proved was that she had no idea what she was doing.

He stepped back, his face thoughtful.

"Well?" she snapped. "Say it!"

"Say what?"

"Tell me I know nothing. Tell me I have no skills. Tell me . . ." She clenched her jaw. She was so angry with herself that she could feel the tears burning behind her eyes.

I hate the way anger makes me want to weep! I wish I could be angry like a man is angry!

"There's little point in me telling you things you already know," Gavan said. He frowned at her. "Now! What would you truly have me tell you?"

She swallowed. "Tell me what I did wrong," she said. "Tell me how to do better."

"Adopt a defensive stance."

She stood as she had stood before, the sword

angled across her back.

He circled her. "Your feet are too far apart; bring them closer. They should be no wider apart than your shoulders. And you stand too heavily; the weight should be on the balls of your feet. Your left foot should be pointing toward your enemy. The right foot should point sideways. Your knees should be slightly bent. You should feel the tension in your calves and in your thighs."

As he spoke, she adjusted her stance to fit his instructions.

"You must achieve three things in the way you stand: mobility, stability, and confidence. You are holding your shield too close to your body; hold it farther away so you can block your enemy's blow sooner. Keep your upper shield arm against your side and the forearm angled upward so your hand is at shoulder height. And hold the shield so that its upper rim is angled toward your enemy. This will help you in punching aside his sword blows."

She changed the way she was holding her shield and instantly noticed the difference, realizing that the disk of wood could be used as a weapon as well as a defense.

"You are holding your sword correctly now," Gavan continued, "but you need to angle your hips a little." He put his big hands on her hips and cocked them so her shield hip was a little higher. "This will help channel the power of your blow," he told her. "When you strike, the power should come from your whole body, not just your arm. Tighten your stomach muscles and your shoulders. Your muscles should speak to you; you should feel them straining, like hunting dogs on the leash."

Branwen tensed as he suggested. It felt strange—as if her body were a drawn bowstring waiting to be loosed. Gavan stood behind her, slightly adjusting the angle of her arm and of her wrist so that the blade of her sword ran from her right shoulder to her left hip. Her arm muscles protested, but she said nothing.

"When you strike, rotate your upper body and let the force of the blow rise up through you. But do not lean forward, or you will leave your neck vulnerable."

"The way I did before," Branwen said.

"Indeed. Now, to block an opponent's sword, you must thrust forward with your shield." He stood in front of her. "Strike at me slowly. As though you were fighting underwater."

Branwen's body was trembling with the tension of her unnatural stance. It was a relief to bring her sword arm over and down, but it was hard to do it slowly as Gavan had asked. She felt as if her muscles were going to burst under her skin. As her sword fell, Gavan's shield came under it at a sharp angle, striking the blade near the hilt, pushing her blow aside and then following through so the upper rim of his shield was against her throat.

"Do you see? I bring the shield in close to your

222

hand so that you cannot trick me by changing the angle of your blow. Also, I can use the shield to strike at your throat. And while you are gasping for breath, I can follow through and finish you off with a strike to your neck or your stomach or your thigh."

"Yes. Yes, I understand," Branwen said.

"Stand ready again."

Branwen stood ready. She could feel every muscle as tense as a fist under her clothes.

"Is your weight on the balls of your feet?"

"Yes."

"Is it hard to keep still?"

"Yes!"

"Good. Do not keep still. Do not let me bring the fight to you. Move around as I do. Let your body flow with the flow of battle." He stepped forward. Branwen danced back, and despite the tension in her body, she felt strangely light and lithe. "Good! Good!"

He lunged at her and she sprang aside, her shield angled toward him.

"Watch my sword, not my face!" he said. "I'm going to stab you, not bite you!"

She almost laughed at this unexpected show of humor.

He leaped forward, his sword slashing down. She punched her shield hard against his sword. The blow jarred her arm and made her gasp, but his sword slipped off the edge of her shield. She let loose with her sword arm, feeling the power of the blow rippling through her entire body. He parried her blow, moving quickly to her left so she had to pivot on her toes to keep facing him. He slashed at her and she bounded back, watching his sword arm. Again he came at her, and again she avoided the blow. They circled each other as if they were partners in a deadly dance.

He shifted his weight as if intending to move leftward, but at the last moment he threw his weight onto his right foot and almost caught her with a low, swinging blow to her waist. She knocked his sword aside with her shield and leaped back out of range. She kept her feet moving all the time, springing back when he came for her and then bounding sideways, forcing him to turn as she circled.

She watched his sword arm all the time. It was up in the primary position again, ready for the next blow. She made a stuttering move to the right and he lifted his shield, but then she brought her foot down hard and threw all her weight onto her left leg. He swung his arm down; but his sword slid off her shield, and she almost caught him under the chin as she thrust the rim at him.

He jumped back, and she saw a slight smile on his face. She had impressed him!

Gavan stepped away. "Do you wish to rest awhile?" he asked.

"No! Why? Are you tired?"

His eyes widened. "A pert maiden, indeed!" he

said, and there was a hint of amusement in his voice. "Come, then, daughter of Alis ap Owain! Let us see who wearies first!"

Branwen knew she had youth on her side, but the old warrior matched her breath for breath and move for move as the morning wore away. Although she was well aware that Gavan was holding back, he out-fought her at every step—pushing through her defenses time and time again, and time and time again striking aside her attacks. But at the end of each move, he would explain what she had done wrong and show her how to parry a blade and how to launch an attack.

They fought together until every muscle in Branwen's body was aching and her heart was pounding like a drum. Still she refused to call for a halt, even though her body was slick with perspiration and her hair was wet and lank on her shoulders.

Often he would make her repeat a particular movement over and over again until she got it right. He never praised her nor condemned her, and she soon came to realize that the real battle was taking place within herself. The battle to keep her concentration steady, to force her aching muscles to respond quickly, to keep her tired legs moving, to hold her sword high and bring it down with all her might even though it seemed to weigh as much as a great forest oak in her throbbing, numbed fist. To use her shield despite the fact it was as clumsy and as burdensome as a wagon wheel.

"You cannot defeat me with strength," Gavan called to her. "Use your agility and your speed. You stumble around like a three-legged ox!"

She gave a yell of rage and flung herself at him. He sidestepped and tripped her. She went headlong into the grass. She lay there, gasping for breath, her head swimming.

He stood over her. "Do not let your emotions rule you," he warned. "The blood may be hot, but the mind must be always cool." He reached down and hauled her to her feet. "That is enough for today."

Branwen scrambled to her feet, dripping sweat and panting heavily. "Why?" she gasped. "Are . . . you . . . too . . . tired . . . for . . . more . . . ?"

"Yes," he said, breathing easily. "You have worn me to a thread." He rested his hand on her shoulder. "You are a brave girl," he said. "And you have a great heart."

"When . . . can we . . . meet again?"

"Tomorrow," Gavan said. "But it must be earlier, and we must not tarry here so long again. I have my duties in the citadel. Go now—I will wait awhile."

She handed him the sword and shield. "Till tomorrow . . . *early*," she said.

He nodded. "Yes, daughter of Alis ap Owain, till tomorrow."

26

"RHODRI? ARE YOU there?" Branwen called as she pushed her way through the trees. She was sure this was the place where she had met him earlier that day, but now there was no sign of him. "I've brought food!"

Tired as she was and aching from the training session with Gavan, she had kept her word and had come back to the forest with bread and cheese and meat bundled up in a cloth.

"Rhodri?"

He appeared suddenly from behind a tree, startling her and almost making her drop the bundle.

She held it out to him. "Food," she said.

"Thank you." He took the bundle and sat on the ground, opening it in his lap. He began to eat immediately, stuffing hunks of bread into his mouth, tearing off pieces of meat with his teeth, gnawing ferociously at the cheese.

Branwen sat at his side. "You were hungry, then," she said.

He nodded, unable to speak through the food crammed into his mouth.

She watched him for a while longer. "When we first met up in the mountains, you said you didn't think we would be traveling the same path," she said. "And yet here we are."

He chewed and swallowed. "Fate plays merry tricks, does it not?"

"You said you were a servant," Branwen prompted. "Who was your master?"

His face darkened. "A Saxon swine by the name of Horsa Herewulf, the saints rot his evil guts!"

"You were a Saxon captive?" Branwen asked in surprise. "When were you taken? How long were you held?"

"You're full of questions today," Rhodri said. "But if it's all the same to you, I'd rather not talk about it. It's something I prefer not to dwell on."

"No, of course not." She eyed him with curiosity, thinking of Hild, wondering if he had been stolen away from his family as the old servant woman had been from hers.

There was a small silence while he dealt with the last crumbs and scraps of his meal. "That will keep me going a good while; thank you, Branwen."

"Does it make up for knocking you off the cliff?"

He smiled. "It does. In fact, I'm in your debt. I have a long journey ahead of me, and food is hard to come by in the wild." His eyes brightened. "I'm going home, Branwen. Home to my father's family. They farm a stretch of land in west Gwynedd. It's by the sea, near a place called Cefn Boudan."

"I've never heard of it," said Branwen. "Is it far?"

"Far enough for a poor, footsore wanderer." He sighed, peering into the sacking that had held his food. "I don't suppose you thought to pack an obedient little horse for me to ride?"

She laughed. "I'm afraid not."

"That's probably just as well. I haven't ridden for a long time."

Branwen looked at him—at his dirty, bruised feet, his raggedy clothes and tousled hair. He must have been on the road for days. "I'm going home too," she said.

"Is that so? And where might that be?" His eyes narrowed. "East of the mountains, I'd guess."

"Would you? Why?"

"You'd hardly declare your intention to be going home if you lived close by," he explained. "I think your home is in one of the eastern cantrefs that border the Saxon lands. Am I right?"

"Now who's asking a lot of questions?"

"A fair point," he conceded. "But you puzzle me, Branwen. The first time we met you were wearing

229

a fine riding gown, and you were being escorted to Doeth Palas. That was the word you used: *escorted.* I assumed you were the daughter of some powerful captain or land-owning noble. But now you're wearing peasant clothes and wandering the forest alone." He shook his head. "That makes no sense to me, unless . . ." He paused, looking intently at her.

"Unless?" she prompted.

"Unless it has something to do with Rhiannon of the Spring," he said, his voice lowering to a reverent whisper. "Was it your meeting with her that changed everything for you?"

"No!" Branwen said abruptly. "She was . . . I . . ." She stumbled over her words. "I will not . . . I am not following her. . . ." Anger erupted in her. "The gods are pitiless and unfeeling. I will not do what they want."

"What did she ask you to do?"

"It doesn't matter," Branwen said. "I will not do her bidding! I will follow my own path." She looked at him through a veil of unshed tears. "I should never have come to this land," she said. "I am going home to fight the Saxons. I am going home to help my parents avenge my brother's death."

There was a pause; and when Rhodri spoke, his voice was quiet and kind. "How did your brother die?"

"He was murdered by Saxon raiders." She looked into his face. "I saw him die. I lit his funeral pyre. Then I let myself be brought here because my parents wanted to keep me safe." Her voice rose as the anger grew in her again. "But it was wrong! I should have stayed with them."

"And now you wish to go back and kill Saxons," Rhodri said. "Trust me, Branwen, I have no trouble understanding that. I hate the Saxons above all things in this world. But what could you do? Anger isn't enough, Branwen."

"No, anger isn't enough," Branwen agreed. "That is why I intend to become a warrior. Then I will fight the Saxons. Then I will avenge my brother."

"And what of Rhiannon of the Spring?"

"What of her?"

He looked anxiously at her. "Do you really think you can defy the gods? How do you run away from a goddess? Where can you hide?"

"I'm not running or hiding," said Branwen. "Rhiannon said I had to choose my destiny of my own free will. I have done that."

"And she wasn't angered by your choice?" Rhodri asked in surprise.

"I don't think so," Branwen said hesitantly. "She said . . . she said there would be a price to be paid if I didn't go with her. She said I would have to choose between two lives, and that someone would die because of the choice I made."

"She means to kill someone to punish you?"

"No, I don't think that's what she meant. I'm not sure *what* she meant."

There was a tense silence.

"So what are you going to do?" Rhodri asked.

Branwen squared her shoulders. "Become a warrior. Avenge my brother. Fight the Saxons."

He nodded slowly but said nothing.

She stood up. "I'm going to be in the forest early tomorrow morning. If you like, I could bring you some more food."

"Food for my journey would be much appreciated, thank you," Rhodri said.

"Dawn tomorrow, then."

"Good-bye, Branwen—and be careful. You've turned away from a goddess. She may have unpleasant ways of paying you back for that."

As Branwen made her way through the trees, Rhodri's warning echoed in her mind. Had she been wise to insult a goddess to her face and to run from the destiny that the Shining Ones wished for her?

Probably not, but it's done now. And if Rhiannon seeks vengeance on me for it, then it will only prove that I was right not to follow her.

27

IT WAS BLAZING midafternoon and the courtyard stones were hot under her feet as Branwen
returned to the fortress.

*I will meet with Gavan tomorrow, and I'll learn all that
I can from him. Then I must go. I can't leave it too long;
Prince Llew's scouts will be back soon, and I don't want to
risk being sent south. I'll take as many of my things as I can
carry, and I'll ride Stalwyn over the mountains and all the
way back to Garth Milain!*

Excitement ran through her as she imagined
her secret flight from the fortress. Her mother and
father would understand. She would make them
understand.

A young man stepped into her path, breaking her
thoughts. It was Bryn, the freckle-faced boy whose
arrow had narrowly missed its target.

"I've been waiting for you," he said. "I thought perhaps you would be interested in a rematch?"

She looked into his face. His eyes were cold and hard, like brown pebbles. "As you wish," she said.

He turned and walked between two long huts. She followed warily, not really trusting him. There had been a look in his eyes that she didn't much like.

Bryn led her to a narrow alleyway behind the huts. She looked around, expecting to see arrows and perhaps a target. There was nothing. She could still hear the everyday sounds of Doeth Palas, but the dusty alley was deserted and invisible from the main thoroughfares. The rampart wall loomed up high above them. An ominous feeling hung in the dry air.

Bryn folded his arms. "Are you as skilled with the staff as you are with that slingshot of yours?" He gestured toward two long wooden staves that were resting against the wall of one of the huts. "Would you like to try your luck?"

His simmering resentment was so strong that Branwen could almost taste it. "You want to fight with me?" she asked.

He smiled, but his eyes were still hostile. "You bested me, slingshot against bow. Are you prepared to fight me on even terms—staff against staff?"

She could tell from his expression that he expected to beat her with ease. And what if she refused his challenge? Then there would be yet another reason for everyone to mock the wild eastern princess.

She nodded. "Very well."

He walked over to the staves, snatching them up and throwing one toward her. She caught it awkwardly. It was almost as long as she was tall, a thin length of hardwood, smooth under her hands but strange and unwieldy. She watched Bryn carefully, seeing how he held his staff, with one hand at the center and the other halfway to one end. He swung it a few times, then brought it pounding down onto the ground so that it kicked up a spray of dry earth.

Branwen copied his grip, trying to gauge the balance of the staff, trying to remember how she had seen other people use it. She eyed him appraisingly. He was big and muscular, and there was something in his face that suggested he was quite capable of cracking her head.

My best chance is if I . . .

Bryn let out a sudden shout and lunged at her, the staff swinging toward her at head level. She ducked as the weapon hissed over her head. He stepped forward, the staff whirling in his hands. She managed to block the blow this time, but the impact almost ripped her own staff out of her hands. He was strong! She fell back, remembering the morning's lessons, flexing her knees, keeping her back straight and her eyes on his staff. Again it came down, and she only just avoided a severe blow to her shoulder.

Swing!

A leap to the side.

Swing!

She blocked the blow this time. The crack of wood on wood echoed between the walls. Branwen's fingers stung from the impact, and her hands felt numb.

The air shrieked as the flying end of Bryn's staff narrowly missed her head. She thrust forward with her own staff, trying to find a way through his defenses. But he was too quick for her, and his staff grazed her knuckles as he struck hers savagely aside. She leaped away as he jabbed the end of his staff at her stomach in a blow that would have doubled her up if it had made contact.

She kept him at a distance, her feet constantly moving as she circled him. But she knew she could not keep this up for long. Already her muscles were protesting, sore and tender from a hard morning of training with Gavan. She had to try and end this quickly, before exhaustion overwhelmed her. Bryn showed no sign of tiring, but she could see the frustration growing in him. He had expected this to be all over with a couple of strikes, and he was getting angry. He gritted his teeth, his eyes burning as he lunged at her again.

She remembered Gavan's advice: *The blood may be hot, but the mind must be always cool.*

"I expected more from you, Bryn," she mocked. "Am I wearing you out? You puff and blow like an old woman!"

Grimacing, he came at her with the staff lifted above his head. She sprang to one side and brought her own staff around to whack him on the rear end as he stumbled past her. He turned, growling, gripping his staff with white knuckles. He ran forward with his staff in both hands. Branwen made as if to dodge to the left; but as soon as the staff came whistling down toward her head, she shifted her weight and bounced to the right.

The staff came down with a shoulder-wrenching crack on the hard-packed earth; and while Bryn was still trying to regain his balance, she brought her own staff around in a wide swing and hit his staff a fraction away from his right hand. He lost his grip, dropping his staff and falling onto his knees. She moved in and kicked his staff out of his reach. Then she stood back, watching as he scrambled to his feet, his face red with rage.

The sound of slow-clapping hands broke out. Branwen turned to see Iwan leaning against a wall, smiling.

"Nicely done, barbarian princess!" he called. "Bryn, Bryn! You should have kept your temper if you wanted to beat her."

"Get away from here, Iwan," snarled Bryn. "This is none of your business. If you choose to swallow her insults, then that's to your own shame."

Iwan lifted his right hand and pulled a thick, golden ring off his index finger. "I'll wager this ring that she'll get the better of you."

"She'll not!"

Iwan chuckled. "Look in her eyes, Bryn. Do you think she's afraid of you? *Look* at her!"

Branwen stood panting, looking from one to the other.

I've had enough of this!

She threw her staff down at Bryn's feet. "This is pointless," she said. "If I offended you this morning, then I apologize. But I'm not going to fight you anymore, Bryn. It's over."

Bryn glared at her for a moment and then turned on his heel and walked away.

Branwen looked at Iwan and gestured toward the fallen staves. "Would you like to try your luck?"

Iwan bowed. "Indeed not, my lady. It would hardly be fair. You look worn-out." He spun the golden ring again. "But one day I may take up your challenge, and then we shall see." He turned and walked away. "Oh, yes, then we shall see."

Meredith was in the bedchamber, sitting on her bed, picking colored beads from a small wooden box in her lap and threading them together into a necklace. Branwen's heart sank. She had hoped to change from her hunting clothes and go to sit by herself on the rampart overlooking the ocean. She didn't need any more confrontations.

"There you are!" Meredith said, putting the threaded beads and the box aside and getting up. There was an odd urgency in her voice. "I've been waiting for you."

"Why?" Branwen crouched by her chest and

opened it. "Have you come up with some new way to belittle me?"

"Not at all."

"Then I'm grateful for that. So, what do you want?"

"We are not friends," Meredith began slowly. "But that doesn't mean I would stand by and let you be hurt."

Branwen sat on her heels, waiting for more.

"I heard Bryn ap Anerin talking to his friends," Meredith continued in a rush. "He's planning to challenge you to a fight because of something you said to him." She frowned. "Why are you always saying things and doing things to offend people, Branwen? I don't understand it. Everything you do is defiant . . . and . . . and so *rude*!"

Branwen looked at her in amazement. "Me?" she said. "I'm not the rude one. You people have made me feel unwelcome ever since I came here."

"That's not true," Meredith said. "And . . . and if it is, well, you deserve it! The way you look at us, as if we disgust you! You make me feel as if everything I do displeases you. Are we really such terrible people that you have to hate us all so much?"

"I don't hate you all," Branwen said, amazed that Meredith should be the one feeling hurt. "It's you who hate and despise me."

Meredith shook her head. "I don't."

"Romney does!"

"Romney is a spoiled child," Meredith said. Her eyes narrowed. "Mama says that your bad behavior is because you're jealous of our wealth and status, because you come from a poor cantref beyond the mountains. But it's not our fault that we have things and you don't, and it's mean of you to dislike us because of it."

"What about that trick that was played on me the first night I was here?" Branwen said. "When Iwan fooled me into challenging Gavan ap Huw in front of everyone? I hope I managed to amuse you all sufficiently!"

Meredith hid a smile behind her hand. "It was rather funny," she admitted. "And the look on your face when you stormed out! And then you snapped at Romney and shouted at Reece ap Colwyn. I thought you were half mad!"

A smile touched Branwen's lips. "That's what we barbarian princesses are like," she said. She stood up. "I'm sorry if I have offended you. Things have not been easy for me here."

"If you don't want them to get even harder, then please avoid Bryn ap Anerin."

"Thanks for the warning," Branwen said. "But you're too late."

Meredith's eyebrows rose. "He didn't hurt you, did he?"

"No," Branwen said with a laugh. "Though I fear for his pride!"

"You beat him?"

"Yes."

"Excellent," Meredith said, her eyes shining. "Bryn is a bully." She looked at Branwen with a furrowed brow. "You should not be angry with Iwan for playing that prank on you. It's his way of showing he's . . . well—*interested* in you." She smiled hopefully. "Perhaps you should be flattered. He's very handsome."

"He is not!" Branwen protested. "He has a face like the hind end of a dead donkey!"

Meredith stared at her. "You are so very strange, Branwen," she said. "You are the strangest person I have ever met!"

28

DAWN LIGHT WAS just beginning to filter across the sky when Branwen slipped away to the forest carrying a bag of food for Rhodri. She had gone into the storeroom of the Great Hall and come away with a few small loaves, some dried fish, salt pork, and cheese, along with a stoppered jug of buttermilk.

Leaving Doeth Palas so early in the morning was not a problem; it was the custom in Brython that the gates of great fortresses should be kept open throughout the night for any wayfarer seeking shelter. Only when danger threatened were the gates slammed shut and the bars thrown across them.

She walked through the trees calling, "Rhodri!" She listened for a reply, then walked on. "Rhodri! Breakfast! Rhodri!"

She had reached the place where they had met

before; she was certain of that. He was not there. She sat under a tree and waited.

A thrush began to sing from the branches above her. The clear, trilling notes filled the air with such a joyous sound that Branwen smiled and looked up, but the leaves were too thick for her to be able to see the bird.

No sooner had the thrush stopped singing than the voice of a jay rang out, its cry like tearing cloth, harsh and complaining. Then came the bright, high-pitched warble of a robin, followed instantly by the chatter of an ouzel.

So many different birds in one tree? And all their voices seeming to come from exactly the same place? Branwen stared up in puzzlement. The guttural croak of a crow sounded from among the leaves.

Branwen laughed. Real birds of different species would not gather together like that! It was someone mimicking birdcalls. "Come down here, Rhodri!"

"Rhodri is not up here," replied a high, thin voice. "I am a pooka of the forest, practicing birdsong."

"Rhodri!"

The branches rustled and bobbed, then two feet appeared, followed by raggedly clad legs. Rhodri dropped out of the tree, grinning widely. "I had you fooled at first, didn't I?"

"You did. How did you learn to do that? It was almost perfect."

"Well, hardly perfect," Rhodri said.

Branwen pointed to the bag of food. "That was as much as I could carry."

"Thank you." He sat cross-legged, delving through the bag. He shoved a hunk of bread into his mouth. "Would you join me for breakfast?" he mumbled.

She sat down. "There's not much point in me bringing food out here for you and then eating it myself. The sealed jar has buttermilk in it. So long as it's not in the sun too much, it should last awhile."

He swallowed his mouthful. "Why are you doing this for me?" he asked.

She shrugged. "To make up for clouting you with a branch when we first met? No, that's not true. I think it's because you're the only person here who doesn't expect anything of me." Her voice dropped. "You're the only person who doesn't know who I am."

He gave her a quizzical look. "Who *are* you?"

"No. That would spoil it."

"Can I try and guess?"

"I'd rather you didn't."

"Then I shan't."

They sat together in easy silence while Rhodri ate. He unstoppered the jug and took a long swig of the buttermilk. Wiping his mouth, he offered her the jug. She shook her head, but he insisted. She drank a small amount of the thick, sweet liquid and then gave him back the jug.

"So," he said, closing the bag, "have you decided when you'll go home?"

"In a few days. I need to plan my escape care-fully." She gestured in the direction of the fortress. "There are people there who mustn't find out. The prince, for one. I'm not sure what he'd do. Tie me to a horse and send me to Gwent whether I liked it or not, probably."

"If they do that, I'll rescue you," Rhodri said. "I'll cut you free, and we'll escape into the forest together." He smiled wryly. "Except that I'm not so good at hunting. Otherwise I'd have been eating better over the past few weeks."

"I'll hunt for the two of us," Branwen said, joining in with the fantasy. "I have firestones and kindling, so we'd be able to eat roast meat every day."

"And in a few months, there will be apples and pears and blackberries and sloes," Rhodri added. "We'll eat like the king of Powys."

"No one will ever find us!"

"And we'll dance by starlight with the pooka of the woods and the goraig of the streams," laughed Rhodri.

Mention of the wood fairies reminded Branwen too closely of other mystical creatures who dwelled in the forest—powerful, dangerous creatures who may be holding a grudge against her.

"Maybe living in the forest wouldn't be a good idea," Rhodri said quietly. "No—we'll make our way through the forest as quickly as we can. We'll be safe from disgruntled goddesses and family duties at Cefn

Boudan. My father's family will adopt you, and we'll spend our days fishing for sea trout." He smiled, trying to lift her mood. "What do you say, Branwen? Shall we start now?"

"I should abandon my own family to live with yours?" she mused. "I don't think so." She put her hand lightly on his arm. "I have to go home."

Rhodri didn't say anything; and when she looked at him, there was a kind of wistful sadness in his face.

"What?"

"Oh, nothing," he said. "Your home is to the east; mine is to the west." He shrugged. "I had it in my mind that we might become friends." He gave a wan smile. "I knew it wasn't really possible. . . . it was just a pleasant daydream. The servants of Saxon warlords don't get to make many friends, Branwen. And runaways even less."

"So, come with me. You'd have nothing to fear from my mother and father."

"You know, I almost—" He broke off, staring into the forest. "What was that?"

"I didn't hear anything."

A large figure burst out of the trees, pushing Branwen aside and coming down on Rhodri like a thunderbolt. Rhodri was thrown onto his back, a broad hand at his throat, a knee in his stomach.

"A runaway servant, is it?" Gavan growled. "We'll see about runaway servants!"

Branwen scrambled to her feet. "Stop it!" she cried. "You're hurting him!"

Gavan got up, dragging Rhodri by the scruff of his neck and pinning him against a tree trunk. Rhodri writhed in his grip.

"Keep still, boy!" Gavan snarled.

Rhodri's struggles ceased and he stood there, his chest heaving and his eyes on Gavan's face.

Gavan turned to look at Branwen. "What are you doing here with this creature, my lady?"

"He's my friend," Branwen protested. "He's done nothing!"

"Nothing, eh?" He glared at Rhodri. "I doubt that!"

"He's escaped the Saxons," Branwen explained. "He's trying to get back to his family. I order you to let him go!"

"You may have fooled her, my fine fellow, but you'll not fool me," Gavan hissed. "Do you think I don't know a Saxon accent when I hear one?"

"*What?*" Branwen gasped.

"The boy's a Saxon!" Gavan said. "A spy, like as not!"

"That isn't a Saxon accent. All our servants are Saxons. He sounds nothing like them."

"That is because the accent you're used to is the Mercian one," Gavan said. "This wretch has a Northumbrian accent—don't you, my lad? You're from the far north, sent here by King Oswald or one of his captains to spy out the land."

Branwen stared at Rhodri. That wasn't true. *It couldn't be.* "His family comes from Cefn Boudan in Gwynedd. And he was the servant of . . ." She struggled to remember the name. "Horsa! Yes, a man named Horsa Herewulf!"

"Herewulf Ironfist!" Gavan cried. "Lord of Winwaed, commander of King Oswald's armies in the west! Is that so, boy? Is Herewulf Ironfist your master? Have you come sneaking over the mountains to do his bidding?" He looked at Branwen. "I tell you true, Princess Branwen, this man is not of Brython; this man is a Saxon spy. And to think that a daughter of the House of Rhys should be found like this with him! By the saints, Branwen ap Griffith, you are lucky that it was I who discovered you! Death is the only reward for those who consort with spies—be they a peasant farmer or a princess of Cyffin Tir!"

Branwen stared at Rhodri, fury rising inside her. The one person she had trusted was a hated enemy! And then a truly horrible thought struck her. She had met him first on the mountainous borders of her homeland. If he had been spying in Cyffin Tir, could it have been Rhodri who told the bloodthirsty Saxon raiders about Bevan's farm?

She stared into his face, trembling. If that was so, then Rhodri was responsible for the death of Bevan's family. And worse even than that: He was responsible for Geraint's slaughter.

"It's back to Doeth Palas for you, boy," Gavan growled. "Then you'll tell us the truth, and hang by the neck when we've learned all!"

Rhodri stared at him with bulging eyes. "I'm innocent, sir," he gasped. "I'm no spy!"

"We shall see!"

Gavan pulled Rhodri away from the tree trunk. The moment he did so, Rhodri brought his fists down hard on Gavan's arm, knocking it away and leaping to one side. Gavan snatched at him; but Rhodri was too quick, bounding away through the trees almost before Branwen realized what was happening. Gavan gave a roar of anger and chased after him. Branwen snatched her slingshot from her belt as she broke into a run, following Gavan into the trees.

Rhodri may be fast footed enough to outdistance Gavan, but *she* was as swift as a deer in the forest: She would chase him down. He had no chance of escaping her.

29

"NO!" BRANWEN HOWLED. "Not again! This is madness!"

This was the third time she had come stumbling out of the trees and into Rhiannon's clearing. The water goddess was not there—but neither was Rhodri, although Branwen had definitely been closing in on him before she plunged into the sunlit glade.

She stared around, frustrated and bewildered and growing ever angrier. It was not natural, the way the forest seemed to turn around her like a great wheel, spitting her out into this deserted glade while her prey flitted away unseen. Some power was hindering her and helping Rhodri.

You will run in a circle, Branwen ap Griffith, and I will be there.

Was this what Rhiannon had meant, that her

footsteps would be endlessly led back to this clearing no matter how she tried to avoid it? Branwen walked into the clearing, looking all around.

"Come on, then!" she shouted. "Show yourself! I know you're doing this."

She peered into the trees, expecting to see a moving white shape. But there was nothing. Rhiannon was toying with her.

She heard a soft *clop* behind her, as if a stone had been dropped into the pool of silver gray water. She turned. Ripples were slowly spreading from the center of the pool. She walked into the reeds, going as close as firm ground permitted. She stared down at the mirrored sky as the ripples faded away.

The reflected sky grew night-dark. There were high stars and a red glow in the air that was like the radiance of unseen flames. Branwen was keenly aware that the sky above her was still clear.

A picture began to form in the still water. She could hear the screams and shouts of a fierce battle and the clash of weapons. And her own face stared up at her, grimed and bloodied from fighting—and she was wearing chain mail and clad with an iron helmet. Her black hair flew in the wind. On her left arm was a round shield decorated with the red dragon of Brython. A sword was in her right fist.

Branwen tried to pull away, but she couldn't move.

The reflection's mouth opened, and Branwen's own voice rang out.

"The falcon is on the roof! Two tongues tell the truth!" the image shouted to her. "Remember this! A life depends on it! The falcon is on the roof! Two tongues tell the truth!"

And then the surface of the pool broke up as if with a sudden storm of rain, and the image shattered into a thousand fragments.

Branwen stood at the poolside, gaping down at a reflected sky of pale blue.

Was this some phantom vision conjured by Rhiannon to muddle her wits? A hint of the possible future? Or another trick?

"I won't do what you want!" she shouted.

You will. You will.

"Never! Hear me, Rhiannon of the Spring. *Never!*"

She was about to leave the clearing when Gavan came running out of the trees.

"Have you seen him?" panted the old warrior.

"No, he outran me," she said. "He'll be deep in the forest by now, curse him!"

"Never fear, my lady. He'll be caught; have no doubt of that." His eyes narrowed, and the muscles tightened along his jaw. "Did you speak long with him, my lady? Did he tell you anything other than lies?"

"He told me his name was Rhodri," she said. "He said he had escaped his Saxon master and was heading west to find the kinfolk of his father." She gritted her teeth. "I liked him. I brought him food for his journey."

"Food, by the saints?" growled Gavan. "My lady, you showed poor judgment in this."

"Yes, Gavan, I know that now. It will never happen again."

"I must return to Doeth Palas and raise the alarm. I shall not tell of your part in this." He rested his hand on her shoulder. "Learn from this, Princess Branwen. Trust only the trustworthy."

She nodded. It was a hard-won lesson, but one she would not quickly forget.

30

WHEN BRANWEN RETURNED to Doeth Palas, she found the fortress in a ferment of activity. Gavan had spread the word about a Saxon spy in the forest. Armed horsemen passed her as she headed up the stone-flanked path. Prince Llew was at the gates, deep in discussion with Gavan and Angor and other captains of the guard. More warriors were mounting up, and the village folk were gathered in anxious knots, their faces grim and fearful.

Prince Llew turned to her as she came in through the gates, his brows knit, his voice sharp. "Branwen, where have you been? The hunt is up for a Saxon spy. You should not be outside the gates alone!"

"I'm sorry, my lord," Branwen said, glancing quickly at Gavan. "I did not know."

Gavan did not look at her.

"Now you do," said the prince. "Lady Elain has told me of your wayward nature and your desire to be alone in the forest. I have not spoken against it thus far, but it ends now, Branwen. I will not risk harm coming to the only heir to the House of Rhys. You will remain within these walls until you depart for the south."

"Yes, my lord."

"Go now. Attend Lady Elain so that she knows you are safe."

"I will, my lord."

Branwen walked away with a heavy heart. As much as she hated the idea of being imprisoned within the high stone walls of Doeth Palas, it was nothing to the emotions that boiled through her as she thought of the way Rhodri had played her with his cunning lies.

Was there no one in the world she could trust?

The evening meal was a miserable ordeal. The only relief was that once Lady Elain had lectured her on how close she had come to having her throat cut in the forest, Branwen was left entirely alone. Most of the men were missing from the Great Hall, and the women wanted only to talk of the depraved Saxon spy and of what swift punishments he would receive once he was caught.

Angry as she was with Rhodri, Branwen did not like to listen to their discussions of the cruel ways in which the truth would be forced out of him, nor of the fate that awaited him once the questioning was done. She sought refuge on the battlements, but the voice of the night-shrouded sea did nothing to soothe her.

Now that her rage had calmed a little, images flashed through her mind. Confusing images that came to her unbidden and unwanted—of Rhodri, the first time she had encountered him, sitting waist deep in a rushing stream with clouds of mist around his shoulders and his blood welling into the running water. She had called him a Saxon swine. *Swine I may be, mistress,* he had retorted, *but don't insult me further than that.*

She had hit him with a branch and sent him tumbling down a cliff face—and he had responded with humor and forgiveness. How could such a person be a Saxon spy? Surely she would have *known*? She remembered his tenderness in healing Fain, and the mischievous light in his hazel eyes when he made gentle fun of her. And she remembered, too, the expression on his face when she spoke of her wish to go home and fight Saxons.

I hate the Saxons above all things in this world.

Had he been lying?

He's a spy. A villainous Saxon!

But was he?

Branwen went to her bedchamber late, hoping that the princesses would already be asleep. Walking through the agitated, wakeful fortress, she heard nothing to suggest that Rhodri had been captured yet. She felt curiously relieved.

The chamber was in darkness.

"Branwen?" It was Meredith.

"Yes," she whispered back, as she slipped into her bed.

"A Saxon spy—isn't it dreadful to think of!"

"Yes. Dreadful."

"Such a man could cut our throats while we sleep."

"Don't worry; they've closed the gates. He can't get in. Besides, I expect he'll be far away from here by now. Don't be afraid."

"You're not scared?"

"No. I'm not scared."

Not scared. Bewildered and torn apart by uncertainty—but not scared.

Meredith said nothing more, and soon Branwen heard her breathing deepen into sleep.

She was awakened by a hand coming down across her mouth and a fierce voice whispering close in her ear.

"Don't cry out, Branwen. I'm not going to hurt you. I need to talk to you."

She squirmed onto her back, grabbing the hand and pulling it away from her mouth. She looked up into Rhodri's face, lit by the faint glow of a rushlight. He looked demonic, his face striped with deep shadow, his eyes mere points of burning light.

"How did you find me?" Her voice was a harsh whisper.

"We must talk, but not here. Will you come with me? Please?"

She could let out a shout that would bring Prince Llew's warriors down on him like an avalanche. He must know that, too, and yet he had come to find her. She had to give him the chance to explain himself—not only for him, but for her own sake as well.

She slipped out of bed and quickly pulled on her jerkin and leggings. At the chamber door, Rhodri doused the light between his finger and thumb. They came out into the hall where the hearth-fire was low and red, the fitful flames sending shadows dancing across the floor.

Branwen and Rhodri skirted the side wall, staying in deep shade. The night sky was sullen with clouds that blotted out the stars. At the back of the long building they paused in a place where animals were penned in wicker stockades. The smell of the cattle was thick in the sultry night air.

"Are you a spy?" Branwen demanded.

"No. Believe me, Branwen. I'm not."

"Then Gavan was wrong about your accent?"

"No. He was right. I'm half Saxon. My father was born in Gwynedd, but my mother is Saxon. I was brought up in Northumbria. But I'm not spying for Herewulf Ironfist. I *was* his servant, and I'm running

x

x

258

away from him." There was anxiety in his face. "Why didn't you tell me who you were?"

"What difference would that have made?"

"Wotan's blood, Branwen!" Rhodri exclaimed. "I could have warned you if I'd known you were Griffith ap Wynn's daughter."

"Warned me of what?"

"Herewulf Ironfist commands King Oswald's army in the west," Rhodri said urgently. "I was a household servant in his camp outside Chester. I heard things. Plans. War is coming, Branwen. The Saxons are almost ready to invade Brython."

"That's old news," Branwen said. "My mother and father have been expecting it since the spring snows melted."

"But you don't know *how* they will come," Rhodri insisted. "They mean to avoid battles as much as they can. They plan on taking down the eastern citadels one by one. Attacking with stealth—striking like lightning out of a clear sky. Murdering everyone, burning the fortresses, and then disappearing again before your people can muster an army to fight them."

Branwen shuddered. In her mind she could see the fortresses burning, bodies consumed by the leaping flames, victorious Saxons galloping away in triumph. "Why didn't you tell anyone about this?"

"Who could I tell?" Rhodri asked. "Who would believe me? You saw how that old warrior reacted.

What chance was I given to speak with his hand at my throat?"

"He would have taken you to Prince Llew. The prince would have listened."

"I'm half Saxon, Branwen. Yes, maybe he would have listened—and then maybe he would have tortured me to try and learn more. But certainly he would have had me killed in the end. Do you think I'm that brave?" There was agony in his eyes. "The courage was beaten out of me long ago, Branwen."

Compassion filled Branwen's heart as she looked at him. "It's a foolish coward who risks his neck the way you have done tonight," she said. "But tell me— how did you know where to find me?"

"I knew that a princess would lodge in the Great Hall," Rhodri said. "I was lucky—or perhaps fate was on my side—because yours was the first room I came to."

"And how did you get into the citadel in the first place? The gates were locked and barred at nightfall."

"I climbed in," Rhodri said. "These ramparts are built to hold back an army of thousands, but they offer plenty of hand- and footholds for a single man."

"Then get out the same way you came," Branwen said. "And get as far away from here as you can; there are men out searching for you. I will tell Prince Llew what you've told me."

"I haven't told you everything yet."

"What else?"

"The name of the first citadel to be attacked." He put his hand on her arm. "They are going to destroy your home, Branwen. They mean to start the war by burning Garth Milain to the ground."

Branwen's heart stopped. "My mother and father will prevent that," she said, but her voice trembled, and the words sounded unconvincing in her ears.

"No, they will be deceived," Rhodri insisted. "The Saxons will come as emissaries, pretending to offer hopes of peace. That is what I heard in Ironfist's camp the night before I fled. That is what I came to tell you tonight. By Wotan's blood, Branwen, you must get word to your people before they die."

31

BRANWEN WATCHED AS Rhodri glided owl-quiet between the buildings, heading for the ramparts. At the last moment, he turned and lifted a hand in a gesture of farewell. Then he was gone, swallowed by shadows.

She had promised to give him some time to get clear of the fortress before she woke Prince Llew with the information he had given her. But the wait was a torment to her. It was agonizing to think of her parents guilelessly opening their gates to the Saxons, only to have their faith in the honesty in men's hearts betrayed by sharp iron and leaping flame.

At least now there would be time for the prince to send riders over the mountains to warn the people of Garth Milain. Branwen felt certain that her parents would survive any Saxon attack once they knew that it was coming.

She sent her good wishes out to Rhodri. He could have lost himself deep in the forest; instead he had risked everything to bring her the news. Whatever he thought about himself, he was wrong to say he was not brave.

She turned, intending to go back into the Great Hall.

A noise stopped her in her tracks.

Shouting.

She spun around, staring into the gloom.

The yells of alarm were coming from the same direction as Rhodri had taken. Several voices were calling out, the shrill, urgent noise cracking the night wide-open.

Rhodri!

Without thinking, she ran toward the sound.

She came to a huddle of storage huts, rough daub-and-wattle structures where grain and hay were kept. The huts were in darkness, but torchlight flickered on the brown walls. There was a knot of hectic movement against one of the huts.

Three young men were punching and kicking a fourth figure that was hunched on the ground with knees up to his chest and arms covering his head. Even though she could see little of him between the flying feet, Branwen knew who was getting the beating. It was Rhodri. They must have caught him before he reached the walls.

The boys surrounded their victim like wolves, their blows raining down on him with a sickening thud-ding sound. Branwen could hear Rhodri's groans and grunts mingling with the shouting and catcalling of the boys. She recognized them all: Bryn was lead-ing the attack; and Padrig was there, too; and Iwan, standing slightly aloof, holding a torch.

"Stop it! Stop it!" Branwen shouted. "You'll kill him!" She launched herself at Padrig, dragging him backward and sending him flying. "Leave him alone!" she howled.

She grabbed for Bryn next, but Bryn's head snapped around, and he brought up his elbow hard into her face. Her head exploding with pain, Branwen stumbled and fell back into the dirt. Shouting, she tried to get up again despite the pain that flared in her cheekbone. But a knee came down on her chest, and two hands pinned her shoulders to the ground.

"Branwen! What are you doing?" It was Iwan, his face close to hers as he leaned heavily over her. "Are you out of your wits? We've caught the Saxon spy!"

"He isn't a spy," Branwen gasped, fighting to get free of him. "I know him. You have to let him go."

"Shut your mouth, you fool!" Iwan hissed. "Do you want to share his fate?"

There was concern for her in his voice. And he was right: She would be in severe danger if people found out that she'd secretly been spending time with a Saxon.

"Let me up," she said.

He pulled her to her feet. By then several guards had arrived from the gate, their white cloaks billowing and their swords ready in their fists. Others were coming, men roused from sleep by the noise, furs thrown hastily over their shoulders. One of the guards pushed the boys aside and dragged Rhodri to his feet. Another took his other arm. He hung limp between them, his head dangling, blood smeared on his face.

Captain Angor strode through the gathering throng of townsfolk. He was fully dressed and armed with a sword, his eyes glinting as he lifted Rhodri's head by the hair and looked into his face.

"How often have you come creeping into Doeth Palas at dead of night, I wonder?" he snarled. "Sniffing like a rat for secrets to take back to your masters. Well, no more, boy." Rhodri's mouth hung open, the blood dripping from his lips. He hardly seemed to know where he was. Branwen ached to say something on his behalf, but this was not the time or the way. Angor would not listen to her; it was best to wait till she could speak to Prince Llew.

"Now it's our turn to seek for answers," Angor continued. "Rest overnight, boy. There's stern work ahead of you in the morning. Can you hear the fires spitting in the braziers? By dawn the gouging tongs and the blinding irons will be white-hot. Be sure of this: Death will be a relief by the time we're done with you." He let Rhodri's head fall again. "Take him away."

The two guards dragged Rhodri off, his feet hardly

able to stumble along as he was hauled between them. Branwen had listened to Captain Angor's threats with growing horror, and she couldn't keep quiet any longer.

"I have to speak with Prince Llew," she told the captain. He gave her a surprised glance. "Immediately!" she snapped. "You will wake him for me, or I will wake him myself. I have information that cannot wait."

He gave a curt nod. "Very well, my lady," he said. "Come. At the very least, the prince will be glad to hear that the Saxon dog has been captured."

Branwen tried not to think of the instruments of torture that he had described. Unless she said something on his behalf, Rhodri would suffer unimaginable agonies when the next day's sun dawned.

Prince Llew sat on his high chair in the Great Hall, wrapped in a fur-lined cloak of purple silk, newly roused from his bed and watching Branwen with doubtful, narrowed eyes. Candles had been lit, and other sleepers had been awakened. Gavan ap Huw was there, along with Captain Angor and many other warriors of the prince's court. Branwen could feel their disbelief growing as they listened to her.

What is this? She's a child! What does she know?

"Garth Milain will be taken by treachery, unless you send riders to warn my father and mother," Branwen finished. "Rhodri is no spy. He was telling the truth. Why should he lie?"

266

Prince Llew's voice rolled like thunder. "You ask why a Saxon spy would tell untruths? For the same reason that he befriended you in the first place—to protect himself and to sow confusion among the people of Doeth Palas."

"What did he tell you of himself?" asked Gavan, his voice less harsh than the prince's.

"He said he was an escaped captive of the Saxons," Branwen said. "He said his family lived in Gwynedd." She looked desperately from one to another of them, hoping for a single sympathetic face. There was none. "He was trying to get back home."

"That was a lie, my lady."

"You don't know that for certain. . . ."

"Enough of this!" exploded the prince. "I do not know what madness possessed you to trust that boy, Branwen, but understand this: If any person other than the daughter of Griffith ap Wynn had given succor to an enemy of Powys, they would pay the price with their head!"

"He was not lying to me!" she shouted. "He risked his life to warn me about the threat to Garth Milain."

"There is no such threat," said Captain Angor. "The Saxon dog risked his life, that much is true, but not to bring you the truth." He looked at the prince. "My lord, if the boy says Cyffin Tir is to be attacked, then be assured, the truth is otherwise!" His eyes glinted. "And I will get at that truth before he dies, if I have to tear it from his filthy heart with my own fingers."

"Then you will not send riders to warn my people?" Branwen gasped.

"A rider will be sent in due time," Prince Llew said. "But there is no urgency. Garth Milain is in no danger, and Captain Angor will learn the truth from the boy." He gave a grim smile. "And more easily, I suspect, after he has had a sleepless night in which to consider his fate."

"If you refuse to send anyone else, then let me go," Branwen begged. "Saddle Stalwyn. I'll ride alone over the mountains if I have to."

"You will not!" said the prince. "News has arrived from the south. The roads are clear and safe to travel. A group of traders will be leaving Doeth Palas early tomorrow morning." His eyes gleamed. "You will go with them, Branwen."

"No!"

"Get you to bed, Branwen ap Griffith," the prince growled. "And think yourself lucky that you are your father's daughter—or a far worse fate would await you when tomorrow's sun rises!"

Branwen took a step toward the throne, clenching her fists. How dare he speak to her like that!

"Enough!" shouted the prince. "Take her from my sight. Put her to bed! Chain her down if need be!"

Gavan was the first to step forward. "Come, my lady," he said, resting his hand on her shoulder. "No good will be served by this."

She allowed herself to be led toward her chamber. "Rhodri is innocent," she said to the old warrior.

"No, my lady. He is not." Gavan looked sternly at her. "Must I put a guard on your door?"

"No," she murmured, her anger draining away. "That won't be necessary."

She walked alone to the far end of the chamber. Shadows flickered on the walls, tormented shapes that writhed around her and filled her mind with dark images of the tortures that awaited Rhodri when the sun arose.

If not for her, he would have been far away by now. In trying to help Branwen and her family, Rhodri had condemned himself to death.

32

THE FALCON IS on the roof! Two tongues tell the truth!
Branwen lay a long while sleepless on her mattress, her eyes full of troubled darkness. She was adamant that she would not do the bidding of the Shining Ones—but for some reason she could not stop brooding over the rhyme that her own voice had shouted to her out of Rhiannon's pool.

"A life depends on it." She mouthed the words silently. "Remember this."

The falcon—that could refer to Fain. But *two tongues*? What did that mean?

What has two tongues? Serpents have forked tongues. Was she to be guided by a snake?

No, no. That makes no sense.

What else could have two tongues?

A man could—a man who speaks two languages.

Branwen's eyes stretched wide in the darkness.

A man who speaks both the Brythonic and the Saxon languages. A man with a father from Cefn Boudan and a mother from Northumbria.

Oh, by Saint Cadog and Saint Cynwal and Saint Dewi! Rhodri!

A life will depend on it!

She sat up. The breathing of the sleeping princesses came faintly to her across the pitch-black room. She knew what she had to do. Rhodri had risked his life for her; now she must risk hers for him.

Drawing her blanket around her shoulders, she groped her way to the door, lifting the latch as silently as she could. The hall was empty now and full of shadows. The stones were cold under her bare feet. She lit a candle from the embers and crept back to her room. She had to risk a small light.

She put the candle on the floor and knelt by her chest, glancing over her shoulder as she lifted the lid. If she was fleeing this place, possibly never to return, there were things she needed to take with her. And if she succeeded in her plan, she had a long road to travel before she could ever present herself at Prince Llew's court again.

She dressed in her hunter's clothes and clasped the leather belt around her waist. Her slingshot was tucked into the belt, and the pouch of stones alongside it. Then she tied her other cherished possessions onto the belt: the pouch of crystals that Geraint had given her, the pouch with the firestones and kindling in it, the comb, and the golden key given to her by her father. She felt a pang of regret that Geraint's knife had been destroyed. A sharp blade would have been an advantage.

She looked over her shoulder again—and saw two eyes watching her from the far end of the room.

"What are you doing?"

"Nothing, Romney, go back to sleep."

"Tell me what you're doing, or I'll run and tell Mama and Papa."

May the floor open up and send the wretch to Annwn!

"I'm doing something that should please you greatly, Romney," Branwen said softly. "I'm leaving."

"Like a thief in the dark?" said Romney, sitting up. "What are you intending to steal that you should want to sneak away in the middle of the night?"

"Nothing!" hissed Branwen. "By all the saints, Romney, I am not a thief. Your baubles mean nothing to me."

"I'm going to Papa," Romney said, getting out of bed. "He'll know how to deal with you."

A different voice sounded from the end of the room. "Romney, you stay here." Meredith got up and snatched at Romney's arm, pulling her back onto her mattress. "If she wants to go, let her go. She doesn't belong here. Wouldn't you rather just be rid of her?" Her voice took on a gentle, coaxing tone. "Then it'll just be the two of us again; wouldn't you like that?"

"Yes!"

"Well, let the barbarian princess sneak off. Who cares about her? Let her go and live like a wild thing in the forest. Among the wild pigs, eh, Romney? Can't you see her snuffling around on all fours like a wild pig?"

Romney giggled. "Yes! Yes, I can!"

Meredith's eyes turned toward Branwen, and she saw a new light in them. It was not friendship; it was not even understanding . . . but it was respect.

"Shall we be rid of her, then, Romney?" Meredith asked. "We can tell Mother and Father about it in the morning."

"When you speak to your mother, tell her I'm sorry I wasn't a better guest," Branwen said, looking at Meredith. "And tell her . . ." Her voice faltered.

"Once a barbarian princess, always a barbarian princess?" Meredith offered with the slightest hint of humor in her voice.

"Yes. That will do very well." Branwen snuffed out the candle. Moments later she was at the door, through the doorway, across the stones of the hall, and out into the night.

She kept to shadows. Braziers were burning on the ramparts on either side of the closed gate. She could see guards moving about up there. Although the Saxon spy had been captured, the fortress was still vigilant.

"So, then," Branwen murmured under her breath,

peering up into the sky, seeking for a piece of darkness blacker than the night. "Where are you?"

Fain came gliding out of nowhere. Branwen smiled. The bird flew low, passing her close by, its eye like a jewel. She followed it, knowing it would lead her true.

The falcon guided her to a huddle of daub-and-wattle huts with peaked, thatched roofs—simple huts deep in the heart of the fortress, under the lee of the sea-facing ramparts and far from the gates. Huts used to store food and other supplies.

Branwen watched as Fain came to rest on the sloping roof of one of the huts. *The falcon is on the roof! Two tongues tell the truth!*

Fain had brought her to the place where Rhodri was being kept. She moved out of cover, keeping close to any shade, slipping from hut to hut.

There was a guard on the door of the prison hut.

She had expected it, although she had hoped otherwise. She put her hand to her slingshot. An accurate strike could fell a small deer—but a man? Maybe a stone into the eye would disable him enough to . . . *no!* She shuddered. The soldier was only doing his duty.

She looked more closely at the guard. It was not one of Prince Llew's burly warriors; the figure at the door was much slighter than that. A young man with light brown hair and a casual way of leaning on the doorframe that was very familiar to her.

She breathed his name. "Iwan."

Was that good or bad?

She took a breath and stepped into the open. She was halfway to the hut when Iwan noticed her. He stiffened, his hand coming to his sword hilt. Then puzzlement filled his face. "Princess Branwen?" he said. "What do you want here?"

Branwen walked up to him, feigning a confidence that she didn't feel. "I want to see him," she said, nodding at the door.

"Really?" Surprised, but still in control. "Why?"

"He made a fool of me. I want to pay him back for that. I assume you've got him tied up in there. Open the door and let me in. I promise I won't kill him."

Iwan raised his eyebrows. "You don't think he's got pain enough coming to him in the morning? I've seen Captain Angor's interrogations before. Those who come to gawk need a strong stomach."

"He's a Saxon dog; why should you care?" Branwen said, making her voice sound harsh and cruel. "A few extra bruises won't show."

Iwan looked narrowly at her. "I'm glad we never became enemies, my lady," he said.

"Will you open the door?"

"No."

"Are you his jailer or his protector?" she spat.

Iwan stepped in front of the door. "I won't let you in," he said. "Even a Saxon spy deserves better than that." He shook his head. "Where's the honor in this, Princess Branwen? Go back to bed. If you want to see him suffer, then rise early in the morning and come to watch the captain practicing his skills."

"I'll go," Branwen said, already half turning. "But remember this, Iwan ap Madoc, before you judge me too harshly: Things are not always as they seem!" She swung back toward him, the heel of her left hand striking him on the chin and jerking his head back hard against the door while with her right hand she pulled his sword from his belt and pressed the point against his stomach.

Anger and pain flared in his face, and he made as if to rush at her; but she jabbed the sharp iron into his belly, stopping him.

"I don't want to do you harm, Iwan," she hissed. "But I won't let Rhodri be hurt. If you make me choose, I'll do damage to you that will take a long time to heal." She glared into his eyes. "Trust me on that."

"I do," Iwan gasped.

"Step away from the door."

Iwan's dark eyes were unreadable as he moved aside. She gestured for him to stand against the wall of the hut, the sword on him constantly as she reached for the bar that held the door closed. She threw the wooden bar down and pushed the door open.

"Rhodri?" she called softly.

"Yes."

Relief flooded through her at the sound of his voice. "Can you walk?"

"I'm bound hand and foot. Wait—I think I can get to the door." She heard grunting and panting, and a few moments later Rhodri's head appeared in the doorway at her feet.

"Lift your hands."

She slashed the rope with a single sweep of her blade. Iwan made a sudden move toward her, but she brought the sword up again in an instant, its point at his chest. "Do not do that!" she warned in hushed tones.

He stepped back again, his hands raised.

"Can you untie your legs?" Branwen asked Rhodri.

"Yes. Give me a moment. But, Branwen, this is madness. Why did you come here? They won't care that you're a princess. They'll hang you for setting me free."

"Hopefully, they won't get the chance," Branwen said. "We're leaving together."

"*What?*"

"I've made my choice. I won't let them kill you."

Rhodri stood up, stamping his feet and rubbing his wrists to get the circulation going again. "The gates are closed," he said quietly. "We'll have to go over the ramparts." He gestured toward Iwan. "What about him?"

"Fair exchange is no robbery," Branwen said. "Let's leave one prisoner to take the place of another. Is there enough rope to tie him securely?"

"I believe so."

"If they catch you, you'll hang side by side," Iwan said grimly. "Branwen, give this up! Let the Saxon die—but save yourself. Why is he worth this sacrifice?"

"It's a debt of honor," Branwen said, as Rhodri circled Iwan to tie his arms behind him. Iwan resisted at first; but Branwen brought the sword point close to his throat, and he quickly became still again as his wrists were bound.

"Rhodri is not a spy," Branwen hissed. "I know you don't believe me, but it's the truth."

Iwan grimaced as Rhodri tightened the rope. "You're a fool," he said.

"Maybe so." She looked at Rhodri. "I'll tie his feet," she said. She led Iwan into the gloom of the hut, the sword steady in her hand. "Sit," she ordered.

Iwan sat down, his legs stretched out in front of him. Branwen put the sword down and tied the remaining rope around his ankles. "I need to gag you," she warned. "I want to be far from here before you are found." There was a scrap of cloth on the ground, a piece torn from an old grain bag.

He stared at her, his eyes bright in the darkness. "I hope we meet again under better circumstances, Princess Branwen ap Griffith."

"As do I."

"One last thing," Iwan said, as she brought the gag up to his mouth.

"What?"

"My sword," he said. "It has been in my family since the time of my great-grandfather. Will you leave it, please?"

She frowned. She had been intending to take it in

case they were discovered. But in reality, how would one sword help them if a band of Llew's warriors came upon them?

She nodded. "I'll leave it outside the hut."

He smiled. "Thank you, " he said. "You're going to have an interesting life, Branwen! I wish I could have shared it."

She gagged him and closed and barred the door.

The night was strangely quiet. Branwen could hear her heart beating as if it were the loudest noise in all of Doeth Palas. "Where's best to climb the ramparts?" she murmured to Rhodri.

"The way I came in," he said. "I'll show you."

She rested Iwan's sword against the wall of the hut. Rhodri looked questioningly at her.

"If we have to fight, we're already lost," she said.

"Very well. Come." He sprinted away through the huts. Branwen quickly caught up with him and ran at his side.

She knew that she was leaving her old life behind her, that things would never be the same again . . . but whatever happened, she had chosen this path herself. This was not a destiny determined for her by Rhiannon and the Shining Ones. In fleeing this land, she was also leaving them behind. Or so she hoped.

Is it possible to outrun gods?

Who could say? But for the time being, Branwen felt at last that she had taken her fate into her own hands.

33

THE NIGHT SEEMED to magnify the sound of the crashing waves until Branwen felt as if her head would crack open. She was standing on a narrow ledge, high above the ocean, with her back pressed to the cold stone. Above her the ramparts of Doeth Palas soared away into a sky teeming with stars.

One arm was stretched out, and her fingers were tightly clasping Rhodri's hand. He had guided her safely this far, but the ledge felt uncertain under her feet and the leaping white foam below her seemed full of voices urging her to jump.

Rhodri's hand squeezed hers. "You won't fall. Edge toward me. I'll keep hold of you."

She slid one foot along the shelf of rock. She pressed down on it, testing it. It seemed firm enough. She transferred her weight.

"You don't need to grip so tight," Rhodri said.

"Sorry."

"We're going to need both hands soon, so I'd rather not have one of mine crushed."

She risked moving her head to look at him. He was smiling reassuringly at her.

"At least . . . we've made it hard . . . for the guards to . . . follow . . . ," she said, attempting to smile back.

"We've done the hardest part," Rhodri promised. "The ledge widens from here."

He was right. A few steps farther and Branwen was able to let go of his hand and walk along the ledge with relative confidence, although she leaned in close to the cliff face and tested each step thoroughly before proceeding. Then there was a final wild scramble up a back-sloping rock face, as cracked and seamed as a mud-track under the summer sun. Branwen stood on the cliff top, the ocean-wind in her hair, cooling the sweat on her face, her arms and legs trembling from the climb.

Doeth Palas towered against the stars, its crown tipped with red flames. How long before Iwan was discovered? How long before riders came pouring through the gates to scour the land and bring the two of them back, bound and helpless?

"We need horses," Branwen said. "We can't walk all the way to Garth Milain." She gazed into the east, where the mountains formed a high, broken, black horizon. "It's a two-day ride," she said. "Less if we rest as little as possible."

"I'm not a good horseman," Rhodri admitted. "I was a servant of the household, not of the estates."

"Will you be able to stay on a horse if we find you one?"

"I'll try," he said. "But if not, then you'll have to ride on ahead."

"There are a lot of farmsteads between here and the mountains. Let's find ourselves some horses before the farmers are awake."

"Steal some, you mean."

"*Borrow* some," Branwen corrected him. "If all goes well, the House of Rhys will repay the loan tenfold." She broke into a run. "Come, quickly," she called. "I want to be a long way from here before the dawn."

The sky was brightening above their heads as Branwen and Rhodri cantered their stolen horses through a field of ripening wheat. They had been lucky, finding suitable steeds quickly in a farm close to the fortress and managing to bridle them without awakening their owners. Branwen had watched Rhodri with concern as he had clambered clumsily astride the horse's back. She did not like the idea of having to leave him behind, although she knew that if his horsemanship proved too poor, that was exactly what she would have to do.

Rhodri sat badly and looked uneasy, but he managed to keep on the horse; and after a while Branwen felt able to take them from walk to trot and finally to canter. Alone, she would have been tempted to gallop the lands like an arrow; but she knew that a galloping horse would tire sooner and need more rest than a horse taken at an even canter, and so she kept her impatience under control and thanked the saints for firm ground under their horses' hooves.

They had ridden hard through the night, heading across country toward the foothills, taking the straighter route to save time and to avoid the roads. Branwen looked back over her shoulder. Doeth Palas was lost behind a fold in the land. The road—a brown curve away to the south—was empty. Luck had been with them so far, but they still had far to travel before journey's end.

She thought of Iwan's parting words: *You're going to have an interesting life, Branwen! I wish I could have shared it.* It was a strange thing for him to have said; she would have expected threats and anger from him. Despite the casual hurts he had inflicted on her, and despite her wiser self, she wished she could have got to know him better. It seemed a shame that she would never see him again—if only for the chance to challenge him to a fair fight and crack him over the head with a staff!

As Branwen and Rhodri moved eastward into the deep glens, they had to slow their horses to a walk. In the deeper clefts, rushing streams of clear mountain water ran through stony beds and tipped over mossy ridges, while forests of birch and elder and oak clung onto the steeply rising shoulders of the hills. The day became warm as the sun appeared over the peaks, and soon the horses' mouths were flecked with foam. Branwen constantly had to sleeve the sweat out of her eyes.

Ever upward they went, urging their horses to climb the steepening slopes and to walk precarious ridges from one high point to another while stones and shale went tumbling into a green gully. Branwen gazed down, her stomach tightening and a cold sweat standing out on her forehead. It was all too easy to imagine plunging headlong into that yawning gulf. Shivering despite the heat, she nudged her heels into her horse's flanks and it moved slowly onward, hoof by cautious hoof.

The farmlands of Bras Mynydd were far behind them now, glimpsed only occasionally between crags and cliffs. Branwen was still unwilling to use the winding mountain road, although she knew that she would have no option once the gulfs became too deep and the slopes too sheer. It was a long time since they had eaten, and Branwen's stomach ached for food. It was too early in the year for fruit or berries; and in their rush to get away from Doeth Palas, neither of them had thought to steal food for the journey.

They came to a high plateau in the middle of the afternoon. The sun beat down on the mountains out of a clear blue sky. A haze was rising. Branwen shaded her eyes against the sun.

"Are you hungry?" she asked Rhodri. "Can you last a while longer before we stop to look for food?"

"Yes, and yes," Rhodri replied tiredly. He sighed as he gazed into the west. "I keep thinking of that bag of food you gave. It's still lying back there somewhere. It seems something of a waste, what with my stomach thinking my throat must have been cut."

"Animals will find it and eat it," Branwen said.

"Ahh," Rhodri said heavily. "Yes. I'm sure they will—and I shall comfort myself with thoughts of fat-bellied squirrels, too stuffed with my food to move."

Branwen almost smiled, but she was preoccupied with the threat of pursuit. At the very latest, Iwan must have been found at first light. Prince Llew would be wild with anger. He would have sent out half his army to recapture them. And it was likely that Gavan ap Huw would be among them. It made Branwen's heart ache that she had not been able to explain her actions to the old warrior. It must look as if she had betrayed all his kindnesses. Perhaps a time would come for her to be able to put things right between them.

She turned in the saddle, staring up at the towering peaks. "Prince Llew is sure to have sent some men this way. That's why I've been avoiding the mountain road." She was aware of Rhodri watching her in pensive silence. "But we can't keep climbing like this. It's getting too dangerous. We have to make for the road now."

"I agree," Rhodri said. "It won't be much consolation to me as I plunge to my death to think how cleverly I've escaped the noose."

Branwen nodded. "To the road then," she said. "And let's hope the saints are watching over us."

Branwen crouched low on a sloping spit of rock that jutted out over the mountain road. This was the last vantage point from which they would be able to look down into the west before the road began the long, twisting journey down the eastern buttresses of the mountains. It was late in the afternoon, and the low sun was pouring golden light over the distant plains; even the shadows seemed to be aswim with dark honey. She could make out few details, except that closer by, she could see occasional stretches of the road as it wound up toward her.

She called down to Rhodri, whom she had left holding the reins of both horses while she scrambled up to check for possible pursuit. "The road seems empty."

"You almost sound disappointed," Rhodri called up.

She turned and slid down the stone to join him again. "I'm not," she said. "I'm just surprised."

"We've been lucky," Rhodri said, handing her the reins. "We had half the night to get a head start on them."

She wrinkled her nose. "We'll ride on a little farther, then I'll catch us something to eat while there's still enough light."

Rhodri looked dubiously at her. "Are we to eat raw meat?" he asked. "I'm hungry, but I'm not sure I'm that hungry yet."

"No, we'll stop for a little while. We need to rest, and so do the horses. I have firestones with me." She looked at Rhodri. "Don't worry, the meat will be cooked."

As the lowering sun sent her shadow spinning ahead of her, she glanced uneasily over her shoulder, unable to shake the growing feeling that pursuit could not be far behind.

34

BRANWEN HARDLY BREATHED as she crawled along on her belly, moving as silently as a snake through the long grass. The big buck mountain hare was sitting on a rock, enjoying the warm evening, its whiskers twitching and its long ears alert. Once killed, skinned, and cooked, she knew from experience that it would make good eating.

She had left Rhodri with the horses, using all her skill and patience to approach the hare from downwind. Now she was ready. She fitted a stone into her folded slingshot. To kill the hare with a single shot, she would need to strike it cleanly between the eye and the ear.

She whirled the slingshot and let the stone loose. There was a swish and a hiss, and the hare was stretched lifeless in the grass. She rose from cover and walked over to the dead creature. There was a small, neat depression at its temple and a smear of blood on its nose. She lifted it by the ears, turning at the slow clop of hooves.

"You're very good at that," Rhodri commented as he approached, leading the horses. "Who taught you to hunt?"

"My brother did," Branwen said, looping her slingshot back into her belt. "He also taught me that taking a life is a solemn thing. We kill to eat, but the death must be quick and clean. To kill for sport or pleasure is a shameful thing, be it fish, fowl, or beast."

> *Child of the Spring*
> *Child of the Wood*
> *Chase flesh, fowl, fish*
> *But spill no blood*

No! I won't think about that. I've left Rhiannon in her sacred grove. I've parted forever from the Shining Ones.

"What is it?" Rhodri asked.

"Nothing," Branwen said, shaking her head. "I was just thinking it's a pity I lost Geraint's knife." She stooped and lifted the hare by its back legs. "This fellow needs skinning and gutting."

"That sword might have come in useful after all," Rhodri said.

"Iwan's sword, you mean? No. A sword would be too unwieldy. But I do need something with a sharp edge." Her hand came to the golden comb in her waistband. "Gold is a softer metal than iron," she said, holding up the comb and looking appraisingly at it. "And the points are not so sharp as a good blade, but it might do the job." She looked at Rhodri. "Gather some dry stuff for a fire and enough stones to make a small hearth." She crouched, laying out the hare belly up on the ground. "Oh, and some good, straight sticks," she added. "To make a spit."

Rhodri was gazing thoughtfully at her.

"What?" she asked.

"Command sits well on you," he said. "You're a natural leader, I think."

"I'm a princess," Branwen said. "I'm used to people doing what I tell them."

"I dare say—but it's more than that."

"Get away with you," Branwen said. "Find stuff to make a fire, or you *will* be eating your meat raw."

While Rhodri was foraging, Branwen got busy making the hare ready for roasting. She had just finished and was cleaning her hands and the comb on some moss when Rhodri returned, empty-handed but with an excited expression on his face.

"I found a cave," he said, pointing back the way he had come. "The entrance is narrow; but so far as I could make out, it opens out into a large chamber. It would make good shelter while we rest." His eyes gleamed. "And there's more. It was too dark to see much, but there seemed to be markings on the walls."

"What kind of markings?"

"Drawings," Rhodri said. "Come and see for yourself. It's not far. I'll fetch the horses."

Branwen followed Rhodri through the deepening twilight. The cave mouth was just a slot in a broken face of gray stone. It appeared suddenly through the trees like a slice taken out of the mountain by a giant's ax.

She peered in at the entrance; it was wide enough to take a horse through, and five times that in height. She was able to make out the gray walls and shaled floor close by; but darkness hid the rest, and she could see no drawings on the walls.

"It's too dark now," Rhodri said, standing at her shoulder. "But I did see them."

"We could make a fire if you'd gathered the things I asked."

"I did." He pointed to a small circle of stones close by the cave mouth. Dried leaves and twigs were piled in the ring.

Branwen knelt and took the two flint firestones and the scrap of dried kindling from the pouch at her belt. She bent double, striking the flints together so that the sparks flew. It wasn't long before the kindling began to smolder. She blew gently on it, carefully feeding more dry stuff in until a tiny white flame sprang up.

She offered more fuel to the flame, and soon a merry blaze was dancing in the ring of stones. It reminded her of similar fires she had lit with Geraint in the forests of her childhood, the two of them vying to be the first to make flame.

Mother! My fire lit first!

Branwen picked a flaming branch off the fire and went into the cave. Rhodri had been right: The cave was huge, stretching deep into the mountain. She swung the sputtering branch. Shadows jumped and crouched like prancing demons.

She let out a long breath as she saw the drawings spread across a wide stretch of the smooth stone wall. The drawings were of animals, daubed in pigments of yellow and brown and red and black. Branwen walked slowly along the unfolding gallery of images, her heart hammering in her chest. She had never seen anything like this! The drawings were all jumbled together, some no bigger than her hand, others drawn so large that she had to step back to take them in.

Although the forms were strangely proportioned, she could make out many familiar creatures. There were deer and cattle, sometimes with their legs spread out as though they were galloping, sometimes standing watchfully still, and sometimes with their heads down to graze. There were twelve-point stags, and wolves running in packs, and bears rearing up on their hind legs, and hares leaping one over the other. And there were fish. Birds. Dragonflies. Frogs. An endless array of beasts crept and prowled and ran and leaped and flew along the wall.

"Who *did* this?" she wondered out loud. "I've never

seen anything like them before."

"Neither have I."

Branwen started at Rhodri's voice; she had not even realized that she had spoken her question aloud, and under the eerie enchantment of the drawings she had forgotten that she was not alone.

"They're beautiful," she said. "But they scare me a little."

"I know what you mean."

Then Branwen saw the people.

They were brown and black, stick-thin humans—hundreds of them, it seemed to her, covering the wall from the ground to the height of her shoulder—and they were dancing under a bloodred disk drawn high on the wall at the very edge of the torchlight. Their jagged limbs were at strange angles, their heads featureless; but every head was tilted back, as if the dancers were looking up at the red disk.

Branwen stepped back, bumping into Rhodri.

I know this! But why? From where?

"Branwen? Are you all right?"

She pointed at the flat, red circle. "What do you think that's meant to be?"

"The sun?" Rhodri suggested.

"Yes, of course." The half memory faded softly away.

"So? Shall we use the cave?" Rhodri urged. "We could bring the horses inside. There's plenty of room."

"Yes," Branwen said distractedly, mesmerized by

the red globe above her head. "Yes, do that, Rhodri. But set the fire on the far side, over there—away from the drawings."

She didn't know why, but she didn't like the idea of being too close to the dancing people. There was a wildness about them that was too intense . . . too passionate. Too powerful.

"How long should we stay here?" Rhodri asked, tossing a well-chewed bone into the fire and leaning back against the wall of the cave.

"I don't think we can risk the mountain in the dark," Branwen replied. "The cave mouth faces east, so we'll see the dawn early. We should leave then. At very first light."

"Time enough for our hunters to catch up with us," Rhodri pondered.

"I don't think so," Branwen said. "They won't risk trying to cross the high pass at night, not if they value their necks and the necks of their horses."

"I hope you're right."

Branwen frowned. "I think I am," she said slowly. "I don't know why, but I feel that our luck will stay with us."

"That's good enough for me," Rhodri said, turning and stretching out on his back with his head pillowed on his hands. "I've slept in worse places than this in the recent past—and in better places with worse prospects."

Branwen licked her fingers clean of the meat juices. The hare had roasted well, and it was good to have a bellyful of warm food. The horses seemed content as well, standing by the wall deeper into the cave, with their reins tied loosely around a rock. While the hare had been cooking, Branwen and Rhodri had left the cave, pulling up armfuls of fresh grass for the weary animals to eat. It was meager fare, Branwen knew, and she promised them oats and barley when they came to Garth Milain; but for the time being, grass would have to do.

"Tell me about your parents," Branwen prompted. "How is it you have a father from Brython and a Saxon mother?"

"I never knew my father," Rhodri said. "He died or escaped or was killed before I was born. The story would change according to my mother's mood. The only thing she never wavered in was that he was a man of Gwynedd, captured by the Saxons in the wars and taken to Northumbria as a servant. Sometimes she would say that his family came from Cefn Boudan; at other times she said he was captured there but lived in some other place."

"And how did your mother meet him?"

"She was a bonded servant. She was no more free than he was." On the surface Rhodri's voice was quite calm, but Branwen could tell that the memories troubled him. "That grim old warrior of yours was a little out in his reckoning with my accent. I was born in

Northumbria, but my mother came from the kingdom of Deira; and it was her accent that I picked up as a child."

"I've never heard of Deira," Branwen said.

"I'm not surprised. It's a little coastal kingdom to the east of Northumbria. It is only allowed to survive because the king pays heavy tribute to Oswald." He gave a grim smile. "Part of the tribute is paid in bonded servants. My mother was one of them. She met my father while working the estates of Herewulf Ironfist—and I was the result. At the age of six, I was taken from my mother and became part of Herewulf's household. I never saw her again." He sighed. "I would have liked to have known my ancestry. Am I of warrior stock? Was he a farmer or a smithy? A charcoal burner or a traveling bard?"

"Is that why you were making for Cefn Boudan— to find out about your family?"

"Partly," Rhodri agreed. "And also to put as much land between me and old Ironfist as I could." He gave a bleak chuckle. "And here I am heading back into his loving arms. What a marvelous sense of humor fate has; it's a wonder we don't all die of laughter."

"We should sleep now," Branwen said. Beyond the stone lips of the cave, the world was black.

She lay down, turning her back to the fire and curling up her legs. The last things she saw before closing her eyes were the dancing folk, capering under the bloodred sun.

35

*N*OT THE SUN—THE *moon!*
   A bloodred moon!

Branwen awoke with a start. She had no idea how much time had passed, but a bright, silvery light was flooding in through the cave mouth.

"You will run in a circle, Branwen ap Griffith, and I will be there. We shall meet again in the place where the men of mud dance beneath the moon of blood. And there you will learn the truth, and perhaps a little wisdom!"

Rhiannon's voice echoed in her mind, bringing her as sharply awake as a splash of cold water in the face.

The silver light filled the cave, illuminating the paintings, making their colors glow and their outlines shimmer. The men of mud danced on under the moon of blood. Branwen looked away from them. The little fire was flickering weakly, and Rhodri was still asleep with his back to her. She stood up and walked into the light.

It was deep night, but Rhiannon was there, standing in a pool of snowy shadow, one hand on the pommel of her horse's saddle, the other held up with Fain on her wrist. She was standing absolutely still, staring into the east with her back to Branwen.

"You brought me here on purpose," Branwen said.

Rhiannon's voice was like water falling under starlight. "No, child. You brought yourself here. I merely foretold it."

"Then why are you here?"

"To answer your questions," Rhiannon said. "Or perhaps to watch the sun rise over Garth Milain for the last time."

Branwen stepped forward, her hands tightening to fists. "What does that mean?"

"In fire did you leave your home, in fire shall you return." Rhiannon turned and looked at her with eyes full of silver light. "Did you think that by running from me you could run from your own fate? The world weaves a tighter web than that, child. Have you not learned that lesson yet?"

Anger flared inside Branwen. "All I've learned is that you did nothing to save my brother when the Saxons cut him down. I will never follow you, Rhiannon of the Spring."

"A life lost, a life saved," said Rhiannon. "Who is to judge the right and the wrong of it?"

"You could have saved both of us!"

"Yours is not the saved life of which I spoke," said Rhiannon. "Not all the stars revolve around your head, Branwen."

This was confusing. "If not me, then who?" Branwen asked. "Whose life was saved?"

"The boy in yonder cave," said Rhiannon. "If not for me, his life would have ended with the coming morn."

"You!" Branwen exploded. "You did nothing! I saved him. I, alone, with no one's help—least of all yours."

A faint smile touched Rhiannon's lips. "And would you have saved him were he a stranger caught wandering in the woods of Bras Mynydd? Would you have saved him were he an unknown half-Saxon vagabond dragged into the fortress of Doeth Palas to be tortured and killed?" Rhiannon's voice grew louder. "I set the events in motion that resulted in you meeting Rhodri."

"How?" Branwen demanded. "How did you do that?"

"I sent the dream that filled your thoughts as you crossed the mountains," Rhiannon replied. "The dream drew you away from the others and left you companionless on the high pass."

Branwen stared at her. The dream of Geraint! *Rhiannon* had put it into her sleeping mind? *No!*

"I created the fog that blinded you all as you crossed the mountains," Rhiannon continued. "And when you were alone and forsaken, I summoned the gwyllion of the mountains to lead you with their lights."

Branwen remembered the thin, white flames in the fog—the phantom lights that took her from the road.

"And when you would no longer follow the gwyllion lights, it was I who sent my falcon to lead you to the boy. And I sent Fain to you once more in the forest that skirts Doeth Palas. Although you wounded him, Fain led you to the boy again. I foresaw the danger the boy was in, and I knew that only a friend would save him." Rhiannon's eyes flashed. "Tell me again, Branwen, how it was that I did not save his life!"

"I didn't *know*!" gasped Branwen. "But why was Rhodri's life more important than my brother's?" She looked apprehensively at Rhiannon. "Does he have a destiny, too?"

"All creatures that live each has its own destiny, child; but I am not the sculptor of human destiny. I merely play my role, as do all things, as did your brother—as do you."

"You mean you were *allowed* to save me, but not Geraint?" she said. "And through me you also saved Rhodri."

"The eyes open and wisdom enters in," said Rhiannon, her voice growing softer. "You have fought me hard, Branwen; fight no more. I am not your enemy. Your enemy comes creeping over the eastern hills even as we speak, cloaked in deception."

"Am I too late?" Branwen exclaimed in alarm. "Is Garth Milain already lost?"

"There is still time," Rhiannon said. "Speed is your only ally now, Branwen. Fly as fast as you can, and you may still save many lives." Her hand reached out in warning, three fingers pointing. "But heed me, child: When the battle is done, for good or ill, you must make your choice: to follow your destiny, or to turn forever from it. But choose wisely, for your decision will seal the fate of thousands. This is my final foretelling."

The silver light began to fade; and it seemed to Branwen that although Rhiannon and her horse did not move, they fled away from her through the trees, growing smaller and smaller.

"I will weep for you," the voice cried as it faded. "A single teardrop of ice to light your way."

"No, wait!" Branwen shouted. "I have to know more!"

"I have opened the floodgates of fate," came the distant voice. "All the waters of the world pour through. Wade into the water, Branwen ap Griffith. Go, find your destiny!"

36

"RHODRI! WAKE UP! We have to go!"

Branwen was trying to pull him to his feet before his eyes were open.

"It's still nighttime . . . ," he gasped, peering blurrily at her. "What's the rush?"

"We have to go *now*," Branwen insisted. "I'll explain on the way. Come *on!*" She ran to the horses, snatching up their bridles as she went.

Rhodri lurched to his feet. "Is it Prince Llew's men? Have you heard something? Seen something?"

"I've seen Rhiannon again," Branwen told him urgently. "The Saxons are on the move. Unless we go now it'll be too late."

Rhodri knuckled the sleep out of his eyes and ran to help her. They led the horses out of the cave. All was dark, but away and away, Branwen could see a thin, gray line—the far horizon—and lurking just beyond it was the sun rising on a terrible new day.

Despite the need for haste, Branwen kept watchful for uneven surfaces or holes in the road as she led them down from the high pass. A hoof misplaced and a horse lamed could ruin everything. They hardly spoke, but Branwen took comfort in Rhodri's presence at her side as the sun rose in the east and the wind blew warm from the south.

They passed a stony plateau under a towering sheet of bleak, bare rock—the very place where Prince Llew's company had halted for the night only a few days earlier. Below them the mountains stepped down in forested ridges into an ocean of trees. Somewhere beyond that final forest, Garth Milain lay in peril. The sun was high in the sky, and still there was far to go.

"The worst is over," Branwen said, wiping the sweat out of her eyes. "The road gets easier now. This is the Great Forest Way." She led Rhodri at a canter along the wide, brown trackway as it wound through the forest that cloaked the foothills of Cyffin Tir. There was a fist in her stomach, but this time it was not hunger. It was desperation—and the fear that she would emerge from the forest only to see Garth Milain already burning.

The horses were exhausted, but she could not let

them rest. Their eyes rolled and foam flew as they sped between the ranks of trees. The wind had picked up; and as it rushed through the leaves, it seemed to hiss with a thousand sneering voices: *too slow, too slow, too slow!*

The first stars were budding in the velvet sky as Branwen came out of the forest and saw Garth Milain ahead of them. Not burning, thank the saints. *Not burning!*

She rode that final stretch at the gallop, leaving Rhodri in her wake, desperate to get home. She sped past the pool where the children had played. She pulled on the reins, urging her snorting horse up the ramp to the open gates.

A guard stepped out. "My Lady Branwen!" he gasped.

"Where are my mother and father?" Branwen called.

"In the Great Hall, my lady, feasting with the Saxon messengers."

Rhodri had been right—her honorable parents had been tricked into allowing the Saxons into Cyffin Tir. Branwen jumped down from the horse as two other guards approached. "Where is Captain Owen?" she demanded.

"He is in the hall with the prince and his lady," said one of the guards. "It is good news, my lady. There is to be no war."

"Go to the hall," Branwen ordered. "Say nothing

of me, but tell Captain Owen that he is needed at the gate." She stared into the man's face. "Do nothing to give the Saxons reason to be concerned. Go!"

The guard nodded and headed toward the Great Hall.

Branwen looked back the way she had come. A dark shape was coming fast toward the hill. Rhodri.

The horse labored up the slope, snorting and stumbling. Rhodri slid from the horse's back and would have tumbled to his knees if a guard had not stepped forward and helped him.

"Close the gates," Branwen said. "Bar them. Now!"

The guards glanced at one another. Then one nodded and they ran to heave the heavy wooden gates closed. The oak bar came down with a reverberating crash.

Branwen turned to see Captain Owen striding toward her. "My lady, what is this?" he asked. "How is it that you are here? And why are the gates closed?"

"How many Saxons are there in the hall?"

"My lady?"

"Quickly, man!"

"Twenty, my lady. But they come in peace. There is nothing to fear. They have no armor, no weapons. They are emissaries sent from Chester to bring a peaceful end to the hostilities."

"No," said Branwen. "They are not. They have been sent to trick us into letting our guard down. No weapons, you say?" She frowned. "Have they been searched?"

"No, they have not. It would have been a great discourtesy to have searched them." He looked uncertainly at her. "My lady, why do you think they are not honest brokers of peace?"

Branwen gestured toward Rhodri. "He was a servant at Herewulf Ironfist's camp—he heard the plans. It is deception and treachery, Captain Owen. Trust me on this, or all may be lost."

The captain looked at Rhodri, his eyes narrowing. "Who is this lad, my lady? How do you know him?"

Rhodri gave a brief bow. "My name is Rhodri," he said. "What Princess Branwen tells you is true. Ironfist has an army encamped outside Chester no more than two days' march from here. He sent these men to do you nothing but harm. They have weapons hidden in their clothes."

"They are but twenty," Owen said. "Were they to make a move against us, not one of them would live to tell the tale." He turned to Branwen. "My lady, this is folly. I cannot go to the prince without proof of their perfidy."

"Ironfist sent these men here to kill and be killed," Rhodri insisted. "They know they will not survive. Their purpose is to murder the lord and lady of this court even though they pay for it with their own lives. Ironfist means to leave Garth Milain in disarray and without leadership when his army comes."

Captain Owen shook his head, his face troubled. "We risk much on the word of a stranger," he said.

Branwen had listened to this exchange with growing impatience. "Enough talk!" she said. "My mother and father are in danger. Believe me or not as you choose, Captain Owen; but unless you act against those Saxon dogs, I will go directly to the hall and put an end to their treachery on my own."

The captain searched her face for a long moment and then turned, a fierce light igniting in his eyes. "Aled, gather every able man not in the Great Hall. Have them all arm and meet here. Emlyn, see that there are guards at every point on the walls." He turned to Branwen. "Our best warriors are within the hall. They have no weapons. It will be hard to warn them without alerting the Saxons." He frowned. "There are many women and young folk there too."

"We need armed men in there," Branwen said, an idea forming in her head. "Captain Owen, return to the feast as if all is well. Tell the Saxons that they will be witness to a display of fine swordsmanship between our warriors. Then pick your best men—ten men at least—and tell them to go and arm themselves for the display. I will speak with them once they are outside. I will tell them to show no sign of what is about to happen until you give the word."

The captain smiled grimly. "A fine plan, my lady. But the Saxons will not have limited their assault on us to twenty men. If what you say is true, there must be more hidden close at hand."

Branwen nodded. "An army, I should think, waiting for the signal to attack. But they will find the gates closed against them. Go, now, Captain Owen, and put on a good show for them."

"By your leave." The captain bowed briefly and then turned and ran back to the Great Hall.

Branwen noticed Rhodri looking at her with raised eyebrows.

"What?"

"Didn't I say you were a born leader?"

"That remains to be seen," she replied, watching as the captain entered the hall. "Many a pot cracks in the firing, Rhodri. I think this will be a long night."

As ever, the doors of the Great Hall were wide-open. Firelight and candlelight and the smells of good food and the sound of laughter spilled out into the night. Branwen and Rhodri stood outside the doorpost with their backs to the wall, hidden from the sight of the people inside.

Branwen's plan was laid. Twelve armed warriors had gone into the hall. She knew them all: valiant, quick-witted men skilled with sword and shield. The moment when the veil of Saxon deception was to be whisked aside was approaching fast. Her heart was beating rapidly, and the blood was surging like an ocean through her temples; but all the same she felt curiously calm, her senses sharp.

She leaned sideways a little, just enough so that she could peer into the Great Hall. The fire dominated the center of the long chamber, roaring in its stone girdle, fingers of flame sending shadows splashing up the walls. Oak logs were piled high in the hearth, and many earthenware food-pots were standing warming among the stones, tended by silent servants.

Inga, the old woman who had packed Branwen's belongings only a few days ago, was carrying bread, her eyes lowered as she moved among the revelers, placing newly warmed rolls on their trenchers.

"What's happening?" Rhodri whispered. "What can you see?"

"There are a lot of people in there," Branwen murmured. "They've moved back to the walls to make room for the entertainment. The whole middle section of the floor around the fire is clear now. I can see some of our warriors with their wives and families; but they're dressed in their best linen, and they have no weapons. There are merchants and craftsmen in there as well, but they'll be of little use if the Saxons put up a fight."

"I can hear children," Rhodri hissed.

"Yes." Anxiety filled Branwen's voice. "Many children. They're playing games, running in and out among the people. I wish there was some way of bringing them to safety before the Saxons are challenged." She remembered the sad little bodies of Bevan's children lying dead in the forest clearing.

"What of the Saxons?" Rhodri asked.

"They're gathered in two groups near the double throne," Branwen whispered back to him. Her stomach tightened and a sick shiver went through her body as she looked at the Saxon men in their hide leggings and long, tan-colored jerkins—clothes loose enough to conceal knives. Their pale eyes seemed to be filled with a wintry malice. Their full beards gave them a fierce and sinister look, their mouths opening red to eat and laugh and spill out their lies.

"Saints preserve us!" Branwen gasped with a jolt of horror. "I know one of those men!" She had seen him before. A man with a white scar crossing his left cheek and—although she could not be certain at such a distance—with one light-colored eye and one dark. "He killed Geraint! I will have his life!" she hissed, snatching her slingshot from her belt.

"Branwen, no!" Rhodri grasped her arm and dragged her back into cover. "You'll ruin everything if you show yourself now! Wait for Captain Owen to give the word!"

Branwen glared at him. But he was right. Agonizing as it was, she must wait. If all went well, her brother's murderer would meet his end soon enough.

Captain Owen strode into the middle of the floor where the warriors were waiting, their swords blood-red from the flames. He stood with his back to the restless fire, his arms raised for silence. "By your good graces," he called, "let the entertainments begin!"

Applause and cheering erupted through the hall.

But instead of turning to fight one another, the twelve warriors split into two groups and ran to either side of the double throne, their faces grim, their swords aimed at the Saxons.

"Beware treachery, my lord!" Captain Owen shouted. "These men are armed—they come to start a war!"

The scarred Saxon leaped up, his mouth twisted with fury, his hand reaching into his tunic. "By Hel and Tiw and Wotan's sacred ravens, death to you all!" A moment later a long knife glinted in his fist.

The other Saxons sprang up, reaching for their hidden weapons.

Women screamed, and men shouted in alarm. Lady Alis leaped to her feet, her hand seeking the golden dagger that she wore always at her waist. One of the Saxons thrust his knife at her, but a warrior's sword came chopping down, severing the man's hand from his wrist before the knife could be thrust home.

"Get the children clear!" Lady Alis cried above the clash of blades and the shouting and turmoil that filled the hall.

Another Saxon came at her, his knife held high, his face contorted with battle-madness. Branwen's mother moved with liquid speed, spinning clear of his lunge and then bringing her own knife up in a blow that sent the blade deep into his chest.

A warrior went down at Prince Griffith's side with

a knife wound in his throat. The murdering Saxon turned to the prince, the bloody knife stabbing toward him. Lord Griffith's arm came up, parrying the blow aside; and while the Saxon was still off-balance, the lord swept the sword from the dead warrior's hand and drove it to the hilt in the Saxon's stomach.

Branwen could hold back no longer. She ripped free from Rhodri's grip and ran into the hall, her slingshot already armed with a stone as she swung it around her head.

"Branwen! Take care!" she heard Rhodri call.

But Branwen was beyond fearing for her own life. Women and children and servants flooded toward the doors, their faces panicked and fearful, their screams echoing to the rafters. Branwen pressed through the frightened crowd, hardly able to keep to her feet but desperate to get to her mother and father.

Now that their deception had been revealed, the Saxons fought with a wild savagery, slashing and stabbing with their knives even as cold iron blades cut their flesh and pierced their bodies. Branwen saw one Saxon snatch a girl-child by the hair, holding her close against him with his knife to her throat as he edged away from the swordsman who faced him. She spun her slingshot and let a stone fly. It hit the hand of the man holding the child, jarring the knife out of his fingers. A second stone struck the man in the mouth, smashing his teeth and sending him reeling back while the child was snatched to safety.

Rhodri was in the hall now, helping the fallen to their feet, catching up a small child in his arms and carrying her along in the fearful human tide. Several of the Saxons lay dead, their blood soaking into the earth floor; but those still living fought with brutal ferocity. Some had taken swords from the hands of dead warriors and were trading blow for blow with Prince Griffith's warriors.

Lady Alis was among them, her golden dagger in her left hand and a sword flashing in her right. Branwen's heart swelled with pride and with fear as she saw her mother bring down a Saxon with a slash to the neck that sent the blood spraying high.

But her *face*! Her mother's eyes were feverish with a frenzied battle-light, and her gentle features were transformed into a mask of wrath. Now Branwen understood the tales she had heard of the warrior maiden of the House of Owain; now she knew why her mother's fighting skills were revered throughout Brython.

Three Saxons managed to hack their way past the warriors. They came pounding down the hall toward Branwen. She stood bathed in the heat of the fire, blocking their path. She swung her sling-shot; and one of the three went down screaming, a stone lodged in his ruined eye socket. The second man wielded a sword snatched from a fallen warrior. The blade slashed toward Branwen, but she didn't flinch. Spreading her feet, she waited as the Saxon bore down on her with his blond hair flying and his face misshapen by bloodlust. As the sword arm came down at her neck, she dropped to her knees. The man's blow went wild; and he stumbled over her, tripping on the hearthstones and falling into the flames with a piercing scream.

She snatched the sword from his fingers as he fell. The fire roared with a hungry voice. Her nostrils filled with the stench of burning hair and flesh. Branwen sprang up, armed now and ready to face the third Saxon.

It was the scarred man—Geraint's slayer. His face was contorted with rage as he ran toward her, a bloodied sword in one hand, a knife in the other. Branwen's heart froze. Screaming filled her head; but whether they were the screams of real people or just phantoms of terror howling in her own mind, she could not tell.

A galloping horse. A whirling ax. Eyes filled with madness.

"No!" she shouted. "*No!*"

A bloodred fog came down over her mind. Fear would not claim her this time. As the hated man bore down on her, she could hear Gavan's voice in her head, feel his guiding presence at her back. She adjusted her stance, breathing slow, feeling the hard earth of her home solid under her feet. She tensed her body, her muscles straining for release. *Soon! Very soon!* She gripped the sword hilt in both hands, swinging the long blade back over her right shoulder until she felt its tip against her left hip.

The man was almost upon her now. She kept her eyes on his sword hand as he hurtled forward, his eyes blazing, his red mouth howling.

"For Geraint!" she shouted. "For the House of Rhys!"

The Saxon slashed at her neck. Springing to one side, she brought her sword over and down in a smooth movement that had all her weight and power behind it. Iron clashed on iron, and his blow was swept aside.

He stumbled, caught off-balance; but even as he staggered forward, he swung his sword arm at her, the blade cutting a long, sweeping arc through the air that would have torn her belly open if she had not leaped back. Roaring with anger, he fell to his knees. Branwen bounded in, aiming a blow at his head, meaning to finish him off before he got to his feet again. But she hurried the stroke; and instead of bringing the sword slicing down from her shoulder, she stabbed from the hip.

Her opponent's sword blocked the weak blow, the collision of iron on iron jolting her arms and almost jarring her sword out of her hand. He was on his feet in an instant, swinging again and again with his sword. Branwen staggered backward, overwhelmed by his strength and savagery. The Saxon's blade struck her own sword close to the hilt, knocking it out of her hands. She looked into the crazed blue and brown eyes and saw her death in them.

The Saxon raised his sword for the killing blow; but as Branwen backed away in defeat, her heel caught on one of the stones that ringed the hearth, and she fell. The Saxon's wild swing unbalanced him; and he toppled forward, crashing down on her, crushing the breath from her lungs. She struggled to get free, her arm reaching out blindly. Her fingers closed around a hearthstone; and she took a grip on it and lifted it, bringing it down with all her remaining strength on his sword hand. He bellowed with pain as the sword was struck from his fingers. But he still had the knife in his left fist. Branwen let the stone go and threw both her arms up to grip the wrist of his knife hand. His face was close to hers, his foul breath on her cheek, his mad blue and brown eyes blistering with rage. She had no strength to throw him off. In a moment the weakening muscles in her arms would fail her and the knife would stab downward and all would be over.

But then a tall figure rose above him, and a long blade cut down through the air. The man arched up, his face knotted with agony. Branwen used her last ounce of strength to tip him off her.

Her mother was standing over them, her gown and her face spattered with gore. She drew the sword out of the dead man's back.

"Mother!"

But Lady Alis didn't seem to hear her. Instead she turned, the blood spraying across Branwen's face as she swung her sword in a great arc and held it high. "What Saxon still lives?" she shouted. "Come, you dogs! Come, you vermin! I am Alis ap Owain! I am the blood-drinker, the wrath of heaven! Come!"

Trembling, Branwen scrambled to her feet. "Mother?"

Her mother rounded on her, her teeth bared.

"They are all dead, Mother," Branwen said. She reached out to the fierce, blood-soaked warrior woman. "Mother—it's *me*!"

Lady Alis stared at Branwen as if she didn't recognize her, then a veil seemed to fall from her eyes. She gave a gasp, dropping her sword and opening her arms wide.

"Branwen!"

Branwen fell into her mother's arms, holding her so tightly that her head spun and her legs threatened to give way under her.

"Branwen? Are you hurt, child?"

It was her father's voice, but for the moment she could not respond. She was lost in her mother's embrace, held by her strong arms.

"She is all right," said Lady Alis, her hand stroking Branwen's hair. "Give her a moment, Griffith."

She heard Captain Owen's voice. "They are all dead, my lord."

"And of our own?"

"Three slain, four wounded. Healers and herbalists have been called for."

"Are the gates secure? The walls manned?"

"Yes, my lord. Lady Branwen ordered the gates closed."

Branwen took a deep breath and lifted her head to look at her father. There was blood on his fine blue mantle, and a cut along his cheek. She reached a hand toward him. "I came as quickly as I could," she said.

"How is it you are here, child?" he asked.

Branwen gazed at him, lost for a simple answer.

"Time for questions later, my lord," her mother said. "It is enough that she is here and we have been saved from a great danger."

Branwen looked down at her feet. A lifeless face stared up at her, one eye blue, the other brown. There was blood on the lips and in the beard.

Geraint's murderer was dead.

She looked around for Rhodri. The floor of the hall was scattered with the remains of the feast. A handful of warriors were checking the Saxon dead. Rhodri was among them, helping to lift one of the bodies and carry it from the hall.

She called to him, and he came over to where they were standing. He kept his head low, and Branwen could see the unease in his eyes as he approached her parents.

"This is Rhodri," she told them. "We have him

to thank for our victory here. He told me what the Saxons were planning."

Lord Griffith brought his hand down on Rhodri's shoulder. "You have our gratitude, lad," he said. "And when time allows, you will tell us the full tale."

"Thank you, my lord; I shall, gladly," Rhodri said.

Lady Alis looked sharply at him. "You are a Saxon, by your voice."

"Half Saxon, my lady. But my allegiance is wholly to Brython."

Lord Griffith turned to Branwen. "Do you trust this boy, my daughter?"

"I do, Father. With my life."

He nodded. "Then so shall we."

Finally, Rhodri dared to look into the lord's face. "I will strive to prove worthy of your faith, my lord," he vowed.

There was the sound of running footsteps, and a guard came stumbling into the hall.

"An army!" he gasped. "A Saxon army comes, a thousand strong. And they bear sheaves of flame, my lord—fire enough to burn Garth Milain to its foundations!"

37

PRINCE GRIFFITH RAN from the hall with Captain Owen. Branwen heard them calling out orders. The Saxon army was coming. Garth Milain would soon be under siege.

"The gates are closed," she reminded her mother. "We can withstand them within the walls, surely, even if they come in thousands."

Lady Alis's eyes were grave. "That we cannot do, Branwen," she said. "If we lock ourselves away within our walls, they will turn and ravage the countryside. Our people will be murdered and their homes and crops burned. You saved us from being cut down while we feasted, but now we must meet their onslaught in open battle."

Beyond the doors of the Great Hall, Branwen could hear shouting and running feet. Lord Griffith's war-horns were blowing, warning the people of Garth Milain that danger was upon them.

"I want to fight!" she said, looking determinedly into her mother's eyes. "Please let me fight!"

Lady Alis rested her warm hand against Branwen's cheek, her face filled with sorrow. "You shall fight, Branwen," she said. "It is clear that fate has brought you to us here at this time. You shall fight at my side." She took Branwen's hand. "Come."

"Wait for me here," Branwen said to Rhodri.

"I shall."

Branwen allowed herself to be led to the door of Geraint's bedchamber. Taking a candle, Lady Alis entered the darkened room and guided Branwen to the chest that held her brother's battle gear. She knelt, opening the chest and drawing aside the gray blanket to take out the bow and arrows.

"I hoped to spare you this." Lady Alis sighed, lifting the dark green cloak from the chest and revealing the leather jerkin studded with overlapping rings of mail. "But fate will have its head, so they say."

"Mother, the man you killed—the man with the strange eyes—he was the one who murdered Geraint," Branwen said in a sudden rush.

Her mother paused and then slowly turned her head to look up at her. "That is good, Branwen. Blood has avenged blood."

Branwen swallowed hard. "I thought . . . I thought it would feel . . . *different*," she said. "Knowing he was dead and that Geraint was avenged."

"And how does it feel?"

"It feels . . . empty . . . ," Branwen murmured.

Her mother nodded. "Vengeance has no flavor, Branwen," she said. "A life taken is not a life given, no matter how just the cause. The slaughter of tens of thousands of Saxons would not return breath to the body of a single one of their victims." She sighed. "That is a truth worth knowing, Branwen."

"Yes, it is. But I'm glad he's dead, all the same."

"As am I."

Branwen stooped and took Geraint's shield and sword from the chest. The round, wooden shield was painted with a red Brythonic dragon on a white field. It felt good on her arm. The sword was old, its leather-bound hilt smoothed by the grip of generations.

"Don't fear for me, Mother," Branwen said. "I can defend myself. And attack, too, I hope. I have learned some fighting skills since I left here."

Her mother looked surprised. "How so?"

"I convinced Gavan ap Huw to help me."

She frowned. "Prince Llew allowed this?"

"He did not know."

Her mother gave a sad smile. "I knew that you had talked Geraint into teaching you sword-play when you thought none saw," she said. "But to have beguiled Gavan ap Huw? I did not know you could be so persuasive, Branwen."

"I am your daughter," Branwen said, a shiver of pride running through her.

"Indeed you are." Lady Alis stood up, the smile gone. "Come now. Put on the mail jerkin, Branwen, and the woolen cloak. It is thick and will protect you from a glancing blow. But we must find you a suitable helmet."

Branwen dressed quickly in her brother's clothes. The chain mail jerkin felt heavy, but she found she was able to move quite freely in it. Her mother clasped the cloak at her daughter's throat and then paused, resting her hands on Branwen's shoulders.

"Are you sure you wish to do this? You have nothing to prove, Branwen. There is no dishonor in prudence."

Branwen met her mother's gaze. "How old were you when you first fought?"

"I was a year younger than you are now."

Branwen smiled, and her mother returned the smile.

"Very well," said Lady Alis. "Let's find you a helmet, and then let us get to the gates. We shall fight side by side, my daughter and I; and the saints willing, we will prevail."

Branwen and Lady Alis stepped together from the Great Hall, with Rhodri just one pace behind them. Branwen felt honored to be walking at her mother's side, wearing her brother's armor and carrying his sword.

Geraint would have been so proud of her!

Torches flared up into the night. Branwen felt the tension thrumming in the air. A battle was coming. Her heart faltered when she saw the warriors gathered by the gates. *A battle was coming!*

Prince Griffith had an army of foot soldiers two hundred strong, well-trained men clad in chain mail jerkins and with iron helmets on their heads. Some carried spears or battle-axes, but most had iron swords and round, wooden shields. They stood silently, their faces grim. Branwen saw a flicker of fear in some eyes, and it comforted her to know she was not the only one who was afraid.

Prince Griffith sat astride his black stallion, Dirwyn, surrounded by fifty horsemen—Garth Milain's warrior elite—carrying spears and axes and bright blades thirsty for blood. A kind of hush hung over the fortress, pierced by the rattle of leather on iron and the sound of chain mail chinking and of horses' hooves thudding on the ground. Beyond the gates, Branwen could hear a growing noise—shouting and howling, the clash of spears beating on shields, the noise of the approaching Saxon army, all the more fearsome for being unseen. For a moment she stared in alarm at the walls. The pales were too thin, like sticks in a windstorm—a child's attempt at a fortress, about to be blown away to leave them all naked and exposed on that earth mound. She felt like a goat in a pen as the wolves prowled by night.

Why fight? Offer your throat to the wolves. Let your end be quick.

No!

You have no courage. You know this.

She gritted her teeth, her fingers gripping her sword until her knuckles flared white.

The ordinary people of the garth stood back from the warriors, mothers with children clinging to them, old men and women with fearful eyes, boys wishing they were old enough to fight.

Branwen turned to Rhodri. "Well, then, my friend," she said. "See where your blabbing mouth has got you?"

He smiled. "When will I ever learn the value of silence?" Then his face clouded. "I've never used a sword, Branwen. I don't know what use I can be in a battle, except perhaps to trip the Saxons up with my dead body."

"Those without weapons will stand on the ramparts and pelt the Saxons with stones," Branwen said. "Go with them—knock a few Saxon heads off their shoulders."

"And you?"

"I'll be with my mother. Quiet now; my father is giving his orders."

The warriors of Garth Milain were packed tight in the space behind the gates, divided into three distinct groups. Prince Griffith's horsemen were in the center under the pennant of the galloping green stallion;

Captain Owen's men formed up under the crossed swords of Cyffin Tir; and Lady Alis's stood under a yellow crescent moon on a field of dark blue.

"The company of Lady Alis will take the right flank," the prince called. "Captain Owen's the left. Let the horsemen engage the enemy while the foot soldiers circle around and strike from the sides and the rear." He stood in the stirrups, lifting his sword high. "May all the saints look down kindly upon us this night," he called. "By Saint Dewi! By Saint Cynwal! By Saint Cadog! *Open the gates!*"

Branwen ran to stand with her mother as the bars were thrown down off the gates.

Lady Alis turned to her. "Remember! Keep close to me!"

"I will."

The gates were swung open into the night. At the same moment a swarm of flaming arrows came hissing over the ramparts, thudding to the ground or striking wood and thatch. But the people of the garth who were not to fight in the battle were prepared for this: They ran to douse the flames, pulling the arrows down from the roofs with rakes and pikes, flailing at the fires with lengths of wetted cloth or heaping earth on them.

As Lady Alis's company began to surge forward, Branwen looked over her shoulder. Despite the efforts of the hurrying people, the dry thatch of several roofs was already alight, and a woman whom Branwen had known all her life was lying in the earth, an arrow jutting from her smoldering back.

Branwen was drawn to the gates by the crush of soldiers. Her shield was pressed to her chest, her sword arm pinned at her side, her helmet knocked as she fought to keep on her feet. Above the mass of people she could see the horsemen moving forward down the steep pathway; but she still could not see the enemy, although she could hear their racket and smell their burning torches.

The surge of soldiers got even worse as they pushed through the gates; but Branwen managed to keep close behind her mother, and soon things got easier as the horses went galloping down the earthen ramp and she no longer had to concentrate on staying upright. Lady Alis's warriors poured down, scrambling and tumbling into the dark dale and flooding along the high flank of the hill.

At last Branwen caught her first sight of the Saxon army. It had gathered in a mass at the foot of the ramp, horsemen and foot soldiers all thrown together, many holding flaming torches for archers to ignite more arrows. The sky above Branwen's head was filled with fire as volley after volley was sent into the fortress.

She thought briefly of Rhodri. Then a horde of Saxons came hurtling into Lady Alis's warriors, screaming their savage war cries and striking out with sharp iron. She heard them shrieking the names of their cruel gods.

"Tiw! Tiw!"

"Ganghere Wotan!"

"Hel! Gastcwalu Hel!"

But the voices of the men of the garth sang out just as loud.

"By Saint Cadog!"

"For Prince Griffith and Lady Alis!"

And Branwen found herself shouting out fit to burst her lungs: *"Death to the Saxons!"*

She had no time to think, no time to summon up her half-learned skills. All she could do was react to save her life as swords and axes came sweeping and thrusting at her and she was buffeted by shields and jostled by friend and foe alike. She had no idea how long the mayhem heaved and pitched around her. The taste of death was thick in her mouth; the stench of blood clogged her nostrils. Men were falling all around her. She stepped on them in her desperation to stay alive, her boots slipping on gore, her face spattered with other people's blood, her sword running red as she stabbed and slashed.

A Saxon towered over her. She was aware of a snarling mouth and of pale, glittering eyes. A double-headed battle-ax scythed down toward her with a force that would have split her from shoulder-bone to belly. She fended it off with her shield, her arm numbed by the power of the falling ax. She thrust blindly and felt her sword cut into flesh. Blood splashed into her eyes. There was a bellow of pain and the man came crashing down, almost knocking her off her feet. She stumbled sideways. Something hit her from behind, sending her tumbling to the ground. Feet stamped all around her; her ears were full of the dreadful clamor of battle, and there was a bitter taste in her mouth.

In a tiny corner of her mind, her mother's words came back to her.

Keep close to me!

She wished that were possible, but she had lost contact with her mother when the first wave of Saxons had crashed into them. She staggered to her feet, dazed and disoriented. At once a heavy blow came crashing down on her helmet. Half stunned, she fell, just managing to keep hold of her sword and shield as she rolled down a grassy slope.

Her face splashed into cold water. Gasping and coughing, she heaved herself to her knees. She had rolled down to the pool that lay at the bottom of the dale. She gazed dizzily around. Impossibly clear above the clamor of combat, she heard a *clop* in the water behind her. She stumbled to her feet and turned to find herself staring down into the black pool.

She let out a startled breath. The dark of the night sky cleared from the face of the pool as if a black veil had been drawn aside. She was looking down into a bright summer's day—and staring up at her was her own reflection.

But not in battle-gear—not with iron helmet and sword and shield. Herself in her marten-skin jerkin and leather leggings. Herself in Rhiannon's glade two long days ago.

Words came to her almost without thought.

"The falcon is on the roof! Two tongues tell the truth!" she shouted down to her own reflection. "Remember this! A life depends on it! The falcon is on the roof! Two tongues tell the truth!"

And then the surface of the pool broke up as if with a sudden storm of rain, and the image shattered into a thousand fragments.

38

BRANWEN TURNED FROM the pool. The battle still raged on the slopes around Garth Milain. Thick plumes of smoke rose from the fortress, their bloated undersides drenched in an evil red light. Branwen's ears ached with shouts and the terrified neighing of horses, and with the clash of iron on wood and blade on blade.

A terribly wounded horse lay close to Branwen, struggling to get to its feet, its eyes crazed and rolling, red foam at its lips. Branwen turned away from the awful sight. A Saxon knelt a few paces away, his face in his hands, blood welling thick between his fingers and blood caked in his long, pale hair. Many men lay dead in the long grass, their bodies ravaged by spear and sword and ax.

Farther away, a close-pressed band of Saxons was

beating its way up the long, steep ramp to the gate; but Lord Griffith's horsemen were among them, swords slashing, horses rearing, hooves smashing down on helmet and chest and limb.

The valiant crescent moon banner of Lady Alis fluttered under the ramparts, surrounded on all sides by a press of Saxons.

"Mother!"

Branwen pounded up the slope.

She felt less terrified now, and she began to remember Gavan's teachings. When a spearman came at her, his arm high, she leaped aside and brought her sword down to hack his weapon in two. She hammered her shield into his body, jarring him backward so his feet slipped on the grass. She never once looked into the wild, bearded face as she drew her sword arm back and then released all the energy in a deadly blow to his neck. There was blood and there was a scream cut short; and then Branwen was springing over the body, baring her teeth, shouting aloud:

"Come, you vermin! Come, you dogs! I am Branwen ap Griffith! Come!"

There was a wild strength flowing through her, and the red mist came down over her eyes again: the battle madness of her people, rich as blood, old as the forests.

"I am the Sword of Destiny," she howled. "I am the Bright Blade! The Emerald Flame of my people!"

A young man with a frightened face and a wispy

shred of beard faced her. She knocked his feeble blow aside, lunging forward with her shield angled toward his neck. Her shield rim caught him under the chin, throwing his head back. His mouth opened in a howl of pain. Pitilessly, she slashed her sword across his throat, and he dropped at her feet.

Another came, huge as a hill, eyes like ice crystals, swinging a battle-ax. She feinted to the left, drawing his blow that way before shifting her weight. She came in close to his side as he stumbled forward. She hacked at his thigh, bringing him to his knees. Then she stood over him, legs wide, as she drove her sword down to split his helmet and his skull.

She fought until there were no Saxons within reach. She had battled her way close to the ramp that led up to the gateway. Her arms felt heavy; her shield was battered and rent, her sword steeped to the hilt in blood. She stared out over the battlefield, sickened by the horror of it. An arrow glanced off her helmet, jerking her head to the side and making her ears ring. She was aware of a spear coming toward her. Another enemy coming to test the mettle of the daughter of Alis ap Owain!

She moved sideways. Her feet slithered on something lumpy and wet. A severed leg. She fell, her elbow striking a stone so that her sword was jarred from her hand. A bearded man loomed over her, his blue eyes glittering. He raised his sword. Branwen hoisted her shield against the blow. The sword came down hard on it, and the shield cracked into two pieces, numbing her arm to the shoulder.

The sword rose again, the man taking the hilt in both hands, the point aimed at her throat. She stared up at the falling blade, her hand groping desperately for her own sword.

A bulky shape came crashing down onto the Saxon warrior, sending him tumbling. Branwen lifted herself and saw that her rescuer was sitting astride the Saxon's chest—and that the Saxon was not moving.

Rhodri got quickly to his feet and reached down a hand to help Branwen up. "I may not have any skill with a sword," he panted. "But I know how to drop on someone from a height!" He gestured up at the high path. "I saw you from the ramparts. . . . You were fighting like a demon, Branwen! But I thought you might need help so I came to the gates, and I was right." He glanced at the fallen Saxon. "I think he's dead."

"So will you be if you don't get back to the citadel," Branwen gasped.

"That's no refuge now. The place is in flames."

A fist tightened around Branwen's heart. Her home was burning! "Stay with me," she said. "How goes the battle? Could you tell from the citadel?"

"Captain Owen is holding fast, but your mother is surrounded."

"Then I must go to her!" Branwen cried. "Rhodri, find a sword. Come with me."

Rhodri wrested the sword out of the dead Saxon's

fingers and followed close behind Branwen as she scrambled along the steep slope. She had not gone far before she heard a terrible sound above the uproar: the scream of a dying horse.

She turned her head; the sound had come from above, from high on the earthen ramp. She saw Dirwyn, her father's stallion, rearing on the very edge of the path with a spear jutting from his chest. She saw the horse fall sideways and her father hurled from the saddle, his sword beaten out of his hand as the enemy swarmed around him.

"Father! No!"

Two choices will you be given—two lives to save; but by your choice will one life be lost.

Two lives to save! Her mother or her father!

A vivid image swam in front of her face. Two fierce, deadly eyes. One blue, the other brown. Eyes with her death in them. Eyes made lifeless by her mother's thrusting sword.

Her heart breaking, and her eyes blinded by tears, Branwen turned away from her father. "Come," she said to Rhodri. "It's done. I've chosen!"

She fought her way through a world of loathing and horror, and even the tears that poured down her cheeks were unable to wash away the red fog that darkened her sight.

But at last she was at her mother's side, and Rhodri was with her.

335

Lady Alis's face was smeared with blood and grime, her cloak torn, her chain mail jerkin ripped and slashed. "Branwen, my child; against all hope, you are alive!"

"Yes, Mother." Branwen wept. "I had to choose you!"

Lady Alis stared at her. "What do you mean, Branwen?"

"Father has fallen. I think he may be dead!"

"No!" Horror filled her mother's eyes.

But the press of the enemy didn't allow for any more words.

A massive, broad-shouldered Saxon warrior was leading a group of men up the slope toward them, his long hair flying, his red cloak snapping in the wind, his bare arms ridged with muscle as he swung a double-headed battle-ax around his head.

Warriors came in from both sides, forming a barrier between Branwen and her mother and the onrushing Saxons. But the enemy crashed into their line, howling like wolves and sending men tumbling into the blood-slick grass. The Saxon leader's ax swung down, and a warrior fell in front of Branwen.

The Saxon roared, his mouth open like the maw of a bear, his red spittle flecking Branwen's face. "*Hetende Wotan!*" he bellowed as the ax swung again and a warrior's head rolled at Branwen's feet. "*Gehata! Bana Hel!*"

"Rhodri, get behind me!" Branwen shouted. She

spread her legs, angling her shield and bringing her arm back sharply, her eyes on the bloody head of the ax as it swished through the air. In the corner of her eye, she saw her mother standing at her side, mirroring her own stance as the roaring Saxon giant bore down on them.

"Strike together!" her mother shouted. "The throat! Strike as one!"

The man towered over them, aiming his ax high to sever their heads from their shoulders.

"Now!" Branwen cried.

Mother and daughter moved as one, ducking to avoid the swinging ax and then thrusting upward together until their swords met in the man's throat. He stood staring with bulging eyes for a moment, the battle-ax slipping from his fingers; then a fountain of blood gushed from his mouth, and he crashed down like a felled tree.

The death of their leader seemed to take the heart out of the others; and Lady Alis's warriors surged in, fighting hard to beat them back down the slope. Branwen and her mother leaped down after them, fighting side by side as the Saxon onslaught crumbled away.

And as they pushed the Saxons back, Branwen saw other warriors of Garth Milain flooding in from the side, Captain Owen at their head and the banner of the crossed swords of Cyffin Tir floating above them. At last, Branwen had a moment to think of Rhodri.

She glanced back fearfully. But he was unhurt. He was standing under the ramparts of Garth Milain, gripping the banner of the yellow crescent moon in both hands, shouting for joy as he waved it wildly.

All around the garth, the Saxons were falling back. Branwen heard a battle-horn blowing from the gate. She turned and saw Prince Griffith's horsemen driving their enemy away just as Captain Owen's men came up hard behind them, cutting them down like corn before the scythe.

Branwen darted away from her mother's side and forced her way up the steep path to where her father lay. He was on his back, his arms at his sides, his torn and tattered cloak spread over his body, blood soaked but mercifully hiding his wounds. His chest rose with short, shallow breaths. Branwen fell to her knees, tears pouring down her cheeks as she looked into his pale face. He was not dead—but he was dying, the light coming and going from his eyes like a candle guttering out.

"I had to choose, Papa," she said, smoothing matted hair off his forehead. "I'm sorry. I'm so sorry."

Geraint . . . I'm so sorry. . . .

First her brother and now her father—was she doomed to stand by and watch all her kinfolk be slaughtered by Saxon invaders?

"Branwen?" Her father's voice was no more than a whisper.

"Yes. I'm here."

"How is my Lady Alis?"

"Alive. Safe."

There was a weak smile. "Then you chose well." He coughed. There was blood on his lips. "How goes the battle?"

"Good, Papa," Branwen murmured, the words like splinters in her throat. "Garth Milain is saved."

The smile widened for a moment; then the light went out of his eyes, and she knew that he was dead. She leaned close over him, her tears splashing on his face, her hand on his chest.

"Good-bye, Papa," she whispered.

The fighting was all but over. The Saxons knew the battle was lost; Branwen could see them breaking ranks and fleeing into the east. She watched the horsemen of Garth Milain pursuing them, cutting many down before they could reach the sanctuary of the hills.

She stumbled wearily down the long pathway, searching for her mother. There were no Saxon prisoners. There were only the dead and the fled. She found Lady Alis standing among the bodies of the fallen, the battle-light gone from her eyes, tears flooding down her cheeks. Branwen took her mother's hand and led her back up to where Prince Griffith lay. They knelt together at his side and wept; and above them, unquenchable flames went roaring up into the night from the fortress of Garth Milain, blotting out the stars with their smoke.

In fire did you leave your home, in fire shall you return.

Rhiannon's prophecy had been fulfilled . . . or almost.

Branwen knew that one more decision lay ahead.

When the battle is done, for good or ill, you must make your choice: to follow your destiny, or to turn forever from it. But choose wisely, for your decision will seal the fate of thousands.

Branwen wiped the tears from her eyes and stared out toward the mountains.

The battle was over.

It was time for her to choose.

39

G ARTH MILAIN WAS on fire. The smoldering gates hung open, allowing the village folk to escape down the pathway. Branwen saw the horror in their faces as they looked out on the dreadful scene. The hill of the garth and the land around it were blackened with bodies, dead and the dying. Men were crying out, some in agony, some with weakened voices close to death. A stench of burning and of warm, spilled blood filled the air. Now began the terrible work of tending to the injured and of clearing the dead, both Saxon and people of Cyffin Tir.

Branwen swallowed her grief and went to help, her mother at her side. It was ghastly work, moving among the corpses, searching by flaring torchlight in the dark night, hoping against hope to find a soul whose life could be saved. All about them there was the rattle and clash of weapons being picked up and thrown together. There was weeping when a woman found her dead husband. There were cries of joy when a warrior was found alive and whole by his fearful family.

The salt taste of blood was thick in Branwen's mouth, the stink of death in her nostrils. She was exhausted, but she refused to rest. There was too much to do. She knelt and closed the lifeless eyes of a young warrior named Emlyn ap Lowri, a gate guard, a friendly, smiling young man she had known all her life. As she gazed down into his dead face, a small, barely heard sound came to her ears. She stood up, pulling back her hair from her blood-spattered face as she stared into the west.

Caw!

A small, dark fleck came winging out of the night. Branwen watched it without surprise, too weary and heart-worn to do more than follow its long, slow flight. As the bird came closer, she saw that Fain had something in its beak—something white that flickered and flashed.

Her mother peered into the sky as the bird approached. "It's carrying something. What is it?"

Branwen reached for her mother's hand. "It's my destiny, Mama," she murmured.

She could feel her mother's troubled eyes on her. "I don't understand," said Lady Alis.

"Neither do I," Branwen whispered. "I hoped I

would have more time." Anguish cracked her voice. "I hoped I would be able to explain everything to you."

Her mother took her shoulders, turning Branwen to look at her. "Explain what, Branwen? What is happening?"

"There's too much to tell. Too much . . ."

Fain arrived in a flurry of wings. The bird hovered above Branwen for a few moments, then opened its beak and let the bright thing drop.

She caught it in her open palm. It burned her skin. A radiant teardrop of frozen white water.

I will weep for you. A single teardrop of ice to light your way.

Fain flew in a long curve and came to rest close by on the helmet of a fallen warrior. Branwen didn't look at the falcon, but she knew the bird's sharp eyes were on her.

"What does this mean?" gasped Lady Alis. "Branwen, whence comes this?"

"From Rhiannon of the Spring," Branwen said.

"No!" Branwen had never heard such fear in her mother's voice.

The teardrop of ice suddenly melted in Branwen's palm, the cold water seeping to the edge of her hand and dripping to the ground. As the droplets struck the earth, a shimmering lacework of white began to grow at Branwen's feet, spinning out like a spider's web of fine, silken threads. The glimmering pattern flowed away in a river of light, crossing hollows and ridges and racing up the hillside. Then, with a final leap of silver, it disappeared into the forest, leaving a shining path that glittered and glimmered like strewn stars.

The battlefield had become eerily still. All around her, Branwen could hear people crying out in alarm and fear. Her mother grabbed her arm and tried to pull her away from the dancing ribbon of light.

"This is ancient mischief," hissed Lady Alis. "Get away from it, Branwen!"

"I'm so sorry," Branwen said with a sudden, strange calmness. "I have to go now."

"Branwen, no!"

She turned to her mother and took her hand. "You can't stop this from happening, Mama," she said. "Please, I must do this." She turned to one of the warriors who stood close by. "Bring me a horse!"

No one moved.

Lady Alis threw her arms around her. "This is the Old Magic, Branwen. It is wild and pitiless. Do not follow this path, Branwen. It will devour you!"

"No, Mama, it won't," Branwen said. "It won't, because I'm part of it. The Shining Ones have chosen me." She looked into her mother's fearful eyes. "They brought me here. They helped save us. Let me go to them, Mama. I'm doing this of my own free will."

Lady Alis stared into Branwen's eyes for a few long moments. Then she dropped her arms from around Branwen and took a stumbling step backward. "Fetch my daughter a horse," she called, her voice trembling.

A warrior led a horse to them, his eyes full of alarm as he looked at the shining path.

"Thank you," Branwen said to her mother. "I don't know where this path is going to take me." She swung up into the saddle. "But I *will* come back, if I can."

Lady Alis came to the horse's side and looked up into Branwen's eyes. "Must you do this? Will you not stay to mourn your father, to help me rebuild Garth Milain and protect our people?"

"I must go, Mama." She tugged at the reins, turning the horse toward the path. "I can't stay with you."

At first she feared that the animal would refuse to set its hoof on the magical way, but it stepped forward fearlessly; and as it did so, the light of the path sprang up like white sparks all around it. She knew that she would grieve for her father, that she would grieve deep and long for him; but right now, in this fleeting moment, she felt only pride that he had died in such great honor, saving his people from their ancient enemy.

Suddenly she was galloping along the path, and the music of high, clear voices sang in her ears. And flying straight and true above the path in front of her was Fain, Rhiannon's companion, messenger of the gods, leading the way. At the eaves of the forest, Branwen's horse paused in a net of starlight, and Branwen turned in the saddle to look back a final time. The flames still leaped from Garth Milain, but it was not that dreadful sight that held her gaze. It was the sight of another rider, moon bathed, sitting his steed awkwardly as it galloped along the path toward her.

Smiling, she waited until Rhodri caught up with her. They looked at each other with glowing eyes.

"Where else is there for me to go?" Rhodri asked. "Or would you rather be alone?"

"No," Branwen said. "I wouldn't."

She pressed her heels against her horse's flanks, and the animal stepped in under the canopy of leaves.

The Old Gods are sleepless this night
They watch and they wait
For the land is in peril once more
And the Shining Ones gather
To choose a weapon, to save the land
The Warrior
The Sword of Destiny
A worthy human to be their tool.

Don't miss Branwen's next thrilling adventure in

Destiny's Path

—— WARRIOR PRINCESS BOOK TWO ——

1

BRANWEN AP GRIFFITH pulled back on the reins and her weary horse gradually came to a halt, snorting softly and shaking its mane. She swayed in the saddle, her long black hair cascading down the sides of her face. Her limbs trembled with fatigue, and her whole body ached. Rhodri's horse went clopping on for another few paces through the trees before it, too, halted. The half-Saxon runaway looked back at her, his brow furrowed, his bright brown eyes sunken in his ashen face.

They had traveled far together, following the magical path of glittering light that had drawn Branwen from her home and all that she held dear, leading her toward the destiny prophesied for her by Rhiannon of the Spring, the ancient earth spirit.

Rhiannon of the Shining Ones.

Branwen had fought long and fiercely against the ominous visions of the woman in white, struggling to free herself of the destiny that gaped like a dragon's maw in front of her, a destiny that threatened to swallow her entire life.

But the foretelling would not be denied. What was it the bard had sung to Branwen—to her alone—in Prince Llew's Great Hall?

> *The Old Gods are sleepless this night*
> *They watch and they wait*
> *For the land is in peril once more*
> *And the Shining Ones gather*
> *To choose a weapon, to save the land*
> *The Warrior*
> *The Sword of Destiny*
> *A worthy human to be their tool*
> *Child of the far-seeing eye*
> *Child of the strong limb*
> *Child of the fleet foot*
> *Child of the keen ear*

Such a weight for a girl who had seen only fifteen summers. To be the savior of her land and of her people. To drive back the rising tide of bloodied Saxon iron. To be a warrior—a leader.

But Branwen had taken up the fearful burden and followed Rhiannon's path. And for friendship's sake, Rhodri had come with her.

She was clad in the chain-mail jerkin and the dark green cloak once worn by her brother Geraint. He no longer needed them—he'd been murdered by Saxons, his ashes blown away on the wind. His sword was at her hip now, and his round wooden shield, white with a rampant red dragon, hung from the saddle. The jerkin and cloak were flecked and stained with dried blood; the shield was notched and dented from the blows of swords and axes. These marks were the result of Branwen's fighting, not Geraint's. Dead too young, her brother had never met the Saxons in battle—had never grown to be the warrior he should have been.

Branwen and Rhodri had ridden through the starless gulf of the night, following the flickering silver path through dense forests and over ridge and bluff, spine and spur of the high hills. With the passing of time, as the mystical moonshine path had waned and its light had bled away into the ground, Branwen's hope and faith had faded with it, replaced by frustration and growing anger.

She turned and gazed back the way they had come.

The distant ridges of the hills were now showing sharp and black against a streak of dreary gray light.

Dawn was coming.

A dawn empty of all magic.

Where was Rhiannon?

Branwen gritted her teeth, a cold fire burning in her heart at the capricious nature of the Old Gods. If the Shining Ones offered her no guidance, no clear path to her destiny, then why should she not simply turn back and fight the Saxons in her own way—on the familiar ground of Cyffin Tir?

Back there, her home was burning. Her father lay dead on the battlefield. An image of the battle-weary, grieving face of her mother, Lady Alis, forced its way into Branwen's mind. She could almost hear the words her mother had spoken as Rhiannon's path had unreeled itself into the night.

This is the Old Magic, Branwen. It is wild and pitiless. Do not follow this path, Branwen. It will devour you!

And she remembered her own reply.

It won't, because I'm part of it. The Shining Ones have chosen me. They brought me here. They helped save us. Let me go to them, Mama. I'm doing this of my own free will.

A fresh wave of anger and disillusionment broke over Branwen as she thought of all she had left behind.

"Who am I, Rhodri?" she demanded as he dismounted and led his horse back to her. "Who do the Shining Ones *think* I am?"

"You are Princess Branwen, daughter of Prince Griffith and Lady Alis of Cyffin Tir," he replied, his face full of compassion as he gazed up at her. "And you're exhausted and ready to drop. We should rest now. For a while at least." He gave a faded smile. "Can your destiny wait a little while longer, Branwen?"

"What destiny?" hissed Branwen, her head swimming. "*Whose* destiny?" She struggled to remain upright in the saddle as she threw back her head, using the last of her energy to shout into the night.

"Rhiannon! Where are you? What do you want of me?"

But the rugged hills and the shadowed forests made no reply.

"I will not go purposelessly into the west," said Branwen. "The shining path has vanished and Rhiannon hides herself from me!" Red anger flooded her mind. "Even her winged messenger has left us. Where is Fain? I will not follow blindly," she continued bitterly. "If this is all the Shining Ones offer, then I will turn my back on them!" A wave of absolute exhaustion struck her, and she lurched in the saddle. "I'm going back, Rhodri," she murmured. "Back to my own people. That way lies the hope for the future. That is the true path to my destiny. . . ." A black fist closed around her mind and Branwen felt herself falling.

She was vaguely aware of strong arms around her and Rhodri's friendly voice in her ear.

"Let destiny go for now," he said. "You need rest and you need food inside you. Just put your arm around my neck. Let's find a soft spot for you to lie down on."

She allowed herself to be carried, one muscular arm under her knees and another behind her back. Her head lolled on Rhodri's shoulder. She could hear his rasping breath as he lowered her to the ground.

She opened her eyes and found herself half lying under a massive old oak tree, its gnarled and twisted

5

roots rising on either side of her like knuckled fingers. Her nostrils were filled with the smell of damp earth and rich mold.

"You wait here," Rhodri said. "I have something we both need." Branwen watched him walk to where the two horses were standing. He led them to a tree and tethered their reins loosely to a low branch. He ungirdled the horses' saddles and drew them off, laying one on top of the other under the tree, then unwound a small sack from his saddle and came back with it hanging from his fist.

"What is it?" Branwen asked tiredly as he crouched at her side.

"Not much, but hopefully enough for our present needs," replied Rhodri. "A hunk of bread and some cheese and a small flask of milk that I managed to purloin from the stores before the battle started. A wise precaution against hunger, if I do say so myself. Providing for an empty belly was a lesson hard-learned on the lean and hungry roads of Brython."

Branwen smiled grimly. "This is more than Rhiannon has given us," she said.

"Ahhh, well . . . *Rhiannon*," murmured Rhodri, sitting cross-legged at her side and handing her a chunk of bread and a piece of ripe yellow cheese. He looked sideways at her. "You aren't really turning back, are you?"

She shook her head. "I don't know," she said. "But this is not what I expected when we began to follow the shining path. I imagined it would take us . . . I'm not sure . . . somewhere . . . *special*. A place where everything would be explained." She narrowed her eyes. "I should have known better. Rhiannon seems to delight in confusing me, in tormenting me with her riddles. . . ." She dug the heels of her hands into her eyes, trying to shake off the lethargy that dragged at her limbs and clouded her mind.

She looked at Rhodri, sitting quietly at her side, chewing the bread, his tawny hair hanging in his eyes.

"If you were me," she asked, "what would you do?"

"I would eat and drink and sleep," Rhodri replied. "Maybe things would seem clearer then. Who knows?" He looked at her with deep sympathy in his eyes. "I've never met anyone with a destiny before, Branwen. What do you think Rhiannon is playing at? Is this some kind of test?"

"Haven't I passed enough tests?" Branwen asked.

Surely she *had* done enough? She had heeded Rhiannon's terrible warning.

Your enemy comes creeping over the eastern hills even as we speak, cloaked in deception. Speed is your only ally now, Branwen. Fly as fast as you can, and you may still save many lives.

She had galloped her horse down the mountain like the west wind, desperate to thwart the Saxons' plans to kill her mother and father and to burn the hill-fort of Garth Milain. She had taken part in the battle that raged at the foot of the ancient mound. She had killed men. And then, despite her efforts, she had seen her father cut down and her home burned. The battle had been won—but at what cost!

Heed me, child: When the battle is done, for good or ill, you must make your choice: to follow your destiny, or to turn forever from it. But choose wisely, for your decision will seal the fate of thousands. This is my final foretelling.

And Branwen had made that decision. She had left her grieving warrior mother standing proud but haggard on the charnel house of the battlefield—had left her home, Garth Milain, in flames.

"Sleep," Rhodri said gently, his hand on her shoulder.

She slid sideways and rested her head in his lap, feeling the soft touch of his hand on her hair as the dead weight of her fatigue finally dragged her into slumber.

IN ONE MOMENT,

FIFTEEN-YEAR-OLD BRANWEN'S LIFE IS

CHANGED FOREVER.

"You can be a warrior, if you choose to be . . ."

She has always been tough, spirited, adventurous, and bold—qualities that have helped her excel as a warrior. But will her training help her when the time comes to save her country and herself?

MAGIC, ADVENTURE, AND TRUE LOVE...

What happens when an ordinary girl is torn between two worlds?

The Faerie Path

Anita was living an ordinary life, until an elegant stranger pulled her into another world. There she discovers she is Tania—the lost princess of Faerie, and the only one who can stop a sinister plan that threatens the entire Realm. Torn between her duty to the throne of Faerie and the Mortal World she can't forget, Tania must choose between her two worlds, and two loves—an impossible decision, with breathtaking consequences.